REGRET

FREQUENCY FIVE | KNOXVILLE

REGRET

ANDREW KRONINGER

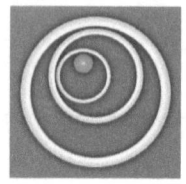

FREQUENCY FIVE

Frequency Five Publications ltd
Farragut, Tennessee 37934

Frequency Five Publications Email address
freq.five.publications.ltd@gmail.com

The Library of Congress has catalogued the editions as follows:
Epub: ISBN 978-0-9916005-9-5
Paperback: ISBN 978-0-9916005-8-8

Kroninger, Andrew
Regret / Andrew Kroninger
Library of Congress Control Number : 2015941598
1. Fiction - Espionage

Physical-related medical information was provided by Dr. Eric Carlson, who remains an invaluable asset to the author's works.

Other medical and psychological information was provided by a trained psychiatrist who I could most effectively thank by leaving anonymous.

ALSO BY ANDREW KRONINGER:

At the Edge of the Storm

Forlorn Hope

If only one page of this manuscript survives, let it be this one.

This book was written for and is dedicated to

Mikaela Faust, A fellow artist

And an amazing person.

Always.

Death is the veil which those who live call life;

They sleep, and it is lifted.

-Percy Bysshe Shelley (*Prometheus Unbound*)

The Edge ... there is no honest way to explain it because
the only people who really know where it is are the ones who have
gone over.

-Hunter S. Thompson

REGRET

PROLOGUE
THE AFFLICTION

Sydney Opera House: New South Wales, Australia – 14 June 2014, 9:45 P.M.

No one spoke to Michael Taggart that night. It wasn't as if he was avoiding conversation; rather, it seemed that conversation was avoiding him. This wasn't an issue for him - his mind was elsewhere.

Taggart sat in one of the many rows that lined the main auditorium, waiting. He behaved no differently from the rest of the audience, apart from one key aspect – his eyes, rather than being fixed on the currently performing singer, were scanning the room as if every detail was of paramount importance.

He was dressed quite differently from any of the other theatre-goers in attendance and had attracted a significant number of strange looks from them as a result. Michael paid this no mind, however. He was there for strictly professional purposes, and if that involved being clad in a faded pea coat and jeans rather than a freshly-pressed tuxedo, he had no complaints.

It was well known to him that his target was waiting backstage at that very moment, only minutes away from making his presence known to the crowd. How he knew this was a mystery to even himself. No schedule had been posted for the evening's singers, no bulletin passed around – Taggart had no proof apart from an insatiable feeling in the back of his mind. After all that he had been through, he knew better than to ignore it.

A hypodermic needle sat in his left pocket, and a loaded, suppressed Sig Sauer P226 X-Tactical filled his shoulder holster. The target could be pacified by either of the implements, but the former of the two would require a great deal more precision and care. The syringe was filled with a local anesthetic. The pistol was loaded with 9x19mm hollow point rounds, specifically chosen to halt a target in its tracks and reduce collateral damage.

Taggart had employed both methods in the past, and neither one proved to be at all simple. He had become a firm believer in Murphy's first and most important law – anything that can go wrong will go wrong. As a result, he had grown more and more wary of any potential complication, and for good reason. Such precaution is fallible, however, as he would learn firsthand in a swift and brutal manner.

His therapist had called it paranoia and his commanding officer had called it a killer instinct, but Michael didn't listen to either of them. To him, it was the only way that he could function. Living in constant doubt was about as unappealing to him as it would be to anyone, but he had been given good reason to have such an outlook.

The onstage performer finished her song to great applause, and Taggart joined in, hardly aware that he was doing so. He was concerned more with the half-illuminated figure waiting in the wings. The man in question carried all of the symptoms of someone suffering from the Affliction – He was breathing heavily, almost to a comical degree; his eyes were stern but unfocused; his limbs had seized up; and he seemed to be wholly unaware of his surroundings. He also seemed to be somehow aware that there was someone who noticed his state, and it wasn't long before he fixed his gaze on Michael. Their eyes locked, the stranger's intense, narrow ones connecting with

Taggart's impassive and calculating ones.

The man made no immediate movement, opting instead to assume an air of complete disinterest. Taggart wasn't a psychiatrist by any means, but he had been around enough Afflicted to know that the anonymous target was still in a frenzied state. He would continue on in the same pattern as all the others, starting with a sudden violent outburst. Detaining him was the ideal outcome in Michael's opinion - he had no desire to kill someone who wasn't in control of his mind.

Unwilling to wait any longer, Michael rose to his feet and was met with annoyed hisses from the audience members sitting behind him. You'll thank me later, he thought as he slid past the people beside him and into the aisle. This action alone seemed to act as a catalyst of sorts, sending the target into a fit of rage. He sprinted from the wing and onto center stage, withdrawing a pistol, which was not at all dissimilar to Taggart's, from the folds of his suit.

The audience gasped, but not out of fear – to them, this was simply an unexpected diversion in the night's production. It was only after they saw the first man fall that their cries were in earnest. Before Taggart even had the chance to reach for his weapon, the target had opened fire on the first row of audience members. Fortunately, he was quite a poor shot, and the majority of the rounds tore up the carpet in front of the audience. Only one man appeared to be seriously injured, blood from a wound in his chest turning his dress shirt a sickly crimson.

Chaos ensued. A mad dash was made for the exits as the perpetrator knelt to reload his pistol. It was no wonder that his aim was lacking – his hands shook uncontrollably throughout, and he seemed to be unable to stop his head from twitching to one side.

By this point, Taggart had unholstered his own pistol and aimed it at the target, but the wave of fleeing theater-goers knocked him on his back. Michael stumbled to his feet and aimed once more, but his own hand was trembling too much for him to line up a shot. This had never been an issue in the past, but he had little time to wonder about it. It was as if his mind was a door that had been shut almost entirely – most thoughts and considerations were gone, but through the cracks of the door he could see the target with perfect clarity.

Conscious thought had been removed; he now moved solely based on muscle memory. The crowd rushing past was invisible to him, but he somehow knew to step over the man who had tripped and to sidestep the woman who had frozen in shock. The target looked up at him, revealing a pair of bloodshot eyes that did their best to focus on his opponent. Michael lifted his pistol and fired, the shots missing their mark by mere inches, but that was intentional. He wanted to frighten the target into a swift surrender. *Why is he not yielding?* he wondered. *Almost everyone has reacted to that in the past...*

Whatever the case, he felt a sense of insatiable anger take hold. His vision blurred, but he remained fully cognizant of the target's every move. Taggart sprinted for the stage and dove onto it, but his lunge fell far short of his prey. The attacker was already making a dash toward the wing from which he had emerged.

Michael gave chase, slipping on the blood that had

collected on the soles of his shoes as he did so. The letters making out the word EXIT above a door backstage were hazy and indistinct to him as he passed them, darting through its open frame and into the balmy night air. He skidded to a halt almost instantly, however, having lost sight of his target entirely. The only things in front of him were several sets of stone stairs leading to an overlook of the nearby cove.

Before Taggart had the chance to register anything more, a hand came swinging across his field of view, a switchblade in its grasp. Michael dropped his pistol and caught his opponent's arm with both hands, twisting it as if he were a fourth-grader giving a particularly vicious Indian burn.

The man howled in pain and dropped his weapon, giving Taggart the chance to make a lunge for it as it fell. Instead of doing so, however, the blade slashed his outstretched fingers and continued to pinwheel to the ground. It was now his turn to recoil in agony.

I'm getting slower... getting older... Come on, Michael!

His thoughts were cut short by an elbow that was sent crashing into the base of his spine. Even more pain followed this, so much so that Michael was forced to collapse to the ground and stare up at the stars overhead. The target began kicking his supine form, mercilessly aiming for the head.

Taggart had little presence of mind left, but he used what still remained to grab his foe's swinging leg and throw the man off-balance. The latter staggered and fell, coming to rest beside Michael with a muffled thud. For a moment, they were able to face each other directly, and Taggart was struck by how normal the man could have looked if he hadn't been infected with the Affliction. His visage was a rotund and almost welcoming one, and he could have very well been a particularly friendly grocery store cashier – one who regular customers tend to gravitate towards simply because of his pleasant appearance and disposition.

Can't get distracted. Damn.

This was counteracted by his diseased state, however, and his bared teeth and blazing eyes were anything but welcoming. Unbeknownst to Taggart, he could have very well been looking into a mirror, as his own expression had transformed into a similarly fierce state.

This moment of introspection was short-lived, with the target recovering quickly and throwing himself on top of Michael. Wringing his hands around Taggart's neck, the attacker began to shout incoherently. Taggart responded with all due force, sending the grappling pair rolling down the stairs. He was only faintly aware of his surroundings by this point, pain taking hold. His field of view was reduced to a repeating loop of sky, stairs, sky, stairs, sky, stairs.

This sensation was alleviated as soon as they reached the bottom, both struggling to their feet beside a guardrail at the water's edge. Taggart tried to wipe the blood from his hands, which only served to smear them further. The target had regained his bearings as well and was once more brandishing his pistol at Michael, who reacted in a surprisingly serene manner. He had become more familiar with the sight of a gun's inner barrel than he would have preferred.

Under ordinary circumstances, Taggart would have made his best effort to reason with whatever gunman might be aiming at him, but ordinary circumstances were anything but ordinary in his experience. He was face-to-face with one of the most vile aspects of the Affliction – reasoning and basic senses no longer were factors. Those were replaced with rage and hostility. Patience and rationality were traded out for paranoia and a complete lack of awareness. Afflicted people were reduced to a state that almost wasn't human at all, and calm discussion has never had much success in conflict with animalistic instinct.

Instead, Taggart feinted to his left and lowered his shoulder into the target's chest, striking the man in the solar plexus. The pistol went flying, and this time Michael's reflexes were up to the task. As it was still clattering on the ground, he kicked the weapon into the water. For a moment, each man froze with his head turned in that direction, watching the pistol sink into the murky depths.

As soon as he was able, Michael withdrew the syringe from his pocket. The target's bloodshot eyes widened. It was unlikely that he knew what was contained within the device, but the Affliction had made it clear to him that it was something to be avoided at all costs.

He began to back away, sending Taggart off of the defensive and into a series of rapid steps in the direction of the retreating opponent. The latter had lost all sense of where he was and what he was doing, apart from the persistent urge to drive the contents of the syringe into that man's system.

Wielding the syringe in his right hand as if it were a

knife, Michael lunged forward, gripping the target's arm with his left. The man was successful in pulling away, but not before the needle had embedded itself in one of the veins on his forearm. His eyes rolled back in their sockets, leaving only bloodshot slits visible, his entire body had gone slack as one, leaving Taggart to catch the shell of a man before his head struck the pavement.

He would recover with time; they all did. All that was left now was to wait until the police arrived. It wouldn't be long now, and Taggart wouldn't have been at all surprised if he were being monitored by a police helicopter at that very moment. The pattern remained the same: Cops would arrive on the scene with their red lights flashing and attempt to arrest him before being presented with his credentials and beginning a series of fervent apologies.

It was all quite tiresome. Michael had long since abandoned all hope of this routine changing; he didn't officially exist and therefore had no choice but to behave that way. His papers bore the name Michael Faust Taggart, but this was only the most recent of his aliases. Whatever his birth name had been was now irrelevant – Taggart was an enigma; just one of the many strangers on their way home from a prolonged journey. The only difference was that his journey's end wouldn't be for some time, and it would no doubt have an abrupt, violent conclusion.

For the moment, however, this particular stranger slumped against the guardrail, waiting for the police to arrive and wishing that he was about twenty years younger.

PART ONE
A RUSSIAN WINTER

"Russia is a riddle wrapped in a mystery inside an enigma."

- Winston Churchill

Obituary taken from *The New York Times*, 12 December 2016

Michael Faust Taggart is presumed dead after a nine-month-long search for the man or his remains yielded no results. A closed memorial is to be held in Brooklyn in the coming week, its attendance restricted to the former co-workers of the deceased (all of whom make up the remnants of the enigmatic group of 'Sentinels'). Due to the inconclusive and mysterious circumstances surrounding the (assumed) death, little more can be disclosed at this time.

Michael Taggart was born on August 28, 1979 in West Chester, Pennsylvania to...

Excerpt from A Study in Psychosis: The Impact of the Affliction *(Section IV; p. 344)*

Though many attempts have been made to identify the exact nature and genesis of 'The Affliction,' none have quite succeeded in doing so. The most accurate accounts liken the state to that of a person suffering from Brief Psychotic Disorder. This renders the victim temporarily delusional and irrational, mirroring what is undergone by a victim of psychosis. Despite this, the two are far from interchangeable concepts. Afflicted persons are prone to being particularly violent and impetuous, almost inevitably creating a volatile situation.

Identification of the Afflicted is a simple enough matter, as has been outlined in Section II of this volume. One key factor not addressed there is the only foolproof method of doing so: Due to a neurological effect that has remained unidentified as of yet, the Afflicted's blood cells will be heavily impacted. As a result, the pigment of the victim's blood itself will have a much darker appearance than that of a healthy person. It will appear with a shade closely resembling that of a ruby.

No definite cure has been identified for such a condition, but many millions of dollars in research and many devoted professionals have netted the medical community a medication that will put such paroxysms of violent behavior at bay. The actions of Afflicted individuals is unlike any other known condition, reducing the victim to their most basic, animalistic instincts.

Bell UH-1A Iroquois Helicopter exiting British Airspace: 12 February 2016, 4:35 A.M.

Colonel Kate Grant was getting too old to be doing what she was doing, plain and simple. She had gone from counting the gray hairs that had somehow found their way onto her head to counting how many hairs were left at all, but she would have sooner donned a wig and pretended to be a decade younger than given her post to one of those wide-eyed Second Lieutenants fresh out of college.

No, she was far too proud of her work for that. Two consecutive tours of duty hadn't earned her the 'privilege' of being relieved by someone who was an infant by comparison, as far as she was concerned. As she sat across from Taggart in the confined space of the helicopter, the realization came to her that this was the very reason that she could stand to work with the man. The two couldn't have differed in age by more than a year or two, and this suited the Colonel just fine.

She had been Michael's handler since the first of the two Bush presidents had taken office, and the two had become founding members of the Sentinels when the president with too much fondness for a certain intern had taken over.

Now, it was with a confused sense of envy that Colonel Grant looked across the helicopter at her old colleague. She had made up her mind long ago that she had taken just about all she could handle in the field – after all, her initial hip replacement had always felt a bit off, and that was nothing compared to the second. That, combined with fragmentation from a bullet wound to the knee, made her more than happy to be sending someone else out on an assignment. Even so, a small part of her felt nostalgic for the time when she herself had been dodging bullets on the ground. The excitement and adrenaline had been rewarding, but along with that came living with a nagging, constant fear, as if danger never truly left – only waited.

Her opinion of Taggart was different from the ones she held for other agents – she actually liked the man. Grant would have been content with merely being able to tolerate those who she worked with, but this was a person who kept his nose clean, kept working, and largely kept his head down. He was also damn fine at what he did. These were standards to which she had held herself, and it was becoming an exceedingly rare concept. In addition, he was living with the fear that she had come to know so well, and she could respect anyone who bore that burden.

The man had a certain air of detachment about him, but that was something which she could understand all too well. The Colonel could see it in the way he carried himself – always looking weighed down, never seeming to make a step or say a word before considering its implications. More than anything, she could see in his eyes that he had been touched by a sensation that is felt by too many. That is, he carried the eyes of one who had killed people simply because he was told to, simply because somebody above him had pointed his or her finger at someone else. How many this was, she didn't know and would never ask, but she could see as plain as the dark circles under his eyes.

"We have a contact on the ground," she shouted over the sound of the helicopter's rotors. "You're to make contact with him for more intel regarding the situation. All we have at the moment is that there have been sightings of several individuals exhibiting all known symptoms of the Affliction. Once you've met with our man on the ground, report back with what you have. We'll let you know what to do from there."

Taggart nodded, doing his best not to get sick. He had never been terribly fond of flying, and the helicopter made a sudden lurch toward the ground. "What does he look like?"

Colonel Grant produced a photograph from the folder on her lap, and Taggart was met with the face of a man who seemed wholly unremarkable. In this line of work, some people would kill just to have one of those faces, Michael thought before setting to memorizing the visage.

The only distinguishing feature that the man possessed seemed to be his eyes, which were dark, almost navy blue. His gaze from the picture was a cold and calculating one, as if he had a deep-rooted mistrust for everyone, even those merely analyzing a picture of him.

Taggart handed the photo back to Colonel Grant, the image of the contact still very much at the forefront of his mind.

"You'll find him in the bar on Petrovka Street. It's a quiet place, and he mentioned that he usually sits alone at a table in the far back corner. We won't be using actual names on this assignment, so you'll know him simply as 'David.'"

He'll only respond when given the phrase, 'Mother died today.' He should respond with, 'Or maybe yesterday. I can't be sure.'"

"How will we be handling communications this time?"

Colonel Grant handed him a cell phone which looked at least a decade out of date. "Disposable mobile phone, courtesy of budget cuts made to our branch. It's prepaid and should last two months, but, more importantly, these are incredibly tricky to trace. All the same, we should keep conversations on it brief and infrequent."

Taggart nodded, pocketing the phone.

"The pilot should maintain a steady altitude in about five minutes' time," Colonel Grant said. "At that point, you'll fast-rope into a forest that sits on the outskirts of Moscow. Interpol has already provided you with enough currency to post up in a hostel for a few months. Preferably somewhere cheap and unobtrusive – remember, you're just another tourist. Any questions?"

Taggart shook his head, eager to get his feet on the ground. It had been too long. At the same time, he spun a wedding band around his finger, an unconscious habit which he had picked up many years ago.

"In that case," Grant said, "Good luck, and everyone at Interpol awaits your next transmission. If we don't hear

anything in two days' time and haven't been notified of
your going undercover for a longer period than that, we'll
have no choice but to pull the plug on this mission and
declare you MIA. Remember, you don't officially exist. As
far as Interpol and the Sentinels are concerned, you're just
another drop in the gene pool."

Taggart nodded again, quite familiar with this spiel.
"Right. Thanks, Colonel. See you on the other side." He
didn't exactly feel impatient, but the fact remained that
he would never get rid of a nagging sense of restlessness
unless he was on the ground and under the influence of
adrenaline-filled stress. Even Michael knew this was far
from being healthy, but it was the only way that he knew
how to live.

Colonel Grant looked up with a grim expression which
betrayed at least a small measure of hope.

"And Taggart…" she said as he prepared to disembark,
"…take care of yourself out there."

He nodded, then slid down the rope and out of sight.

Outskirts of Moscow, Russia – 12 February 2016; 6:15 A.M.

There was a narrow, dirt path which wound through
dense undergrowth. This was the more unkempt side of
one of Moscow's parks. Taggart kept a swift pace on the
trail, just another aimless citizen exercising in the cool
morning air. It had been only two months since he had
been told that his next assignment would lead him to the
frigid streets of Moscow, but in that time, he had gained
a basic comprehension of the Russian language. It was by
no means adequate in terms of his establishing an airtight

cover, but he could now portray himself as a functioning member of society.

He also had a rucksack slung over one shoulder, and it switched back and forth when its strap became too heavy to be comfortable. In the pack was a laptop computer, several army rations that Interpol had scavenged for him, basic toiletries, and his disassembled pistol – a customized Sig P226 X-5 Tactical.

Where an ordinary person might have had a family heirloom or personal gift as their most prized possession, Taggart had this weapon. He had chosen it from a lineup containing dozens of selections, and it had since been modified to suit him personally. Its grip was contoured to fit his hand, the sights adjusted to suit his style of aiming, a suppressor and subsonic ammunition made it whisper-quiet; the weapon had even been confirmed as operational after being submerged in water. It had been tailor-made to improve Michael's shooting efficiency, and he felt as comfortable with it as he did with his own skin.

The P226 remained in the rucksack for the moment. It wouldn't, however, remain there for long; Taggart had learned early on that being armed was like traveling with a spare tire: not always necessary, but indispensable when needed. He was certain that it would be a necessity before long.

It was with a harried disposition that Michael made his way through the park and into the heart of the city. While wanting to appear as normal and unobtrusive as possible, he couldn't escape the feeling that everyone around him knew that he didn't belong.

The streets were almost vacant at this point in the morning, and it created an eerie atmosphere – almost as if the city had become a reincarnation of East Berlin before the wall fell. Taggart kept his view fixed on the sidewalk in front of him, careful to avoid eye contact with any passersby. The less attention that he attracted, the better.

Petrovka Street. What a mess. What parts of the thoroughfare weren't covered in scaffolding and construction equipment were run down compared to the surrounding area. Parked cars that looked as if they hadn't been driven in years dotted the sides of the road. Most nearby storefronts were empty and dark, with discarded bits of wood and other refuse littering the interior. Boards crisscrossed over what must have once been bustling businesses.

One exception to this was a bar that was so dimly lit that it looked to be abandoned as well. Its front door reflected this aesthetic perfectly, with a rusty bell hanging from the top and a faded sign in the window reading 'Free Beer Tomorrow.' The place was a dive, just inconspicuous enough for Taggart and his contact to avoid the prying eyes of the public.

The bell jangled when he entered the bar, but the heads of everyone inside remained lowered, seeming not to notice. The room itself was a dingy affair, with several mismatched chairs and tables laid out beside a bar that was so uneven it must have been impossible to set a drink on it that wouldn't slide away. On the far wall was a row of booths, all of which were partially concealed in the bar's dim lighting.

Taggart's contact wasn't immediately identifiable among the customers, but one of the patrons in particular made an extra effort to ignore the newcomer's presence. While most of the barflies at least raised their eyes to view Michael, the hulking individual in the corner had his gaze fixed on the newspaper in front of him, his eyes not moving an iota.

Taggart stood several paces from the man's booth, looking down at him and hoping that his instincts served him well. Until recently, they had - without fail.

"Mother died today," Michael said.

The stranger sighed and folded his newspaper, seeming reluctant to respond. "Or maybe yesterday. I can't be sure." He folded his hands over the table and gestured for Taggart to sit opposite him. The man had a thick Russian accent, but it was clear by his enunciation and grammar that he had no trouble speaking English (even less so than some native speakers, in fact).

"What do you have for me?" Taggart asked, throwing a glance behind him in case anyone was eavesdropping. No one seemed to be.

The contact opened his newspaper and withdrew a manila envelope from it. He pushed it across the table and Taggart slid it into his bag. The exchange was smooth and natural, the mark of two professionals. "A man who goes by the name of Daniil Kudrin. He's been operating in the area for a few months now. He gets special attention because he's shown all of the major symptoms of the Affliction." He began ticking them off on his fingers. "Unprovoked irritability and aggression, a generally restless and volatile nature, and brief periods of physically violent behavior… But from what I've been told of your work, you already know far too well about those."

"Far too well," Taggart agreed, still guarded toward David. He had never been quick to warm up to people, but this instance was proving to be an exception. This man gave him an innate, pleasant feeling – much like how some waiters and waitresses seem to be more personable and relatable than others and would tend to earn better tips from customers. More than anything else, David seemed to be personable and warm. Taggart valued that all the more since those qualities had become more and more scarce.

"Fair enough. We want to keep Interpol's presence in Russia as low profile as we possibly can, with their government being as… unpredictable as it is. Having agents poking around in their country isn't exactly copacetic." Taggart nodded and felt his lips twitch with the beginnings of a smile. His opinion of David continued to be affirmed. "Anyway, I'm just a pair of eyes for the Sentinels, and I have zero field experience, so that's where you come in. I advise that you tail the man for a while and see if you can pinpoint the source of his Affliction, if he even has it at all. Most of the higher-ups would write this off as being a coincidence, but somehow I know better. Just a gut feeling. Something's off with this guy.

"You'll find a photo of him and his last registered address in the folder. Also, you should probably order a drink before you leave. People around here tend to remember faces better if they feel like they get shortchanged."

With that, David returned to his paper, looking just as

nonchalant and disinterested as before. Taggart rose to his feet, shouldered his pack, and reached for his wallet. After asking for "whatever's on tap" and receiving a warm beer in a filthy mug in return, he paid and turned his attention from the surly bartender to the depths of his drink. It was an easy thing to become lost in, and it wasn't long before he was absorbed in thought.

This sensation had no linear pattern, no cohesive structure, but it for the most part revolved around a sense of overwhelming fatigue. The cause of this was a mystery that even Taggart didn't have the time or inclination to solve. In any case, it was a disturbing change from his usual energetic nature. Because of this, Taggart's eyes never really refocused as he put his hands into his coat pockets for warmth and pushed the door of the bar open with his shoulder.

Taggart let the wind bite at his face, not minding. It kept him awake; kept him alive in a way. Just to feel the impact of nature against his body made Michael feel more connected to the world around him.

Walking aimlessly through the streets, he passed more Russian citizens, none of whom paid him a second glance. The aftertaste of the beer stayed with him, and its repulsive state paralleled that of the Moscow roadways. Even though the area had become more livable over time, these improvements were mostly superficial. It was in one of these areas that Taggart found a hotel, the condition of which was not much better than that of the bar. As for the interior – he could only hope.

Excerpt from "Darkest Secrets of Interpol Revealed" (Published 2054)

The Sentinels were a by-product of the rising number of catastrophic incidents involving individuals suffering from the once-prevalent disease known as the Affliction. Not officially acknowledged by their governing body, very little has been disclosed regarding this group of under a dozen individuals. Even the year in which the task force was founded remains unclear, but reliable estimates place it shortly after the Second Gulf War.

Sentinels were tasked with the pacification or elimination of Afflicted people who posed a threat to any citizen under the umbrella of Interpol's protection. This was a behemoth task for such a small group, so, understandably, many incidents persisted unchecked.

The most notable member of this organization was a man referred to as 'Michael Taggart,' who excelled at his craft until events of a tragic nature…

Moscow, Russia: Nikolskaya Street – 12 February 2016, 7:27 A.M.

Cold. Feverish. Taggart should have felt both of these sensations from standing in the unrelenting Moscow snow, but he was preoccupied with the sight in front of him. Ahead stood a modest hole-in-the-wall hotel that could have been described as anything but imposing. This was exactly the image that Michael himself intended to embody, so he stepped inside.

The interior complemented this aesthetic perfectly – it was on the more run-down side, but the room possessed a quality of being meticulously looked after despite its downscale furnishings. Taggart let his eyes wander across the space, noticing how an employee was dusting a chair that appeared to have no dust on it whatsoever; all of the papers on the front desk were stacked so that the top-left of each one rested in the exact same place. Even the uniforms of the staff contained no wrinkles or blemishes to speak of. Professionalism to its highest extreme – Taggart welcomed the sight. A sign even hung below the front desk, and he was able to discern part of its message. It came across as a polite yet stern request that a quiet, respectful atmosphere be maintained at all times.

He made his way to the desk, the dusting employee looking up and nodding respectfully as he passed. Michael returned this and shifted his focus toward the aging man standing behind the reception desk. He regarded his guest with an open smile, seeming to radiate hospitality. The man even stepped around the desk to shake Taggart's hand, doing so vigorously and speaking with a gravelly voice and a welcoming manner.

"Welcome! It is good to see a man who displays his dignity and class simply through his entrance to a humble establishment such as mine!"

Michael was taken aback. The thought crossed his mind that this may be the carbon-copy, standard greeting for all hotel guests, but he wouldn't have minded even if it had been.

"Thank you," Taggart managed in his best Russian, "it is good to meet someone with your excellent manners."

"I endeavor to convey myself as such," the man said, inclining his head toward Taggart. "I mean no disrespect by this, but by your speech I am able to discern that you are a foreigner. Am I correct?"

"Yes; I spent most of my childhood in Ontario, Canada. The climate there seems to be comparable to yours, and I tend to enjoy the cold."

English-speakers were regarded with a great deal of suspicion, and if he had disclosed his American nationality, every eye would remain on him during his entire residence in the country. Even tourists had taken to identifying themselves as non-Americans to avoid a bevy of suspicious and judgmental stares, and Taggart employed this tactic for the exact same purpose. Even his identifying paperwork listed him as a Canadian, and he had no issue with abandoning the eagle for the moose and beaver.

The man laughed in a manner that was either genuine or simply a well-rehearsed imitation. "You've come to the right place! Tell me, how long do you intend to room here in Moscow?"

Taggart hesitated, choosing his words carefully. "Longer than a day and shorter than a lifetime. That's all I know at the moment, at least."

Another jovial laugh. "Fair enough, friend! I'm sure that you'll find the rates here quite reasonable. I have a room for one that you should find suitable..."

Excerpt from the Memorial Service Bulletin of Catherine Gwyn Taggart

Saint Peter's Lutheran Church – Pottstown, Pennsylvania
In loving memory of Catherine "Cathy" Gwyn Taggart
May 16, 1982 – October 7, 2002

Organ Prelude

Remembrance of Baptism (LBW p. 206)

Hymn: "Great is Thy Faithfulness" (LSB 809)

Eulogy: Delivered by her widower, Michael Taggart

Readings

Philippians 4:8-9

Isaiah 41:9-12

Gospel Lesson

Matthew 12:18-21

Sermon

Choir Anthem: "A Mighty Fortress Is Our God"

Apostles' Creed (LBW p.209)

Hymn: "Abide With Me" (LBW p.272)

Postlude

Nikolskaya Street: Moscow, Russia - February 12, 2016

After a brief discussion regarding housing arrangements for Taggart, the landlord, who identified himself as Nikolay Pavlovich, led him up several flights of stairs and into a room that was roughly the size of a walk-in closet. A door adorned either wall, presumably leading to the kitchen and bedroom. It was furnished much in the same way as the lobby (that is, sparse and archaic in nature), but its confining space had a distinctly cozy feeling associated with it, and Michael was perfectly satisfied.

After shaking hands with Nikolay, he was left to his own devices, immediately opting to shut the door and gaze out of the living area's only window. Through the flurry of snow that was drifting past, Taggart could see a vague outline of Red Square and St. Basil's Cathedral, two landmarks where his target had been sighted on a regular basis.

He fell into the chair that adorned the corner of the room and threw his head back. The mission dossier remained on the table beside him; it could wait. In a way, Taggart was steeling himself for the weeks to come. It was doubtful that he would get very many moments of peace such as this one. In a manner that had become a ritual of sorts, Taggart was preparing to face the reality that his thoughts and emotions would need to be suppressed. They were irrelevant. Everything was, aside from his actions and their consequences. It had been difficult for him to come to terms with this reality, and, though he never fully agreed with the premise, Michael knew that the people controlling his actions had humanity's best interests in mind. He hoped so, at the very least.

When he had encountered these emotions in the past, Taggart had conditioned himself to suppress them. This had been changing gradually over time, and this change brought along with it the sickening reality that the past few decades of his life had been misused and dictated entirely by others. Taggart shelved this thought in his mind for the moment, promising himself that he would return to it later. The notion remained, however, that this procrastination would end like most others – left to the wayside until absolutely necessary. He hoped that it wouldn't be too late.

The United States and Russia had shared an interesting relationship following the Cold War, to say the least. It was as if they were two friends passing by each other on a sidewalk, sharing a friendly nod and a wave – except the nod would be forced and insincere, and the waves could have just as easily have been guns pointed in each other's direction.

It was because of this that Taggart kept his nationality and his business to himself. It was two days since he had checked in, and he had already taken to walking the streets of Moscow as an aimless mind-clearing method.

Despite the need to maintain anonymity, Michael was able to observe the city's landscape and culture from within. It was soon apparent that Russia differed greatly from Western society in terms of what was considered venerable. Nikolskaya Street, where Taggart had been staying, was in the older portion of Moscow. Rather than having "old" colonial buildings from the eighteenth century, this area had architecture which had been around for many more centuries. Buildings whose walls had witnessed the rise and fall of numerous Czars, fires to ward off the forces of Napoleon, and eventually survived dozens of bombings.

Michael felt small and isolated when faced with the history around him. So much history had taken place there, history which had helped to shape the world as he knew it. This sensation was paired with one which made him shiver. It wasn't from the cold, rather, it was the shiver that one gets when presented with the knowledge that they can be a part of something monumental.

Even if it would lead to heroism, success, and a world where everyone knew his name, Taggart knew that he would never want that on his shoulders. He had never viewed himself as a person who could handle enacting so much change or impacting so many people. This didn't prevent him from coming to one simple realization, however - those who had changed the world in the past had all possessed the same mindset. They didn't set out with the intent of writing history with their own hands. Rather, they had situations forced upon them and adapted as well as they could. If he was in the same situation, Taggart hoped that he could follow their example.

His observations of the area were broken up by occasional visits to the registered address of the suspect, Daniil. A complete stakeout would have almost certainly alerted the quarry if he was observant at all, so Taggart resorted to riding on a bus with a route which passed the residence. This gave him ample time to reconnoiter the area while remaining inconspicuous, and, invisible to the other pedestrians walking by.

It was after one such ride with typical, fruitless results that Michael happened upon someone who caught his eye. She wasn't necessarily odd or bizarre, but she seemed to be inexplicably out of place.

Standing on a street corner adjacent from his apartment, he could see a middle-aged woman who had dark red hair and was clad in a heavy coat staring at him. Her gaze shifted from him to a nearby storefront each time he looked back. He lit a cigarette and pretended not to notice. After all, he himself must have looked out of place.

Michael was ready to disregard this as paranoia, but,

instinctively, something about this woman caught his attention. Where people had been absent or refused to step in, his instincts had remained. To Taggart, betraying them would be akin to treason.

Keeping his eyes fixed straight ahead, Taggart crossed the street and pretended to be enamored by a newspaper in a receptacle by the side of the road. In truth, he understood only bits and pieces of the text, but the woman in the coat didn't need to know that. In his peripheral vision, he could see that she was still standing in the same place, seeming to have no particular place to go. She was the only stagnant figure among dozens of bustling figures. It was as if she wanted specifically to draw attention to herself, and this concerned Taggart quite a bit.

Careful not to jostle his way past anyone and attract angry glances, Taggart moved closer to his quarry, not knowing what he would do or say if he made it all the way to her position. This was taken out of his hands, however, when the woman set off in the opposite direction at a swift pace. Taggart had to jog to keep up, his mind now fully alert. She repeatedly patted her thigh, as if ensuring that it was still there.

She's armed.

The weight of his pistol in his own coat was reassuring. He was preparing to defend himself, and it was a familiar yet intense feeling. His opponent was a woman who was half his size, but neither of these facts gave him cause to underestimate her. It was a distinct possibility that she could hold her own if necessary.

The familiar sensation of conscious thought slipping

away was very much present with him, and he welcomed the release from the rest of the world. His focus narrowed. It was only he and the suspect. The rest of the world was empty.

She was sprinting now, and Taggart followed suit. The others on the street gave them both confused glances as they passed, some looking concerned. Each step was deliberate and calculated from Taggart, and, because of this, the crowd did little to slow him down. The woman noticed him closing in and darted across the street. Michael squeezed between two parked cars and followed, thankful that there was no traffic in the way.

The red-haired woman threw a glance over her shoulder, but it wasn't one of fear or concern – in fact, she seemed to carry a triumphant expression. A confused Taggart shouted, "Wait a moment!" in Russian, but she didn't seem to hear. She was still running full-tilt away from him, now rounding a corner into the narrow gap between two buildings.

Ready to draw his pistol, Taggart followed. His heart was pounding, but he felt calm – almost unnaturally so. The sounds of the city had been replaced by a rush of wind, and the only thought in his mind was that he needed to catch up with this stranger. He didn't have the faintest idea of why he was doing this, but his mind would allow for nothing else.

Taggart rounded the corner to find the woman standing quite still, her back turned to him. Trying to account for every possibility and variable, Michael reached out his arm to tap her on the shoulder, ready to catch her arm should she try to grab at his.

Even as his hand was almost cupping her shoulder, she still hadn't moved. It was almost as if she had been in shock, and Taggart was mystified. It was then that he felt a wind on the back of his neck that wasn't wind at all. It was warm.

Taggart tried to spin around and got halfway there. A blow collided with his head, sending him to his knees in pure agony. Another blow sent his mind reeling, and yet another left him almost unconscious. It took all of his strength to turn around in an attempt to catch a glimpse of his attacker, but he only caught a sidelong glance at a jagged piece of metal hurtling toward his gut. Fear joined Taggart's pain. He couldn't breathe, and trying to do so only made his condition worse. He lowered his head and writhed on the pavement. Unconsciousness was close, and it seemed ever so merciful.

The last thing that he saw before he blacked out was the feet of the woman, running into the distance.

Psychological Analysis of Michael Faust Taggart (Transcribed, incl. Doctor's Notes in parenthesis), Questioned by Dr. Gerald Moran

Moran: *Hello, Mr. Taggart. I am Dr. Moran, and I've been asked to speak with you on behalf of Interpol.*

Taggart: *Hey, Doc.*

Moran: *I'm about to show you a series of cards with specific ink blots on them, the 'Rorschach Test.' I take it that you're familiar.*

(Subject appears agitated at this point, seems impatient with level of conversation. Perceived condescension?)

Taggart: *We might as well, while we're here.*

Moran: *Precisely. Now, here's the first card. Please take your time and tell me what you see.*

(Subject approaches first figure without hesitation)

Taggart: *A pair of boots. Men's. Or just large ones. Stepping on something.*

(This card is often used to gauge the subject's view of authority. Owing to Mr. Taggart's militaristic background, this response is normal and expected. The only concerning factor is his assertion that the boots are stepping on something. This could very well symbolize his lack of input in his work and an overbearing presence from his superiors. This is merely conjecture; however, sources closer to the Sentinels will be able to verify this on their own time.)

Moran: *Excellent. Moving on, what do you see in* this *card?*

(Again, subject responds immediately)

Taggart: *Two people… they seem to be fighting hand-to-hand. It looks like blood from both of them is there, too. They're evenly matched, it looks like.'*

(In the case of the second ink blot, many have theorized that the subject's attitude toward violence can be inferred based on how they respond. In this case, Mr. Taggart has shown much in few words. He made a quite in-depth description of such a simple image, showing his analytical view of conflict. Commonly, subjects have given one of two responses:

> **a.** *A statement of peace or reconciliation "Two people with hands clasped"*

> **b.** *A brief statement regarding aggression (i.e., "People fighting")*

Mr. Taggart differs from scenario 'b,' in that he made an in-depth description of the situation ('fighting hand to hand' over simply 'fighting,' and so on), and deemed the combatants "evenly matched." This shows his emphasis on violence (because he neglected scenario 'a' and noted the red splotches on the page resembled blood), but a tendency toward thought and planning because of his assessment of the situation.

Moran: *Interesting. Here's another; this will be the last one for the moment. What do you see?*

(Subject gazed at this final card for over a minute, an abnormally long time even for the most indecisive of subjects. His eyes remained focused throughout, as if he was in deep contemplation. Upon answering, Mr. Taggart seemed to remain unsure.)

Taggart: *It's... another set of two people.*

(Subject hesitates)

Moran: *Go on, Mr. Taggart. When you're ready.*

Taggart: *I'm not exactly sure. It looks like they're carrying something. Bags, maybe. Like they're about to part ways. And the red splotch in the middle... That could be a heart being split in two.*

Moran: *Thank you for your patience, Mr. Taggart. Your answers have been quite informative. You are free to leave whenever you'd like.*

(The subject's response to this final card is intriguing, mostly due to his reluctance to make any comment. In most cases, it is immediately identified that there are two human forms present on the card. A delay in coming to this conclusion might indicate a similarly tentative approach toward social interactions. Again, this is merely conjecture. The unreliability of the Rorschach methodology is well-documented, but it has been known to carry some degree of merit in extreme cases such as that of Mr. Michael Taggart.

He has exhibited signs of much suppressed anger, but I am forced to accept the reality that most, if not all, human beings also retain this trait.

While Taggart shows no behavior warranting immediate concern, it must also be stated that he carries with him a series of mental difficulties which must not be ignored. Through this test and others conducted on Mr. Taggart, it can be safely determined that the man possesses the beginnings of acute psychosis. While sporadic in nature, the behavior which he has exhibited includes symptoms of depression alongside anxiety, general withdrawal, and a distinct lack of concentration. Again, there is no immediate cause for concern or drastic action, but his mental state should be closely monitored for worsening symptoms over the coming months. No medication advised at this time. I can only hope that this will not prove to be a dangerous oversight in the future.

Moscow, Russia - Alleyway off of Nikolskaya Street
February 14, 2016

Pain. Pain and confusion. This is all that Taggart's brain would register.

Beside him lay a bloodied pipe of some sort. A note was attached to it by a rubber band; Taggart struggled to a sitting position to read it. Scrawled in red pen was 'Держитесь подальше от Даниила.' He was still disoriented, but after a few minutes of confused mumbling, he was able to make out the phrase 'Stay away from Daniil.'

His eyes rolled back in his head, and he slumped against the wall. Someone obviously wanted to warn him off of his lead, and, because of this, Taggart knew that he was on the right track. Rather than deterring him, the attack had prompted Michael to redouble his efforts. The pain inflicted must have been incentive for Taggart to leave well enough alone, and it was, admittedly, a convincing method. He reminded himself that pain was temporary, but this is of little solace to a person whose body has been abused with such ferocity.

The thought occurred to him that he could report the incident to the police, but Taggart immediately disregarded it. Something told him that asking for help from the country that he was spying on would be a less-than-intelligent idea.

But damn did it hurt. Bruises lined his side, some of them bleeding, all of them searing in pain. No bystanders had happened upon his body to wonder at what had happened, and Taggart was grateful for this. He was content to remain a passed-out bum in their eyes, just as long as they didn't draw unwanted attention to him.

For a man who had performed the action countless times, it took Taggart quite a while to rise to his feet. Each muscle in his body ached, and it was a wonder that he didn't collapse after each step. He looked up at the sky and noticed that it had become quite a bit darker; he had been out for quite some time. The afternoon hadn't yet faded into evening before he was attacked, so he could only assume that he had been lying in that alleyways for at least four hours.

Need to pay more attention, he thought with more than a little bitterness. What's happening to me? This never would have happened before. Don't let it start now.

As he stumbled back onto the sidewalk, Taggart recalled the sensation that had overcome him as of late. It was something akin to an adrenaline rush, or it at least supplemented one. While it did heighten his awareness, it also replaced any conscious reasoning in his mind, and this scared Taggart more than any back-alley threat.

Feeling even more sickened with himself, Michael pushed this thought out of his mind, knowing that it was important but putting it to the wayside for the moment.

For the moment, Taggart thought. Sure.

Suspicious and confused glances were the appropriate reaction to a bloodied man walking down a sidewalk, but they bothered Taggart nonetheless. Each person's eyes seemed to be filled with contempt, and Michael couldn't avoid the notion that he was becoming steadily more paranoid. For the average person, this would have been a non-issue, but for Taggart, it was downright alarming. Even so, paranoia was on some level necessary, given the events of the past few hours.

Regardless, he kept a swift pace back to his apartment, where he found the lobby to be mercifully empty. The journey upstairs was a blur, and, before he knew what had happened, Taggart stumbled into his room and collapsed onto the floor, missing his bed by inches.

For three days, the door of Taggart's room remained shut. The only noises that could be heard from the other side were footsteps, steadily pacing in the earliest hours of the morning. This was broken up by incoherent phrases, muttered too quietly for anyone else to hear. Self-rehabilitation was a necessary evil for Michael, and it was taking its toll. The first thing that a hospital would have done if he had visited would be throwing questions at him, none of which he could answer. Instead, he opted to let his injuries run their course. Like any sick person, he was grateful for the respite but uncomfortable and restless all the same.

Michael would have much preferred a recovery period in which he could continue on with his life. One where he could grit his teeth and work through the pain. He had never been a "macho man" who insisted on passing off his injuries as minor inconveniences. All the same, he couldn't stand being confined to such a small space. It was like a prison for him, one which he would only be released from when he felt able to function again.

Watching the world move on without him was an unsettling feeling, to say the least. It was as if he was a long-time actor who had recently retired and was now confined to a seat in the audience. In a way, not having to exert himself was a blessing, but he could not stop convincing himself that he should be out on the stage. From where he was, as a spectator, Taggart had no control over how successful things went. He didn't enjoy this detached view very much, and it took all of his patience to wait until he was once more under control.

As they usually did when Taggart was left alone, his thoughts strayed to his wife. She had represented to him the vivaciousness that life could bring. Ever since she had passed away, that optimism had become much harder to come by. This wasn't from feelings of sadness or despair, rather, Michael only felt apathy. When emotions did manage to surface, they were rarely positive ones.

Something which made him despise himself even further was the fact that he didn't feel sadness after she had died. They had shared a loving relationship and a close bond, but when it ended, it came to a sudden, harsh stop. Taggart knew that he had begun to isolate himself afterward, and the current circumstance brought back feelings of far too many consecutive days spent indoors. The guilt which had plagued him for so long reared its ugly head in Moscow. Too tired to be frustrated with this, Taggart welcomed the feeling back as an old, nagging acquaintance.

Throughout everything, he had left the wedding band on his finger. It held some sentimental value, but Michael kept it mostly out of routine. The outside of the ring had become tarnished with age and lack of cleaning, but the inner portion remained gleaming. This was probably due to his nervous habit of taking it on and off, which he had been doing for quite some time.

Sighing at the futility of these thoughts, Taggart placed the ring with the rest of his belongings with the intent of keeping it out of sight and out of mind. Even after doing this, however, he found himself returning to it and placing it back on his fourth finger. Lying blatantly to himself, he resolved to discard of the ring soon and leave the past alone for good.

During this time in solitude, Taggart slept for a grand total of fifteen minutes. The battle being waged in his head combined with the discomfort from his injuries made it exceedingly difficult to fall asleep, as if he was putting the wrong key into a lock. No matter how long he kept his eyes closed, his brain refused to shut down.

This period would have gone on for quite some time if it wasn't for an envelope which was slid underneath Taggart's door on the morning of the third day. He had been re-reading the mission dossier for the fifth time when he noticed movement in the corner of his eye. Without waiting to see what it was, Michael drew his pistol and rose to his feet, aiming at the door. His eyes rested on the envelope for only a moment before he cracked the door open, his pistol hidden behind it.

The hallway was empty and silent; even the messenger's retreating footsteps remained inaudible. Heart still pounding, Michael shut and chained his door before turning his attention toward the envelope on the floor. One hand still clutching his P226, Taggart tore the envelope open and found a note inside, along with a small brass key. Written in English was a carefully penned note:

Dearest,

I loved our date the other night, and I can hardly wait to see you again! I think our relationship will be a wonderful one for us both. What do you say we go to the theatre? There's a show playing in a lovely old place near Teatralnyy Street. See you there tonight at 9? The play is supposed to be a wonderful one, even if it is typical fare. I would have invited your new friend, but... Oh, we can talk about that later, sweetie. He's no fun anyways. He might have even skipped town by now! Fair enough for us, though.

Come see me in my private box – you know the one. The same number as the number of beers you drank on the night we met, you old dog. To think we met in a bar! I look forward to talking about that night again, and I count the minutes until I can see you! Be there soon; our time is so short!

--Your darling love

Taggart shook his head in disbelief. The message was so subtle, so direct, and yet it would mean nothing to anyone but him and its sender. It was clear to him that David had sent this, knowing that it would be subject to prying eyes. Michael scanned the note for abnormalities in cadence or tone, and he found several. One coincidence in particular seemed too forced to be accidental, and this is what he focused on. The words 'fare' and 'fair' were unnecessary to the rest of the letter, and, where an outsider may have written this off as being a lack of cohesiveness on the writer's part, Taggart knew better.

Between the homophones was a phrase regarding his "new friend," who could only have been in reference to Daniil. It made more sense, after all, that he might have skipped town, as Michael had seen no trace of him.

The rest of the letter was far less ambiguous, and it provided far more to go on. It seemed to Taggart that he was being called to another meeting, but it was the last sentence of the letter that concerned him.

Be there soon; our time is so short!

This added a sense of urgency to the note, and in Michael's experience, urgency was based on desperation, and desperation was never ideal.

The theater that David had mentioned was only a few blocks from the bar in which their first meeting had taken place, leaving him plenty of time before the meeting with his "darling love."

Taggart moved to the bathroom and splashed the sink's grimy water on his face, wondering how long it had been since a plumber had inspected the place. Once he had packed his things and ensured that everything was accounted for, Michael shouldered his bag and left his room. Sleep would come later, and he could wait.

Opinion Piece from The New York Times: October 23, 2017, Written by Stan Mitchell

This supposed illness known as "The Affliction" has been a topic of conversation and debate for quite some time, more so than necessary. And yes, I do realize that I am contributing to this amount of press, but only as a means to hopefully end it.

One of the greatest and most erroneous misconceptions about the "disease" is a quite simple one – the general public is actually under the impression that it exists. The number of dissenters has grown over the past few years, and that is a welcome shift. This "Affliction" is nothing more than the collective imagination of paranoid sensationalists. They seek a scapegoat for irrational people, blaming it on a chemical imbalance rather than the truth: simple human nature. So many armchair psychiatrists have stated that it carries validity, but it is the invention of government institutions, solely to incite terror within...

Moscow, Russia: Teatralnyy Street; February 19, 2016

An ornate, yellowed building stood in front of Taggart that evening, looking more like a government building than a theatre. In front of it was a statue of an old man in an overcoat, staring down at him in a manner which could have been described as anything but welcoming.

Nevertheless, Taggart strode past the figure and into the building. It took quite some time for his eyes to become accustomed to the dim interior, but when they were, he was met with display cases housing costume-clad mannequins.

They were laid out underneath a chandelier that would have been at home in the Palace of Versailles. A ticket-taker stood at the end of this foyer, looking as ornamental as his surroundings. His expression remained blank as he waved Taggart by, indicating a hallway which was painted a deep blue. The latter gave an appreciative nod and followed this corridor, feeling as if he was somehow underwater.

The uneven decoration continued as he passed other patrons on his way to David's box. The walls turned from blue to crimson, and it was becoming more and more apparent that this theatre had been the site of many renovations over the years. It seemed to be just as much of a museum as it was a theatre; portraits of people who must have acted there in the past lined each wall, and more costumes and props were on display throughout.

Up a short flight of stairs to his right was a door emblazoned with a bronze 4, and Taggart continued down the hallway until he reached box 1. He knocked once and entered when a familiar voice beyond beckoned him to do so.

"Glad you could make it," David said as Taggart entered the booth. "The lights are about to go down, so we'll have to keep our voices low. Probably better that way."

The box itself was overlooking the right wing of the stage from a great height, complete with curtains which could be drawn in front of them. Michael took a seat beside David in a cushioned chair which gave a foreboding creak when he put his weight on it.

Moments later, the auditorium's main lights went out, leaving only a spotlight on the center of the stage. Taggart looked over at David as if to begin speaking, but the latter seemed to be transfixed by the play itself for the moment. It was to be a production of Pisemsky's A Bitter Fate, which was exactly what Michael wished to avoid, if at all possible.

It was only after a half hour that David turned his attention away from the play and toward Taggart. "I'm sure you know by now, but your contact has gone missing. Even the address which I provided you with was a front." Taggart opened his mouth, but David silenced him by holding up his hand. "There is good news. Some of our eyes in the city have spotted a man following the same pattern as your suspect. He looks completely different, everything from his hair to his height. What tipped us off was the fact that his mannerisms remain completely the same. He might have the greatest appearance-altering equipment in the world, but lucky for us, he's not the most intelligent. That's why we need to find out who he's with. I doubt that we'll find a much better way into the affairs of who else is running around with the Affliction in Moscow."

His gaze still fixed on the stage, Taggart said, "He's still not worth underestimating, though. No one is." He recounted his experience with the red-haired woman and the warning note.

"No shit?" David breathed. "Well, nobody would judge you if you wanted to pass this mission off to somebody else, but something tells me that you wouldn't dream of it."

Taggart shook his head.

"Anyways, completely disregard the photo of Daniil that I gave you before. I have a new one, but it's grainy and underexposed. We're probably better off with the updated description that our cells in the area have compiled."

"You mentioned that his height was different. How so?" Michael asked.

"It's a very long and painful process. We had last seen the man quite some time ago, and in the meantime, he must have undergone a surgery in which a doctor breaks open their patient's legs and places a rod in place of the bone tissue. From there, the leg is stretched at the pace of one millimeter per day. From our estimations, the man 'grew' from five feet ten inches to six feet even. The process of physical therapy might not be over, so you may be able to identify him by his uneven stride."

Taggart nodded, feeling his confusion mixing with disgust. He had been familiar with facial reconstruction and things of that nature, but tearing apart a body to grow back more of it was something else entirely.

"Something tells me that this won't slow him down. Do you know where I might find him?"

David's eyes were back on the actors, but they showed some level of concern. "Yes. For the most part, he travels alone. This is very good news for you, since this will make him far easier to track. Our agents have sighted him on the southeast side of Red Square every Tuesday at noon. He stands at the bus stop but never boards when it comes by. Apparently, the man just stares at it and waves the driver on to let him know that he won't be coming on. From there, he makes a long, roundabout walk through the city. He's quite good at losing anyone tailing him; we have no idea where he goes after this. That's where you come in.

"We need you to find out where he's going, who he talks to, where he eats, where he sleeps, how long he brushes his teeth every night, boxers or briefs; whatever you can find out."

"I'll be all over him like a cheap ushanka," Taggart said, finding himself smiling for the first time in a long while as David did the same. He hadn't given it much thought, but Michael was of the opinion that human beings were designed to be around other like-minded human beings. This was a necessity for basic function, at least for him. In his line of work, not much value was placed on this, and perhaps this was one of the roots of his emotional turmoil.

Hoping their voices would be inaudible from their place on the balcony, Taggart said,

"Tell me something, David. You've had to use your weapon on assignments like this, right?"

David, who had been staring down at the performance below, turned to face Taggart with a weary expression. This was in stark contrast to his usual light manner. "I try to avoid it when I can, but yes. I have."

Taggart nodded, feeling the same way. "How do you justify it with yourself? I mean... Well, I'm not really sure what I mean now that I'm saying it. It's not that I want to criticize you for doing it, because that would make me the biggest hypocrite. It's just..."

David's expression reverted to one of conviction. His features became more intense as he said, "I know that I must think like you, darling, because I know exactly what you're trying to say. Even with just a few fragmented thoughts, I know. This is something that I've fought with since I started doing fieldwork. I think all people like us wrestle with this. That may be surprising, but something tells me that these thoughts have been kept to yourself as well." He looked at Taggart expectantly, and the latter nodded. "I thought so. What you need to understand about killing people is that it can't be a psychological thing. If it is, it'll tear you apart. You aren't a religious man, are you, Taggart?"

"I've always found it hard to believe in any religion, really. I mean, just look at Jerusalem. Christianity, Judaism, Islam... the three major religions come from there, and it's one of the most violent places in the world. One without much regard for humanity at all. To answer your question, though, I never have been very devout in anything. My wife was, and I suppose that influenced me to some extent. Beyond that, not really."

David nodded, focusing once more on the stage as he spoke. "This takes away the biggest obstacle - objection to it from a fundamental, moral point of view. The other main thing that might leave you ill at ease is wondering how your life could possibly be worth more than the person's at the other end of your gun.

"I mean, this needs to be taken on a case-by-case basis, but it's usually pretty easy to judge the repercussions of putting a bullet in someone. The way I see it, killing someone who has ill intentions for others - it disproves pacifism." Taggart raised his eyebrows, interested.

"This might seem like an odd thing to say, and I can't really argue with that," David said. "It's just that people who call themselves pacifists call for the end of war, the end of violence itself. The fact is, violence has been around since Cain beat the tar out of Abel. I'm not religious either, but that seems like a good starting point. It's gone on constantly since that point, and it hasn't slowed down since. People have only made it faster and more efficient. Hm. We could have refined and mass-produced so many things for humanity, and we've put that into making instruments of war.

"I digress. The point that I was trying to make is that pacifists want people to not be killed. Well, by taking away people's ability to protect others is doing the exact opposite. Dismantling armies and agents like us might seem like a good idea - to someone who has no idea what they're talking about. Killing one or a dozen people in the defense of millions… That's what pacifism should be. If world peace doesn't happen tomorrow, which it won't, violence is necessary to prevent genocide. We are necessary to prevent genocide.

"In a really roundabout answer to your question, I justify killing folks because I fear the alternative. I fear people dying because I failed to act. It doesn't make it any easier when I have to finish someone off. Not even a little bit, but it just makes sense to me. There's less weight on my conscience when I remember that I'm doing this for a reason. If it got the point where I enjoyed doing it… that's when problems would start to come up."

Taggart, who had been staring intently at him, pondered these words for a moment before speaking. "I see what you mean. It's just…" He sighed. "Like you said, it doesn't make it any easier when you're actually doing it. Part of me envies the people who can do it without emotion, without remorse. Hell, I don't know if those people even exist outside of my mind. And what you mentioned about enjoying it bothers me more than I'd like.

"Don't get me wrong, I'm not homicidal, and I definitely don't relish the opportunity to kill people. When I'm hunting them down, though, it's like my body is loving the sensation. I feel sort of... driven. It's more than that, but I go through times where I don't think I'm in control. It hasn't ended with me doing something I regret, at least. Not yet. Losing control of my senses like that, though... It makes me worried that something in my nature has to have that rush that comes with fighting someone else. I think it might be warping me into someone else, and I have no control over it."

Where many would have been taken aback and left speechless by Taggart's sentiments, David responded without a moment's hesitation. "I wouldn't worry about it that much. Not great advice on its own, I know. But morality is something that everyone has control over, at least for themselves. If what you're talking about isn't something you can prevent or handle, then there's no reason to feel guilt over it. That's just how I feel, but there's no sense in wearing yourself out about it."

Michael appreciated these words, trying his best to convince himself that they were correct. Even so, he would not be left at peace. Thoughts of an alarming and irrational nature were weighing on him still, and they showed no signs of stopping. As per usual, however, Taggart shoved the thought out of his mind and returned to pertinent matters. David, who seemed not to have noticed the silence, smiled down at the performers.

The pair watched the play progress, but Taggart couldn't pull himself to focus on the production. His thoughts were elsewhere, and it was only when the intermission came that he snapped out of his reverie.

"They're really on point tonight aren't they?" David commented.

Michael shook himself out of a daze. "Pardon?"

"The cast! I've seen the same actors in different plays before, but everything seems to be running so smoothly tonight. Even the set changes and soundtrack cues... You know, that really is art. People tend to take that for granted. The stagecraft and technology side of theatre, that is. It truly is art, isn't it?"

Taggart nodded vaguely, caught between deep pondering and persistent exhaustion. David stood up and stretched, watching the crowd below mill about. His focus continued to return to Michael, however, and he asked, "What do you think of art?"

"In what sense?" Taggart could tell that his friend was trying to re-engage him in the world outside of his own mind, and he decided that he was willing to play along.

"Well... What do you think art is? As far as I know, no one really agrees on a definition for it. In fact, I must have heard a hundred different answers to this."

There was a long pause as Michael collected his thoughts. "I think you're asking me to define something undefinable, but I'll give it a shot. Heck, I've tried to do harder things in my life. First of all, I think you're right.

Art is different for everyone. I've put a lot of thought into this, mostly because this line of work gives me a lot of time with only myself for company.

"Regardless, I think that art is something that gives feeling to someone. I know that's vague, but it's the only way I can think of to describe it. I don't think that dance is art, even though a lot of people do. That's the great thing about it — that's okay. Everyone's opinion and definition of art is different, and, no matter how similar two people's view of it might be, no one's art is exactly the same.

"People say that it's something that makes you think or feel a certain way, but couldn't something be art if it doesn't make you think? If it doesn't make you feel? Who's to say that that isn't art, too? It's so abstract, and I really think that art is very closely connected to the idea of a soul. They're both undefinable, intangible, and essential to a person's life."

David had re-taken his seat and was now studying Taggart with his chin resting on a clenched fist. "I like the way you think. That is to say, you actually think about things in-depth. It's a pretty rare thing these days. One ting is bothering me, though."

"Hm?" Taggart said, already lapsing back into his contemplative state.

David, who was doing his best to prevent this, continued, "If art really is different for everyone, like you said, then is it always essential to someone's life? Couldn't art be so minor in their opinion that they really could do without it and be fine?"

It was over a long period of time that Taggart

considered this question. He had never claimed that his logic was airtight, but, then again, he had never thought that it would contain such a major flaw. Even though many would consider this conversation to be insignificant in the grand scheme of things, Michael felt the need to have as much clarity as he could.

When he felt satisfied with his own reasoning, Taggart said, "I guess it's fair to say that. The only thing that keeps me from agreeing completely is the fact that art can come from anything. It would be so hard to escape completely.

"I mean, one thing I think about is windy nights. As random as that might seem, I think about those nights when it's perfectly dry but feels like rain could come at any moment. Those nights when leaves are swirling around as if they were being pushed by an invisible hand. The same nights when it feels like there must be someone hiding in the bushes, ready to jump out at you with a knife or something.

"To me, even that's art. Almost a hundred percent of people would say that it's just the ramblings of a paranoid guy who has a dark mind, but those thoughts give me feeling. I have no idea what that feeling is, and that might be why I think it's art. When small, out-of-context ideas like that can have such an impact, I don't think anyone can escape art. To be honest, it's a mystery to me why anyone would want to escape it."

David looked thoroughly impressed. "Bravo! The man has a heart in him after all! You know, I have to agree with you on that. It's a different outlook than most people have, but I'm sold. How did you end up getting into government work, darling? You know, the philosophy field might not pay very well, but you might have found your calling."

Taggart gave a wan smile and a shake of his head. The performance had resumed by this point, so he continued in a lowered voice. "All of that time spent thinking? I'd probably go insane in less than a year. Nah, I'll have to pass. I spend enough time in my own mind already." He sighed. "To answer your first question, I was more or less coerced into working with Interpol. I hate looking back on that time, mostly because of how short-sighted I was. I fell for the war movies, the documentaries that made a life 'fighting for the rights of others' look so perfect.

"'Regular' people, the ones who go to work from nine to five and can sleep easily at night… They don't realize how damaging war propaganda can be. No matter how subtle or hidden it might be, it recruits people into something that no one should have to go through. Only if you take the bait and join, like I did, do you really see what it does to a person. The physical strain is one thing, but what they put your mind through… The things they've made me do and expected me to cope with… No. It just isn't normal. I was already messed up and on a dozen prescriptions when they found me, and they tossed in another dozen psychotropics for good measure.

"I've been asking myself something for a long time — why the hell am I still doing this? Then the answer comes to me: It's a drug. Just like the drugs they pump into my system. I've gotten too accustomed to the adrenaline and excitement. Yeah, I've gotten very attached to those but never really got used to the sleepless nights and self-doubt that also comes with the package."

David had averted his gaze and only turned to look at

Taggart once the speech was finished. It was clear that these were things he had never considered before in his own life. His face took on a disturbed expression, and the next time he spoke, it was as if Michael had never mentioned his motivations.

"You know, you are a strange man."

Taggart wasn't fazed by this, having considered that fact many times. He only sighed. "Yeah, I know. I've had professionals, amateurs, and everyone in between try to figure out what exactly it is that makes me so strange. I've just sort of accepted it as being true."

"Do you mind if I offer my thoughts?"

"Feel free. I'm always open to self-discovery, even if it means being more concerned about my sanity."

David gave a half-laugh and said, "I hope a fresh perspective will be useful to you. From what I can tell - now, know that I am saying this only knowing you for a short time - you feel alone. That's what the rest of my thoughts are based around, so I should probably ask you: Do you feel alone?"

"This is starting to sound like one of my appointments," Taggart said good-naturedly. However, he was much more comfortable discussing it with a man he could relate to rather than another judgmental, demeaning 'professional.'

"To answer your question, though," he continued, "I really do feel like I am. It's not a topic that I feel like going into, but once my wife left... yeah. I've never quite been around many people who make me feel included."

Surprisingly, David didn't express sympathy about Taggart's misfortune. In fact, he didn't express much emotion at all. It seemed as if the analytical side of his personality had taken over. "Fair enough. Back to the original topic, why you feel strange, I think that everyone is that way, to a degree. Everybody feels like they're strange because they all have different ideas about what is normal. Funny enough, it's pretty hard to find anyone who would think of themself as normal.

"And it seems like your loneliness could be a big factor in this. You said that you don't feel included, and I take that to mean that 'inclusion' means being among those who fit a sort of mold. People who are normal, whatever that means.

"Just remember, there are countless other people who feel the same way as you do. You're a smart man, darling, but you're wrong to feel alone."

Taggart was paying rapt attention now, and it seemed as if David's fresh perspective really did have an impact on him. "What do you mean, though? Why am I wrong?"

At this, David only laughed. "Friend, I'm sorry, but that is something I won't tell you. It's important for everyone to find that out themself, I think. And besides - what fun would it be if I just laid everything out in black and white?"

Michael was disappointed by this response, but only a little bit. "Fair enough, I guess. If nothing else, it'll give me something new to think about instead of when I'll finally get to sleep again."

"Now, that's the spirit!" his friend replied, clapping

Taggart on the shoulder. "Always be thinking about something new. Always."

"You said that I should look into philosophy, but it seems like you would be more suited to it than I would! I had no idea that you had developed all these thoughts about me so quickly. I haven't met many people who put that much thought into things."

"You'd be surprised. You really would. Most people have deep insights, and a lot of them are really worth hearing. They're especially good if they don't agree with you; a conversation where you don't change an iota is a wasted conversation, plain and simple. All it takes is some free time and a good place to talk." He raised his head for a moment, looking around the theatre. When he refocused on Taggart, he was grinning. "Well, I guess it doesn't have to be a good place, considering we've missed most of the play."

As quickly as David had adopted his grin, he dropped it without preamble and returned to a brusque, businesslike manner that caught Taggart off-guard.

"I hate to cut this short, but my paranoia is getting the better of me. Talking for too long in one place is a good way for someone else to hear sensitive information. It's time to become strangers again. Make absolutely sure that this man is unaware of you following him. It has taken us far too long to acquire this lead for us to lose it. I'm starting like you, Taggart. Even though I don't think this'll be an issue, please don't make that be a misjudgment."

Michael rose to his feet to follow David out of the box, but the latter held his shoulder down. "We'd better leave at different times in case someone's keeping an eye on either of us. If you need to speak with me directly, you'll find me back at the bar on most days. I'll contact you again through different means if I need to talk to you again, darling."

With that, he left Taggart to mull over this new information and watch the rest of the play. He was hoping that having immediate, direct orders to follow would curb his restlessness and frustration. It was a desperate hope, and he could do nothing but wait to see if it would be fulfilled. Stretching out in the chair, he tried to focus on the production to ease his mind. It was at that point that he realized just how the pleasant, warm air of the theatre was and how comfortable his chair had been. He thought faintly that he might be able to finally fall asleep that night before slumping over and doing so on the spot.

Telephone Interview With Colonel Kate Grant (Ret.) about the life of Michael Taggart: Taken From *ON PATROL* Magazine (Summer 2017 Ed.)

Q. Thank you for taking the time to answer our call, Colonel. We are all mourning the loss of Spc. Taggart, but it must be all the more difficult for someone who knew him as well as you did, on such a personal level.

A. I appreciate the sentiment, but I didn't know Taggart on a personal level.

Q. But... you were his handler in the field and worked with him on numerous occasions. Surely you must have had some sort of personal connection.

A. I worked with the man, but I didn't really know him. I knew his work, and I knew it was damn good. Some might say that it wasn't good enough, but sometimes… sometimes the best are put in situations that nobody should be made to deal with. I blame the leadership, and that happens to be me.

Q. Thank you for speaking so candidly with us, Colonel. Our readers are interested to know more about Michael Taggart himself. If you caught any glimpse of his true nature and would be comfortable sharing it, we would be very appreciative.

A. (lengthy pause)

Q. Colonel? Are you still there?

A. Yes. I… The thing that your readers, and everyone, needs to understand about Taggart is that he tried to be everything he could for everyone he could. This came at the expense of him being able to take care of himself. Sure, he remained in excellent physical shape in order to do what he did, but… But that was only for the sake of being a means to an end. He even refused to take leave, things like that. He was open to speaking with our psychologists, but if you read their reports, they became even more confused about his nature than when they had started with him.

Q. Fascinating. Do you —

A. Just a moment. I have one thing. One thing to say.

Q. Of course.

A. He tried to hide this fact from everyone for the longest time, and I think on some level he carried some resentment toward me for ever figuring it out. Michael — Taggart, rather, cared. He really cared. He was fulfilled by what he did, somehow. Most people don't see how risking your life every day could be a fulfilling lifestyle, but those are the people who haven't been there. The people who haven't experienced what Taggart has. It becomes a lifestyle, like when someone makes a point of cycling to work every day and giving it their all. Taggart... Taggart... He gave his life to our agency, and that's in more ways than one. We owed a lot to him, and we still do — except that we now owe it to his memory.

Moscow, Russia: South Nikolskaya Street – February 20, 2016; 11:54 A.M.

A man stood beneath the bus stop, smoking a cigarette and grimacing as if someone was pinching his Achilles tendon. He had dirty blonde hair that was slicked back in a style which was outdated by about two decades, and he glared at each passerby who made the mistake of establishing eye contact. His hands were shoved deep into the pockets of his overcoat, which was finely tailored and in pristine condition; a brand-new sheen of polish was still visible on its surface. Reflected off of his coat were his shoes, which were muddy and worn-down. This contrast was unnoticed by most, but even a casual glance at him would have revealed an athletic form which could likely take severe abuse before shutting down. His gaze flitted between pedestrians in front of him and a roadway to his left, which was partially obscured by a building.

Impatience seemed to radiate from this man, and it was apparent to those around him at the bus stop. A circle, several feet in diameter, had formed around him, nobody willing to come too close. The only person on this block who was not off-put by his presence was Michael Taggart.

Taggart found him to be unnatural, even to a comic degree. Perhaps it was simply the fact that he had trained his eyes to observe a great amount of detail, but the

man's legs looked to be too long for his torso, which was
dwarfed in comparison. This might have aided the man in
athletics simply by virtue of an increased stride, but it did
little to improve public appearances. He was simply too
conspicuous, even if he had changed completely from how
he had looked before.

Nonetheless, the next few minutes progressed just as
David had predicted they would. The bus came and went,
with Daniil's gaze not leaving it for a moment. Some
others embarked, while he remained where he was, staring
at the driver with interest. Once the vehicle was out of
sight, he turned on his heel and strode away from Red
Square.

He was followed at a distance by Taggart, who made
a point of keeping a great many people between them.
Daniil kept a leisurely pace, and he continually glanced
at the area around him, as if he was already sure that he
was being followed. A quiet panic dominated his features,
each movement sudden and unpredictable. The Affliction
showed itself in this man, its impact visible in the faces of
those around him. A look of uncertainty and almost fear
crossed over them before disappearing once the man was
a good distance away. Even Taggart himself felt the effects
of this sensation, and it was one that made him feel cold
– almost as if the man was taking all of the surrounding
heat and trapping it within himself. Daniil also carried the
expression often worn by people who find interaction with
others to be irritating and undesirable, one which piqued
Taggart's curiosity about what other traits the man might
have.

Following the man at a distance was proving to be a
difficult task. It wasn't that he moved at a swift pace –

quite the contrary. Each step was careful and measured, as if his movements had been choreographed. It occurred to Taggart that the suspect must have planned carefully to ensure that he arrived to his destination on time, or else had no deadline at all.

Whatever the case, Michael hoped that his observations were going unnoticed by his quarry, but the latter showed no sign of awareness. He continued about his business, which seemed to be a leisurely stroll away from Red Square and away from Taggart's apartment. It was only when foot traffic thinned out and the city began to regress into its more run-down section that Daniil picked up his pace, continuing to throw furtive glances over his shoulder. Michael stayed as far away as he dared, knowing that it would take ages to reacquire his target if he lost him this time.

Street names blurred together, and with all of the Cyrillic characters, Taggart lost any sense of where he was. This was likely Daniil's intention, and Michael was bitter, cold, and wondering how much longer he could pursue this man without being spotted. This question resolved itself when the suspect approached a building which looked like it might have once been a hospital of some sort. Before entering through a door which was missing its top half, Daniil turned around with such rapidity it caught even Taggart by surprise. The latter, who had been watching from across the street, instinctively ducked behind a parked car and held his breath. He could feel his target's eyes fixed on the other side of this bright orange car, as if it had been highlighted to grab his attention.

With his eyes half-closed in desperation, Taggart was oblivious to almost everything until someone cleared his throat close to his ear. Far too close. He opened his eyes and was met with the sight of an old man staring down at him from a car window, breath smelling like cheap liquor.

Taggart hesitated for only a moment before rising to his feet in a nonchalant manner and getting into the backseat of the cab.

"Where you going?" the driver asked in slurred Russian.

"Just drop me off around the corner."

"What?"

Michael, who was still keeping his eyes fixed on the hospital, handed the driver a five hundred-Ruble note and received no more questions. As the taxi was shifted into drive and rolled onto the street, Daniil followed it with his gaze, and, for one tense moment, his eyes locked with Taggart's. There was a coldness present in that stare Michael had never before experienced. It carried with it a loathing toward Taggart himself, and it even seemed to extend to the rest of humanity. It was a coldness that could never be matched by any Russian winter, and it looked to be ten times fiercer.

Taggart turned away and slid down in his seat until only the top of his head was visible through the window. Michael's heart was pounding and his hands had begun to sweat, and he did his best to come to terms with the reality that he would have to come in contact with the man again. Next time, however, it would be a more direct encounter. Somehow, Taggart had no doubt of this. The only justification that he had for this hunch was the intense sensation of clarity and attention during intense situations, and that same sensation was warning him of a definite return. Either that, or he was letting his mind run away with him. Even Taggart had no idea, but he held onto the hope that it wasn't the latter.

So happy with his new fare, the taxi driver ran through a stop sign and skidded around the corner, coming to a halt in an area which had markings which clearly prohibited parking. Shaking his head at this lack of subtlety, Taggart exited the vehicle and waited a moment before peeking around the corner at the hospital. Daniil was gone, and everything appeared normal. Yellow caution tape surrounded the building, and it looked as if either construction or demolition of the place would soon be underway.

Taggart jogged across the street once he was sure that it was clear, pausing just outside of the hospital's perimeter. After all, the last thing that he wanted to do was attract attention, and he was sure that breaking into a decrepit building would do just that. Also, he was certain that Daniil had noticed him and at least guessed at his intentions, and this left him feeling uneasy.

With the practiced nature of a pitcher, he threw caution straight into the wind and stepped over the caution tape. He felt his pistol through his coat, just to reassure himself with its presence. The front door of the building was locked for some reason, so Taggart reached inside the fragmented door. He half-expected someone to grab his arm from the inside and pin it in place, but no one did.

As quietly as he could manage, Michael turned the lock and opened the door. While in reality this was no louder than a whisper, it felt to him like the taxi's tires screeching on the road. He glanced in both directions before stepping inside, but no one else on the street seemed to take any notice.

In contrast to what Taggart had expected, the interior was in almost pristine condition. This would have been completely true if it wasn't for the fact that nothing had been cleaned or maintained in quite some time. Everything still seemed to be in its right place, however, juxtaposing the decay with a sense of tidiness.. Taggart found this strange for a building which was undergoing construction, but he had little time to dwell on this.

The lobby was a spacious one with a full waiting area sitting before a front desk. Among the things sitting on the latter was a computer which was outdated by several decades and a card catalog which might have actually been more efficient.

Beyond this reception area were two hallways, each one veering off in a different direction. There was a faint echo of footsteps down one of these corridors, but it was impossible to identify which one. Taggart chose the left side, making his own footsteps as quiet as he could in the process.

Disused gurneys and other medical implements lined the walls, and, like Moscow itself, the farther Taggart went, the more decrepit things became. Walls faded from solid colors to chipped masses which revealed several layers, each with its own color. Some were decorated with graffiti, most of which was too garbled for Taggart to understand. What he could distinguish was far from optimistic.

Debris littered the floor in lieu of a carpet, and Michael had to take care to not slip on its surface. In addition, there were no interior windows, making the atmosphere and the temperature chilling. He could still hear the footsteps ahead, and they had become more uneven as the terrain worsened. On several occasions, they stopped completely, leaving Taggart to halt in his tracks, waiting a few tense moments before the other person resumed.

They hear something, Taggart thought. It's nothing. Just the wind. Or the hospital settling. It's nothing.

Whether it was due to these subliminal messages or not, the quarry gave up on stopping to listen after a few attempts, instead opting to slow down. Their steps echoed in the long hallway and soon began to fade. Upon rounding a corner, Taggart realized why this was – the suspect had reached the end of the hall and begun to descend toward a lower level.

Michael took a breath to steel himself before following, well aware that he could be walking into a trap. The stairs descended into what must have once been a storage area of sorts, now reduced to stacks of warped cardboard boxes and rows of filing cabinets. Voices could be heard beyond these, and Taggart used this ambient noise to mask his footsteps as he ventured forth.

Peering around the corner of one of the filing cabinets, he could see no less that fifteen men gathered around Daniil. They were standing in a cleared-out area of the basement, their attention focused on one man in particular. This figure was far and away the most well-dressed of the group, and he carried with him an air of authority as potent as Daniil's coldness. Most of his face was obscured in shadow, but his mouth remained in the light, and it twitched every few seconds. At the same time, his hands were clenched in fists, but they were shaking ever so slightly.

He was flipping a coin with his right hand in a sort of unconscious manner, and it looked as if he had done this hundreds of times. Eyes fixed straight ahead, he continued to snatch the coin out of the air with a rapid movement. After several minutes of this, the coin slipped through his fingers and fell to the floor with a rattling sound which echoed throughout the room. All eyes fell upon it and the man who had dropped it, but this lasted only a moment. As quickly as they could, everyone snapped their heads forward as if acknowledging what had just happened was unacceptable. The man who had dropped the coin kicked it into the corner of the room and lit a cigarette with his still-shaking hands. He looked at the others to ensure that none of them were being snide about his mistake. The man must have known about their momentary lapse, as he furrowed his brow and adopted an even more stern expression.

The group was surrounded by the boxes that littered the entire hospital, but these were… different. Some of them were sealed with fresh duct tape, and the frayed edges and corroding corners were nowhere to be found. One of the strangers was sitting on one such box before he was berated by the man with the coin, who appeared to be the leader of the group.

"What do you think you're doing? Those are our lifeline, our income. You know this!"

The voice was slow and deliberate, causing the other man to jump up from where he was sitting in alarm, apologizing hurriedly and straightening the box. While he

did so, Taggart was able to catch a glimpse of its contents
– stacks of rifles, each one gleaming and looking as if it
had never been fired. Michael's mind was reeling, and he
already had the words in his head that he would use for his
status report to Colonel Grant.

Daniil and the others looked at the culprit with
condescending expressions, and Taggart knew that each
one would deny ever being so clumsy if called out by
their boss. He commanded the presence of someone
who others respect mostly out of fear, yet others still
desperately sought the approval from him.

Judging by his appearance, the leader of this group was
one that few people would consider questioning. He was
not a tall man by any means, but he made up for this with
one of the most inherently hostile faces that Taggart had
ever seen. His most striking features were a jawline which
looked like it could cut diamond and large, piercing eyes
surrounded by wrinkles.

The others took seats on a bench that adorned the left-
hand wall and sat at attention. The strangers' focus was
complete and impressive, but this was likely due to the
fact that they would face severe consequences if they gave
anything less.

The leader's expression seemed to soften, if only a little
bit. He walked around the room as he spoke, addressing
his followers one by one. "Now, friends. Remember to
relax! And remember that we are, in fact, friends!"

He gripped one man by the shoulders, shaking them
and giving a smile. The man in question didn't look
reassured. Nonetheless, the head of the group presented

a warmth which the others gratefully absorbed. It was as if they were looking for a reason to like him, and it didn't matter if his kindness to them was only intermittent.

"Now to business," the leader said, returning to his original demeanor. He addressed those around him with a voice which implied mutual respect, but Taggart had heard this enough times to know that it was nothing more than a weak façade. Nonetheless, the group was enraptured and seemed to be hanging onto every word.

"We will be conducting a small-scale experiment with the weapon in three days' time, and following its success, we will begin the transaction to our new allies." He said the word with a biting sarcasm, and his inferiors burst into laughter that didn't seem quite genuine.

The man who had been called out for sitting on the weapons stood up and said, "But Nikolai, how can we be sure that they can be trusted? Their track record is one of the worst…"

The man who was called Nikolai silenced him with a glare. "Our buyer is of a kind that will not dare cross us. They are a people who are quite concerned with honor – even to a fault. You are already on thin ice, Andrei. Ensure that you don't try my patience again. I don't think I need to go into detail about what will be done to you if you ignore this advice.

"As I was saying, we are prepared to conduct our controlled experiment in three days, at one o'clock exactly. Kudrin, is everything in readiness?"

Daniil responded immediately, much like a student who was far too eager to impress his teacher. "Yes, yes, it is!

There is a bus route which passes through a fairly secluded area which I have been monitoring for several months. This is the prime location for our test, and I have no doubt of the positive results." He said all of this very quickly, leaving him out of breath by the end.

"Good." Nikolai's lips twitched into the beginning of a smile. "We have yet to find a suitable candidate to be our test subject, so one of the passengers will have to suffice. Better yet, use someone waiting at the stop that you mentioned." Daniil nodded.

Taggart was left in wonderment, hoping that the conversation would become less vague. It was clear that they were a terrorist group of some sort, but what kind? What was their goal? And what weapon would they be testing?

While these musings ran through his head, Taggart dared to take his disposable phone from his pocket and use it to take pictures of the area. Even though the photos were of a low resolution and fairly dark, he still managed to capture the faces of Nikolai and Daniil. Michael pocketed the phone and made a mental note to send the pictures to Colonel Grant when he had the chance.

The meeting seemed to already be at its conclusion, with some of the men turning their attention toward sorting the weapon boxes and others moving toward the exit. Michael crept back toward the stairs as quietly as he could, hoping that the others were too preoccupied to notice an uninvited guest slipping away.

As he made for the exit, Taggart couldn't help but let his mind stray back to the discussion that he had just overheard. The leader – Nikolai – made several references to testing 'the weapon' soon. Surely it couldn't be the arms that were stockpiled in the crates? Testing those would be a quick and painless task, not requiring much planning at all.

There was also the fact that Nikolai himself seemed to be impacted by a very severe Affliction, one the likes of which Taggart had never seen. The man's every movement seemed to occur without his consent, despite the fact that his mental faculties remained intact. It was a wonder to Michael that such an erratic person could command the respect and dedication of so many other people. He wondered, that is, until he recalled a man by the name of Adolph Hitler.

Regardless, Michael picked up his pace as soon as he knew that everyone else was out of earshot. Shards of plaster and drywall gave way to linoleum tiles, which in turn gave way to the streets of Moscow. It was there that Taggart blended into the midday crowd, feeling weary and cold. The coldness, however, wasn't from the weather – rather, it was a lingering sense that he himself had become cold. There was no escaping the sensation that he was alone. This was not in a sense of wishing for a romantic relationship; he had long since decided that he couldn't support someone else emotionally when he himself was under such a mental strain.

Rather, he felt more detached from the world around him, and along with this came the disturbing notion that he had no desire to change this. Even though this was a miserable state of being, Taggart felt that fighting it would be so much more exhausting. Somewhere in his mind, Michael knew that this wasn't true, but he remained his stubborn self and left things as they were. For the moment, that would have to do.

Personal Journal of Michael Faust Taggart, February 21, 2016

Interpol's on-call therapist suggested that I would function better if I put my thoughts down on paper, so here's the result. I was never great at writing things, and coming up with topics has always been one of the struggles for me. I just don't know what to think. Or even if I should think. That's what seems to always get me into trouble – things getting out of hand get that way because I over-think things. It must be better than under-thinking, but… I don't know. I just don't know.

I probably shouldn't leave this entry without putting anything down that has real substance to it, but my thoughts feel like they're too scrambled to decipher, even for people who are trained for that sort of thing. The one idea that seems to make sense and keeps coming back to me – in dreams, in random thoughts that hide in my mind until they decide to jump out – is that people were designed with a "breaking point." Meaning there is only a certain amount that one person's mind and body can do, and for some reason it's considered a positive thing if you push yourself dangerously close to that breaking point. Tougher. Manlier. Better. I had always thought that, but now I'm sick of it. I say that you should be whoever you damn well please, and if it's enough for you, it should be enough for everyone else. If it isn't enough for them, they have things of their own to sort out. It just makes me wonder how I get by from day to day. How I can live this way and stay sane. I'm not so sure anymore…

Moscow, Russia: South Nikolskaya Street – 23 February 2016, 12:58 P.M.

Something was wrong with the man waiting at the side of the road. He seemed harried and nervous, but his mannerisms were quite different from Nikolai and the other Afflicted persons who Taggart had seen. This stranger looked as if he was preparing to do something regrettable, or nerve-wracking at the very least. He was wringing his hands in a manner which looked downright painful, and he couldn't seem to stand still at all.

Watching this scene from the bus was Michael Taggart, who took in every detail as he had been conditioned to do. He fixed his gaze on the newcomer as the man paid for his fare with trembling hands. None of the other passengers had given him any cause for suspicion, but Michael was at the ready nonetheless. Again, he unconsciously patted his jacket where he had concealed his pistol. It occurred to him with sad humor that this P226 seemed to be one of the only constants in his life, despite his desperation for real, meaningful contact.

Taggart did his best to push these thoughts out of his mind; they had grown all the more intrusive and frequent lately. His focus was split between the task at hand and a multitude of issues going on in the background of his mind. Even though the former was far more pressing and dangerous, the two felt almost equal in importance.

The new passenger staggered to the back of the bus, and, after finding no open seats, held onto one of the ceiling-mounted supports. It looked as if he would collapse completely as the bus lurched into motion, but by some miracle, the man kept his footing.

Traveling to the next stop ordinarily took only five minutes or so, but this seemed to be too long for the nervous man. With a hand that was shaking worse than an introvert forced into a social situation, he grabbed the stop-rope above the windows and gave it a surprisingly firm pull. The driver reacted almost immediately, swinging the bus to the side of the road. All of this was met with annoyed and curious reactions from the rest of the passengers, all of whom locked their eyes on the nervous man. He was already making his way to the front of the bus and was fumbling with something in his hip pocket as he did so.

It was then that Taggart drew his pistol, keeping it low and out of sight – not that it mattered. Everyone else was studying this strange passenger, transfixed. Seeming to ignore this attention, he withdrew a transparent cylinder from his pocket and held it aloft. In the split second that this object was in the air, Taggart could see just enough of it to discern what it was – a gleaming syringe filled with a dark-red liquid.

Michael raised his pistol and aimed, but he was a second too late. The rest of the passengers had already risen to their feet in alarm, blocking Taggart's line of sight. A panic had arisen, during which the nervous man seemed to vanish entirely. The rest of the bus funneled toward the exit, but one man blocked the exit, presumably the one who had been injected with the syringe.

He was a balding, elderly man whose cheeks and eyes were sunken to an almost comical degree. The eyes themselves looked unnatural, however – they had rolled back in his head, their whites so bloodshot that hardly any white remained. He carried a cane, and it was shaking in his hand more violently than the stranger's hands had been. His narrow frame blocked the only exit, leaving the driver and other passengers at a loss for what to do; none of them wanted to be the first to push an old man out of the way.

Any illusion of innocence that the man may have presented was cast aside at once when he raised his cane above his head and sent it crashing down onto the driver's skull. Before anyone could hear the sickening craaaack from this, he was swinging at everyone else. Throughout everything, Taggart had kept his pistol held aloft. This created even more panic among the passengers, but they seemed to be less frightened of him – perhaps because the image of the old man's blazing eyes was still imprinted in their minds.

With each passing moment, the man became more and more dangerous. He showed no signs of fatigue and no intention of stopping his assault. Passengers were moving around in the confined space, leaving Taggart with no clean shot that he could take. He had equal chance of hitting his target or hitting some hapless citizen. Shifting to the side for a better view, Michael pressed his shoulder against the window, held his P226 in front of him, and began to squeeze the trigger. The crazed man was in his sights, and Taggart had the presence of mind to aim for his chest – incapacitating him would mean less paperwork, and, more importantly, more intelligence gained and one less life lost.

He could feel the resistance from the trigger as he pulled it back. All at once, the target's profile was obscured by that of a small girl who could have been no more than a year old. She had crawled into her mother's arms, both of their faces stricken with fear. Taggart let go of the trigger and nearly dropped his pistol in alarm, thanking God that he had adjusted that weapon so that it would require more pressure to fire.

Seeing no other option, Michael stepped back into the

aisle and began to push his way through the frightened crowd. The old man was swinging his cane in a wide arc, smashing some of the windows and causing everyone within reach to duck. He turned toward the mother, who was cradling her daughter's head in her arms. She looked more indignant than frightened, seeming to be irate that someone would dare endanger her child. Releasing her daughter's head for a moment, the woman rose to her feet and sent a kick toward the crazed man's groin.

The attacker howled in pain, an inhuman sound which elicited a collective shiver from the passengers. He gathered himself and approached her again, this time with, if possible, even more rage. When he again wielded the cane above his head and prepared to send it crashing down, Taggart had pushed his way to the front and tackled the old man, sending them both tumbling down the stairs at the front of the bus. Michael's vision had once again narrowed, and all of his senses were focused on fighting this man. His actions were based on muscle memory, blocking the punches that his opponent threw and sending a few in return. Even though he was a decrepit man, the stranger's energy never wavered.

Feinting a punch with his left hand, the man used his right to grab Taggart's pistol and yank it toward him. Michael held the weapon with a viselike grip, shoving it toward the old man's chest. This time, he squeezed the trigger firmly and watched his target freeze momentarily before crumpling into a lifeless heap. Blood stained his shirt, and it was dark, almost black – far darker than blood should be.

Barely registering this fact, Taggart pulled on a lever beside him which slid the bus doors open. Turning to face the streets, he was able to catch a glimpse of someone's back as he darted across the block and into a waiting car. He had no doubt that this was the man with the syringe, but he had neither the energy nor the means to pursue him. In retrospect, Michael was thankful that the terrorists' weapon had been a syringe instead of a bomb of some sort, as he would have stood no chance having been on the bus. But, he reasoned, why would you need to specifically test it here? And why would they be so eager to sell it? They've got to be a dime a dozen if you find they knew what they were using.

It was time to stumble home, away from the prying eyes of the public and police. They were sure to arrive soon. More concerning was the fact that his cover had been blown for certain this time, adding quite a bit of paranoia to an already paranoid man. More than anything else, Michael felt weary. He stood on the bottom step of the bus for a few moments that rest would come, but it would be quite some time until then.

As Taggart stepped off of the bus, he felt a tiny hand grabbing at his coat, and he knew without turning around that it was the infant daughter who had been attacked. By instinct or whatever chance, she just had to feel the presence of the man who had saved her – just to touch the hem of his garment.

Moscow, Russia: Nikolskaya Street – 23 February 2016, 1:44 P.M.

Taggart was running. With each footfall, he felt more fatigued and out of breath, but he ran down the sidewalk, minutes away from where he had been living. One thing was certain – he wouldn't be staying there any longer.

As he stumbled into the lobby of the hostel and gripped the doorframe for support, Michael expected the manager to come rushing over and ask what was going on, but he wasn't there. The room was barren, devoid of even the employees who had almost always been cleaning or straightening up the area. In fact, everything looked as if it had been left in a great hurry, quite unlike the orderly atmosphere that the place usually held.

Pausing only for a moment to register this, Taggart stumbled across the room and up the stairs, clutching at a stitch in his chest. Each step that he climbed to his room provided another sharp pain to his gut, but he pressed on until he was unlocking his room and had stepped inside.

Securing the door behind him, Michael collapsed into his chair and closed his eyes, rubbing the fatigue off of them. His belongings were strewn across the room, and it would take far longer than he would have liked to pack them. Nonetheless, he began to throw things in his shoulder bag.

Taggart felt that he could afford to rest for a few moments, and this time was spent lying on his bed. He had propped himself against the wall, facing the door and holding his pistol loosely in his right hand.

All of him ached, and it was all that he could do to keep his eyes open. Being back on an assignment after being away from his work for years was exhilarating, but that didn't prevent it from being exhausting. Michael felt that he could hardly afford to wait around for someone to burst in on him and finish him off, but his weariness was holding Taggart back from doing anything else. Each day, he convinced himself that he would have time to have a restful sleep in complete safety. When each of these days ended, Michael had been left paranoid and restless. He had been living such a life for quite some time, but he never had gotten used to it.

He was on the verge of drifting off when a series of noises caused his eyes to snap wide open. They were bloodshot and his vision was blurred, leaving him with the appearance of an angry drunk. The only thing which distinguished him from this was the fluidity with which he slid off of the bed and readied his weapon.

There was a frenzied pounding on the door, and Taggart could hear the landlord shouting at him from the other side. Most of his words were vulgarities or downright indistinct phrases, but from what Michael could gather, the man was referring to rent and missed payments.

Taggart had crossed the room and was on the verge of unbolting the door, but he stopped short upon seeing the shadow that was cast through the crack underneath it. Without a sound, he dropped into a prone position and confirmed his suspicion – no less than three sets of boots stood on the other side.

When he considered the situation more carefully, a multitude of red flags rose to full mast in his mind. Not only had he been prompt with all of his payments up to that point, the landlord was contradicting the hotel's policy about maintaining a respectful silence in the interest of all tenants – a policy which had, to this point, been followed without exception.

Michael rose to his feet and fastened the door's chain, knowing that he wouldn't be able to prevent the men from entering sooner or later – he could only delay their arrival. He dashed to the window in two strides, only to find it sealed shut.

The pounding on the door was only becoming more intense, and, before long, it escalated to a series of impacts that seemed to shake the room itself. The chain rattled in its place, but it seemed to hold strong -- for the moment.

Taggart threw all of his weight against the window, but it remained as immovable as ever. His eyes darted across the room, now displaying great concern. The bedroom and the bathroom were the only other areas available to him, so Michael hastened into the latter, locking the door behind him. Moments later, Nikolay and the men with him could be heard stumbling into the main room, the unhinged door preceding them.

Panic began to take hold, and the entirety of Michael's body seized up as it did. Muffled voices could be heard on the other side of the door. A heavily accented one came across the most clearly, and Taggart was able to understand the gist of what was being said. He still was reeling from the realization that the landlord had turned on him so quickly.

"The bedroom is empty." The bathroom door lock rattled as someone said this, and it seemed for a brief moment that it would swing open regardless of its deadbolt. "Wait a moment. I'll make short work of him."

Taggart would never be exactly sure of why, but that phrase caused him to throw himself onto the floor's filthy linoleum tiles, white-hot aggression taking hold of his senses. This sensation was far from being a new one, but it remained unsettling nonetheless.

As he was falling, bullets screamed by above his head, creating a cacophonous echo and sending bits of wood and plaster cascading onto his back. The automatic fire reverberated painfully, but Taggart had no complaints -- he knew from personal experience that temporary deafness was preferable to a well-aimed shot.

All at once, the firing ceased, leaving Michael to roll over and survey the room around him. It was a veritable disaster area. The pendant light swung overhead, threatening to come crashing down at any moment. Bullet-holes adorned everything from the now-shattered bathtub to the wall that connected to the adjoining apartment.

Taggart scrambled to his feet, grabbing one of the larger pieces of the bathtub as he did so. Without a second thought, he slammed it into the wall, expanding one of the bullet holes in doing so. Relentlessly, he repeated this process until the detritus he was using had become little more than dust and his palm began to bleed from the impacts. Michael felt no pain from this, however, and his expression remained stern as he continued the process with a new piece of debris until a hole about half of the size of a window had appeared.

The voices continued on the other side, seeming to be arguing about who would be forced to finish Taggart off, and he caught a fleeting glimpse of the door being kicked inward before he managed to wriggle through the gap he had created.

Sharp edges of the drywall cut into his back and chest as he forced his way into the adjoining room. It was with sharp pain in both areas that he collapsed into what appeared to be the bedroom of an apartment identical to his own. With some difficulty, Michael lifted himself from the floor and was met with the sight of a bewildered, alarmed couple that seemed to have been interrupted in the midst of amorous activities.

The couple moved to cover themselves with a sheet, but Taggart was already across the room and at its doorway. Grinning, he turned to them before leaving, gave a wave of his hand, and said, "Pardon me."

After ducking back into the hallway and out of sight of the bemused tenants, it was apparent to Michael that he hadn't even come close to losing the landlord and his 'friends.' He could hear them tripping over each other in their attempt to reach Michael once again.

The latter lost no time in exiting that floor, taking the stairs three at a time on his way back to the lobby. The entryway he had so closely scrutinized during his first visit passed by in a flash, barely registering in Taggart's mind. He had no idea where he was going; that detail could wait. At the moment, the most pressing issue was distancing himself from angry Russians with guns – making him feel oddly like a Ukrainian.

The streets were empty as he burst out of the hotel; nothing moved save for the steady falling of snow. Running came by instinct, and instinct felt to Taggart like the only thing he could rely on. Because of this, when he came upon a sedan that was partially on the sidewalk and looked as if it had been parked by a particularly inept student driver, there was no doubt in his mind that this was to be his means of escape. Three of its doors had been thrown open and had remained that way, so Taggart slammed them shut before taking his place in the driver's seat. Then, for a sickening moment, it seemed that his instincts had failed him entirely – the key wasn't in the ignition, as he had hoped.

Swearing under his breath, Taggart searched the car with shaking hands that were, like the rest of him, overcome with anxiety-filled adrenaline. A familiar feeling came over him, one of insatiable determination as control of his actions and emotions was lost entirely. With alarming speed, Michael's head snapped to attention, gazing straight ahead as his hand reached for the sun visor above him. After a few seconds of searching, his fingers closed around what he was looking for. No sooner was the key in the ignition than Nikolay and his cohorts emerged from the hotel, each one scanning the street around them.

Taggart, lowering his head in preparation for the bullets that would surely be sent his way, made a first attempt at turning over the car's engine. And a second attempt. And a third. There was no reaction save for a few strained groans from the vehicle's internals.

His rational thought was still very much absent, but his state still allowed for a memory to flash through his mind. Without warning, Michael wasn't in Moscow at all – he was in West Chester, Pennsylvania, and he was behind the wheel of an entirely different car.

His father's Plymouth Duster was being pushed by two of his friends as he steered; all of them were terrified of their parents' reaction to the fact that their curfew was a distant memory. The car was notoriously unreliable, but it wasn't as if they couldn't have been home hours earlier if they had made the effort. Their only option was to roll into Taggart's neighborhood with the headlights out and the car in neutral, but they would have to push-start it in the meantime–

Taggart was back in Moscow. His actions replicated almost exactly what he had done all of those years ago and on so many occasions when he was a teenager. Within seconds, the emergency brake was disengaged, the clutch pressed in, and the sedan was in second gear. It picked up speed on the sloped pavement. Taggart remained hunched over behind the wheel, waiting for the right moment to release the clutch. Muscle memory took over, and when he moved his foot onto the gas pedal, the car let out a deep growl and shot forward in a manner so violent it alarmed everyone around, not the least of whom being Taggart himself.

The Russians had already taken up firing positions in front of him, and it was with a deafening sound that they sent a wave of lead in the direction of Michael's recently acquired vehicle. One of them had taken a position in the middle of the lane and was on the verge of diving out of the way, but Taggart wasn't about to allow that to happen. The gas pedal was scraping the floor, and the car's rear wheels spun faster than they were designed to spin as he flew toward the fleeing man.

Radiator grille, windshield, roof, pavement – these all came into contact with the Russian in short order, but Michael was already speeding out of sight and hoping that no police officers would take notice of the spiderweb-shaped crack in his windshield or simply dismiss it as having fallen victim to vandalism. All things considered, the latter idea wasn't very far from the truth.

Personal Journal of Michael Faust Taggart (No Date Provided)

Well, I'm starting to like this journal. For something that's forced upon me, it actually serves a purpose for me. I'm not really sure what that purpose is, but I guess it could be that I have someone to talk to. That sentence seemed a lot more normal in my head, but I guess it still applies, in a way. It's a way to get my thoughts into the world without talking to myself and seeming even more insane. I mean, people will probably find me to be somewhat crazy no matter what happens, but it's nice to have the peace of mind that I still have some sanity left.

Near Nikolskaya Street - Moscow, Russia: 23 February 2016 - 1:07 P.M.

There was one order of business to take care of before he could pursue Daniil – David had to be warned that he had been compromised. He ran the risk of the trail growing cold, but leaving his friend in the hands of angry, sociopathic men wasn't an option.

Daniil had said that he might be back at the bar on Petrovka Street, and Taggart hoped that the landlord and his friends wouldn't be able to trace them there. The car grinded along, barely able to maintain 40 miles per hour. Nonetheless, Michael kept the pedal to the floor, scanning for police all the while. A speeding ticket would have been less than ideal at a time like this.

Running through each stop sign he came across, he cut across Moscow until he came to a screeching halt on Petrovka Street in front of the derelict bar. From where he was sitting, Taggart could see that the glass in the front door had been shattered, along with the sign that had read 'Free Beer Tomorrow.' Something had gone wrong, and he had a sickening feeling that he already knew what the scene inside would look like.

Pistol drawn, Taggart threw open his car door and sprinted across the street. He skidded the last few feet over black ice, then abandoned all pretense by kicking the bar door open. Its interior was dim, save for a flickering light emanating from the booth where he had first met David. Michael's view of it was blocked by another booth, but he was able to distinguish an arm hanging limply toward the ground, blood slowly dripping into a pool on the floor.

"Ah, shit. Shit. Shit!"

Holstering his pistol, Michael tore across the room and was met with the sight of David – rather, what was left of him. Splotches of red adorned the man's torso and neck, each one accompanied by a deep, round wound.

David looked up at Michael, who moved to apply pressure to the man's injuries. There were far too many to keep track of, however, and he found himself releasing his hand from one bullet-hole just to cover another. It was as if he was trying to stop water from passing through a strainer.

The most concerning of these injuries was the hole in David's neck, and his breath came out in rasps which seemed to count down his final seconds. Throughout it all, the man smiled. This was the first time that Taggart had seen this expression from him, and it created a feeling of happiness, however grim the circumstances. As his eyes lost focus, David whispered something too quietly for Michael to hear. The latter leaned closer in time to hear his friend whisper,

"Find him. Please. In Ostrov. I wish I could have helped. I'm so sorry, dearest."

Michael felt David go limp in his arms, but he held onto him nonetheless. The thought crossed his mind that he could try to administer CPR, but there was no doubt that his friend was gone. The man who had opened his features to a smile was gone, and all that Taggart could do was collapse in agony and do one of the noblest and most sentimental things that a person can manage – he cried over the death of a dear friend.

Taggart's senses were so overcome that he failed to notice a figure emerging from behind the bar. It wasn't until that silhouette was halfway across the room that he raised his head to meet the gaze of a completely unexpected face – it was the woman from the bus, carrying her infant in one hand and a pistol in the other. It would have been a comical sight if she hadn't been so damn intimidating. The woman was several inches taller than he was and had been staring at him from behind pale blue eyes, which were set in a very fair face and surrounded by a curtain of short, brown hair.

She leveled the pistol at him, speaking from behind it in Russian which was so fast that Taggart had difficulty discerning each word.

"I apologize for breaking up your special moment, but there's work to do. Get up." She said this in perfect English and with only a trace of an accent, as if she had been trained to do so. Taggart was also struck by the look in her eyes; it was one of profound sadness. Everything about her seemed to be world-weary, even more so than Taggart himself. There wasn't even a touch of anger in her expression, and that made it all the more difficult to meet her gaze.

Michael's own eyes, tears still coating them, flicked for a moment toward his own weapon, which was resting on the table, very much in his reach. The woman seemed to know what he was thinking, because she said in a low voice,

"I'm holding a Russian-made MP-443 Grach, and others have made the mistake of thinking that I don't know how to use it. It's loaded, and the safety's off. If it misfires, I have a combat knife in a hip sheath. Get up, and don't do anything you might regret."

Taggart met her gaze, and, unflinching, said, "Listen, miss. Every day for me is full of regret. You shooting me right now would be the least of those. It would be a relief, really. But I have the feeling that if you were here to kill me, you already would have."

The woman lowered her weapon, but only by a fraction. "Who do you work for?"

Taggart's response was calculated, and he looked intently at her to gauge how she responded. "I work for my uncle. He has some business in Moscow."

It was clear to Taggart by her eyes narrowing and body tensing that she wasn't at all satisfied with this answer, but she knew that trying to gain anything more would be a waste of her time.

"Because you won't say anything, I will. My name is Emelia Kotova. I am an agent of the Federal Security Service; you would think of us as the new KGB, and that wouldn't be very far from the truth. I was assigned to a task force that is investigating patterns of odd behavior which seem to occur at random but with very similar circumstances surrounding each incident. Simply put, I am no longer with that agency, and I need your help, Michael Taggart. Not only have I observed you for long enough to know your name, I also know that pointing a gun at you isn't the best way of enlisting your aid, but I am short of patience and short of time."

"You're very… forthcoming with this information. I would have thought that your agency wouldn't want you to reveal all of this."

Emelia Kotova laughed mirthlessly, rolling her eyes at the statement. "My agency? Fuck my agency. They abandoned me just as quickly as my husband did once they learned that I was pregnant. They never would have let me continue on this assignment if they knew. I had Alexey four weeks ago. There was no way to hide him from them, so I refused to report in regularly. As far as they're concerned, I'm dead.

"And my husband… He was the only person who I told. He said nothing and looked at the floor for a very long time. Then he raised his head, looked me in the eyes, and told me to leave. He never wanted children. In that regard, he shouldn't have had sex with me in the first place. But try telling that to this man, full of delusion and hubris. I have no doubt that you are the same way."

"Listen," Taggart said, casting a wary glance at the barrel of Kotova's pistol, "I know that I'm not really in a position to negotiate, but there are a whole lot of people looking for me who would have already pulled the trigger if they were in your position. Why do you need my help?"

"You have the same goal that I do, Michael Taggart. What you call 'The Affliction' is causing a great deal of trouble in my country, worse than the authorities are letting on. You are more conspicuous than you think, tramping around as loudly as you are. I distrust and fear men as a general principle. I've been given no reason to feel any other way. But, as it stands, I am alone. All my life, I've been abandoned by men, and here I am asking one for help.

"You see, Michael Taggart, I believe in Russia. I believe that the Russian people are some of the finest and most forward-thinking in the world. The government, however, I do not count among the people. I did before, and after being shut out by them, I have decided that I can stand up for what I damn well want this world to be, not what someone else wants. I don't care if you feel the same way; I just can't do this alone. I'd be fully capable of doing this myself if it weren't for the fact that my back is against a wall. I want this disease stopped because it preys on people like me, who are already downtrodden and not given a fair chance at success as it is. Call me an idealist, but my mind has been made up."

In the growing confidence that Kotova didn't intend to shoot him, Michael rose to his feet, never breaking eye contact. "Okay. In all honesty, I'm not too fond of how my uncle is having me go about this matter either, so joining you is probably the best choice that I've had in a while."

For the first time in this encounter, Emelia looked taken aback. "Just like that?" she asked, lowering her pistol to her side.

"Just like that," came the response, Taggart shrugging as he said this. "I feel like I've reached a point where my life has no real direction, and it's my job to change that, and this might be a start."

Kotova pondered this, saying nothing. It was after a long pause that she sat in the booth beside the one where David's body was still resting and invited Michael to do likewise. She kept her attention split between looking at Taggart with her brow furrowed in mild mistrust and rocking her baby gently in her arms. Little Alexey was still fast asleep.

When Emelia spoke, however, it was without lowering her tone, as if the baby was already accustomed to being around quite a bit of noise. "I arrived here, following one of the men that the Federal Security Service had been eying for quite some time, a political dissenter of some sort. A blond man, very tall and unnatural-looking. I saw him shoot your friend from the front window of this bar. By the time I could get inside, you came charging in and I decided to hide.

"This man left a 'forwarding address' with your friend. He gave you part of it, and I heard the rest through the window. He said that he would be waiting for someone – I suppose he was referring to you – in the large manor house on Pskovskaya Street, Ostrov. I've never been there, but I know of the place. I can tell you right now, it's a trap. This character would never be one to agree to a fair fight, and he's making you face him on his terms. I would really recommend that you lie low for a while, then try to pick up his trail from someplace else."

Even before she had finished speaking, Taggart was

shaking his head. "I can't. I've spent too long waiting for things to happen and letting them get worse in the process. I've reached the point where I really don't care about the risk of all this. That's what lets me fight Daniil on my terms. He's afraid of dying. I'm not."

Emelia Kotova didn't say a word. She knew what he meant better than most people would, and she knew better than to disagree - it would get her nowhere. Instead, she rose to her feet and ushered Taggart toward the exit. When Michael looked back at David's body, she said, "Don't worry about him. I'll make sure this incident doesn't draw any attention. I still have some government connections, and I can call in a few favors. I'll make sure he gets a proper burial, too.

"I respect you, Michael Taggart, because you've earned it. I respect you, but I don't trust you. Now get out of here before your 'friends' catch on to what's happening. I'll be in touch." She handed him a scrap of paper with a carefully printed telephone number on it.

With that, Taggart turned his back on the scene, leaving Emelia and Alexey to their devices. He pushed the bar's front door open and made his way back into the bitter cold. In all honesty, he didn't trust Kotova either, but he had no doubt that this meeting wouldn't be their last.

Rejected Edit from Wikipedia.org Due to Lack of Verifiable Content: 'Michael Taggart: Bio.' Author Unknown.

While so much has been said of Michael Taggart's success in his career, one critical component of this man's life has been overloked [sic]: The man was a nutcase! Even a brief look at his psychological profile would show that his life consisted of strange, twisted, and deranged behaviors which are not acceptable in normal people, apparently only those who are good at killing people. [citation needed] *From what has been discovered of his personal life, Michael was as emotionless as they come and was an inhuman creature which we should fear and hate the memory of, not celebrate it.* [citation needed] *We* [who?] *must take action against such a damaging antihero becoming a person who our children view as a role model. This is the beginning of America's degridation [sic], and it must be stopped.*

Route E22 (On the outskirts of Moscow, Russia): 23 February 2016; 5:45 P.M.

Traffic was light, and Michael Taggart's heart was heavy as he made his way down the E22 highway. In truth, he had only a vague idea of where he was going, but, even after several hours of driving, his instincts remained in total control.

Ostrov. That's what David had said with his dying breaths, and it was all that Taggart needed. Night had fallen, and the lights from the few cars in front of him had blurred together as a result of him straining his eyes. Each time Michael blinked, focus and clarity returned, but it only took a few seconds for things to go out of focus again. Pulling over for the evening was not an option. Even if he could afford to let his target's trail grow a bit colder, passing strangers would likely respond less than positively to the bullet holes in the side of his car if he decided to stop and rest.

He was a man on the move: angry, determined, and dangerous. Given the choice, he would be a man sleeping soundly or a man drinking excessive amounts of coffee to help him stay awake, but it wasn't often that Taggart's line of work afforded him such luxuries.

Another unfortunate aspect of his occupation was a feeling that didn't occur very often, and it would have been all the more unbearable if it did. This state of mind reserved itself for moments where there was little for Taggart to do but think, and the long, monotonous expanse of road in front of him provided precisely such a moment. It has been said of people who encounter danger on a regular basis that being so close to death is the only thing that makes them truly feel alive, and this was largely true of Taggart – Or, at least, it had been. Once the adrenaline rush provided by his escape from Moscow had abated, he felt drained. This was a natural feeling in such circumstances, much like a crash that comes after the effects of caffeine wear off, but it was far from natural that Michael was always left in the depths of a severe depression. It was unknown to even him what the cause of this was, but, every time, it centered on dissatisfaction with everything and everyone.

It is true of clinical depression that it plagues its victim with a sense of isolation, and Taggart's was all the worse in that he felt isolated from only one person – himself. As he tried to maintain a constant speed and rested his eyes for a moment, this sensation hit him with an abruptness similar to that of the car's erratic start back in Moscow.

How is this worth it? Why am I doing this?

These questions had been lying dormant in his mind for quite some time, and it was on the highway that they took center stage in Taggart's mind. He knew full well what he had signed up for when he joined the Sentinels, but hindsight made his feelings then seem like empty sentimentality and foolish enthusiasm.

Why am I doing this?

Try as he might, Taggart could find no answer that he could be satisfied with. In his exhaustion, Michael had let his mind wander, and it had landed upon the lyric from a song that he hadn't heard for more years than he could remember.

Something about not doing this for the money… for my health… not for the wealth…

Taggart wondered what *he* was in it for.

Meatloaf. Dad loved that band. Was that Bat Out of Hell Part 1 *or* Part 2? *What does it matter? Get a grip, Taggart. Shit. Shit. Shit. This isn't normal. Where is my mind going? I can't even control where it goes anymore. I need to stop. I need to stop. I can't. Focus.*

Part 2. It was Part 2. Everything Louder Than Everything Else. *That's what it's called. Track 8. No! Stop. Just stop. It doesn't matter. Focus. I can't. I can't.*

I'm okay. I'm okay. I'm lying through my fucking teeth, but I'm okay.

There was a battle raging in Taggart's mind, and he was losing decisively. He sent the car across four lanes and onto the shoulder of the road; there was nobody behind him to honk their horns at him. The car rolled to a stop, but Michael had the presence of mind to leave it in neutral to avoid having to go through the process of starting it again.

Seatbelt unbuckled, he rested his forehead on the steering wheel. He had to remind himself to breathe, and the breaths that he did manage were sporadic and forced. There was no room for sadness or frustration, or any other emotion for that matter – his mind almost was too full of pure agony to allow for anything else. Those feelings managed to seep through over time, however, and Michael could feel tears trailing down his cheeks. He didn't bother wiping them away, lacking even the energy for that.

This period of anguish was broken for a moment, when Taggart unconsciously lowered his foot on the accelerator, causing an angry growl from the engine. This momentary shock was enough to bring him out of a totally overwhelmed state, but it wasn't nearly enough to stop his trembling.

It was at this moment that Taggart realized something about his life that he had tried to suppress for as long as he could remember – he had become nothing more than a shell of a person, wandering from one place to the next for the sake of those around him. This was a bittersweet sensation, but the bitterness of it was undeniably the dominant feeling.

It was difficult to find much comfort in the fact that he had to exert only a small amount of energy into his decisions; after all, Michael would have been too emotionally fatigued to do even that. This brought him an empty satisfaction and left him with one less choice to worry himself with.

However, the thoughts, the feelings that went into determining his course were not his own, and this made Taggart physically sick to his stomach. He had tried so often in the past to force himself to believe that he had some say in where his life was taking him, but he realized now with a painful bitterness that this had never been the case.

Using all of the willpower available to him, Michael shut down his mind. He forced all of his thoughts and insecurities out of it. They kept creeping back to the forefront, but he pushed them back away each time. He did this by imagining a blank piece of paper, nothing more than a plain white surface without blemish or defect.

The world around him was doing its best to take over his mind, but Taggart fought back dozens of times until he was only aware of the car's vibration and the cold, leather seat that was supporting him. Everything else was irrelevant, everything else was gone.

I'm... I'm gone. I'm nowhere.

It takes the right kind of person with the right kind of mind to make the world disappear, even for a moment. Escapism, in any form, requires one to deny the existence of everything around them. This is the easiest part of it, and most can get that far.

The thing holding the masses back from truly getting away is the concept of denying their own existence. The fact remains that it is far easier to block out others than it is to block out one's self. Taggart was one such person who could shut himself out, but the strain that this process brought made each escape painfully brief.

In this instance his feelings of passivity were cut short by a difficult reality – he had no choice but to keep moving forward. This was at the expense of his personal happiness and sensibilities, but leaving his responsibilities behind now would lead to charges of defection and all of Interpol joining the Russians to ensure that his existence ended as quickly as possible.

"If you're going through hell... keep going."

Churchill. That's Churchill. Dad liked him.

Hated the British, but liked Churchill. I wonder —

Focus. Focus. Breathe. Come on.

A wandering mind is often a difficult thing to control, but Taggart was able to rein his in, at least for the moment. His breathing was still heavy with emotion and exhaustion, but he was able to lift himself into an upright position and put the car in gear. The engine assumed a more steady thrumming at that point, creating a rhythm that was somehow comforting.

Defying his common sense, Taggart switched off the heat and rolled down his window. The bitter cold snapped at his nose and ears, but he met this with a smile. The chill had sharpened his senses quite a bit, and he felt ready to drive to the ends of the earth.

Even if he did know in the back of his mind that this was just a temporary distraction from the emotional war being waged in his head, this was what Taggart needed. Emotion could wait. For now, he needed to do what he did best, and that was hunt down the Afflicted. In this case, the only person he wanted to find on this route was Daniil.

As he drove on, the face of Emelia Kotova wouldn't leave his mind. This wasn't from infatuation or anything of that sort, rather, he hadn't met anyone so captivating. She was unlike anyone who he had worked with in the past, and, strictly speaking, he probably would have been removed from his position in Interpol for associating with an operative without consent from his superiors. Even so,

Taggart couldn't have cared any less. It was a liberating feeling to finally have things on his own terms.

If contentment would always remain out of reach, Michael was somewhat satisfied by the fact that he was the best at what he did, and that was the one thing that he could take comfort in. For now, that would have to be enough.

Personal Journal of Michael Faust Taggart, 24 February, 2016

No matter what I write in this journal or how many specialists I visit, I'm getting worse. More sick. I've never understood how my mind works, but I expected a professional to. What if this is something that nobody's ever seen before? Or been diagnosed with? Have I created Taggart's Disease? As melodramatic as it might sound, I just want to be a normal person. A balanced person. I want that so badly, but there's really no point in hoping for it anymore. It's almost as if whatever is going on in my mind wants to prevent me from getting better, or even trying to make things better. It's fighting me, and I'm losing. Badly. Self-reliance is bullshit. I've relied on myself until now and have reached this point… Then again, relying on others sometimes never helped me anymore than when I've tried to go it alone. No matter what, I'm always left with the idea that death isn't the great terrifying tragedy that everyone makes it out to be. To me, it would be a lack of life and just no more existence, but… On some level, that seems preferable to a litany of pain beforehand. What's the difference if you get there sooner?

I don't feel by any means suicidal, and I don't have a plan, and I'm not just writing this sentence to satisfy the psychologists who screen my journal entries. There's something intangible keeping me here, and the more I think about it, the less sense it makes. Something about waking up each day and overcoming it has an appeal. The work ethic involved is rewarding, but the price of that is a sense that I have nothing left to give to the world. I never wanted to be seen as a selfish person, but it feels like it's high time that the world gave me something back. I can't keep going if it doesn't. For some reason, I'm sticking around with the hope that it will.

Life as we know it is something that people say we take for granted, but what if it isn't granted to us in the first place? It's not like we would be disappointed about missing an opportunity to be alive – we wouldn't even be around to know that this possibility even existed! We'd be none the wiser, and we wouldn't be put through so much pain. I can't see why struggling through every day is something that I should prefer. Maybe it's the small hope that I might get better. It's one of those far-off hopes, but somehow it's been enough to keep me going so far.

I hope that I can look back at these ramblings later and make sense of them. Or at least some brilliant psychiatrist does and can cure other people going through it, if there are any. God help them if there are.

Route E22: 23 February, 2016; 6:32 P.M.

Arriving at the outskirts of the city of Ostrov was about as exciting and monotonous as mowing a lawn, and Taggart could now say that he had done both.

At a glance, it seemed as if the residents there weren't familiar with the concept of mowing lawns at all. Michael was reminded of pictures of the Chernobyl disaster, with everything overgrown and left for the plant life to regain control of things. Less than ten hours away from the site of that disaster, he felt that the two could have been sister cities.

There was nothing to separate this municipality from

the others that Michael had passed on his way out of
Moscow, apart from the fact that a terrorist was said to
be hiding there. Michael wove through the narrow streets,
making his best effort at tracking down the address that he
had written down on one Nikolai's business cards.

A river flowed to his left, a bridge passed overhead, and
houses passed by, but the target's residence was nowhere
to be found. Keen to spend as little time as possible in the
bullet-riddled car, Taggart withdrew his phone from his
pocket and opened its GPS. Using a civilian technology
that some had never imagined possible even for the most
high-tech government agencies, Michael was able to map
out a route to the address, which seemed to be a remote
manor on the outskirts of Ostrov.

The few pedestrians that passed by kept to themselves,
heads down and pace swift. This was more than fine with
Taggart, who was rounding a corner onto a street marked
'Leningradskoye." He lowered the accelerator, scanning the
house at the end of the road. It was unnecessary to read
the number on its mailbox – he knew that this was the one.

The familiar sensation returned; most of his senses
dimmed, and Michael was hit with a feeling of white-hot
rage. His every action was dictated by muscle memory,
and all of those actions were calculated with the utmost
precision. The house loomed closer, an ornate building
that hearkened back to the Imperial era and surrounded
by a low stone fence. Its windows were sealed; that is, all
but one of them. Eyes narrowed, Taggart observed a long,
narrow cylinder protruding from an upstairs window – the
barrel of a rifle.

His motions instant and deliberate, Michael swung

the wheel to the side in order to minimize the target
that he presented to the sniper, expecting to slide to a
stop parallel to the stone wall. Instead, he was met with
a sickening drop in his stomach as the car lurched to
the side, responding to a sharp craack that split the air.
Without seeing it, Taggart knew what had happened – the
target had fired on the front wheel of the car instead of
him. This, combined with the slick nature of the road,
sent the sedan into a roll which resulted in Taggart being
suspended upside-down and in the sniper's direct line of
fire.

Dazed but conscious, Michael unbuckled his safety belt
and landed on the roof of the car before kicking its door
open and staggering into the brisk, open air. His pistol had
fallen out of its holster and onto the ground, so Taggart
picked it up, praying that it would still fire.

There was no doubt that the sniper's weapon would
keep firing, leaving Taggart caught neatly in the ambush.
Using what strength he had remaining, the still-stunned
Taggart made a dash for the wall surrounding the house,
counting on the bullets flying overhead to miss their mark.

Each shot was an ear-splitting warning of the imminent
danger that he was in, and there were far more warnings
than Michael would have preferred. He dove behind what
little cover he could find, feeling a sharp pain in his back as
he slammed into the wall. Snow kicked up beside his prone
form, some of it landing on his back. This was ignored by
Taggart; he remained in a state of total concentration. He
knew full well that the sniper would need to reload before
long, and he had to be ready when that time came.

Six shots had been fired according to his count, but he

had to factor in the reality that he had been quite distracted while attempting to keep track of this. The firing had ceased for the moment, and the air around Taggart was silent. There was no thump-clack of magazines being exchanged. The sniper wasn't reloading yet – he was waiting. Rather than risk giving up a clear shot at his target, the attacker had decided to wait for Michael to exit his cover.

A period of attrition had ensued, and neither party was willing to make the first offensive move. Taggart adjusted his position so that he was lying on his back, staring up at the gray sky above him. He shook his sleeve aside to reveal a battered watch. Its hands had long since stopped moving, and Taggart had no intention of replacing the batteries. He simply wore it because he had done so for such a long time, leaving him feeling naked without it.

In this case, however, it served a quite different purpose. Michael stared at its glossy surface, not taking his eyes off of the reflection on it as he raised his fist over the wall. With a bit of adjusting, he was able to see the window from which he was being attacked, and, sure enough, there was a figure standing in it, aiming a long-barreled rifle in his direction.

If it weren't for his heightened senses, this would be the extent of what Taggart was able to see. His perception had been extended to an extreme degree, however, and this feeling had taken control. As far as he could see, the sniper was holding an H&K 416 with a telescopic sight. 5.56x45 NATO rounds fired from a 10-round box magazine. It was being fired as a semi-automatic, but from the length of the barrel it was likely to be a variant that also included full-auto. He could discern all of this from a reflection on his wristwatch, and even he was taken aback by this thought.

Regardless, even an outstretched hand seemed to be enough of a target for the Russian, who fired another shot, this one splitting the air beside Taggart's arm and coming closer than the latter ever would have preferred.

That's seven shots. Three more to go. Maybe.

Drawing fire from his opponent was an inherently dangerous prospect, and the most Michael could do was minimize his own risk. In that moment, everything was a percentage to him, and it was out of the question to put the odds of this shootout into the Russian's favor by making any rash or hasty action. As time progressed, however, he felt that he might not have much of a choice in this instance.

It was at this point that the standoff ended - at least for a moment. Taggart stayed where he was, knowing that the sniper was still aiming in his direction. Not knowing if it would have any effect, Taggart cupped his hands around his mouth to prevent his breath from rising above the cover and giving away his position. Now able to take his time with the relative safety of the wall, Michael crawled to the side on his stomach.

As this was happening, he was fighting against the rage that seemed to always overcome him in such situations. His experience with this phenomenon was akin to that of someone who a person who was having their first experiences with alcohol. The first few times were miserable, with lack of familiarity leading to a great deal of discomfort and frequent hangovers. This learning stage was necessary, however, as one began to build up a tolerance to these effects. After many such occurrences, the taste of the alcohol was only a bit more tolerable, but it kept coming back because it was a part of life. Taggart's periods of rage mirrored this phenomenon, with the main difference being that his loss of reality was never a pleasant one.

Wishing that he had had the foresight to wear gloves, he clenched his fists and dragged himself away from the car. This was in an effort to misguide the sniper, but the futility of this plan was proven when yet another shot cut through the air and chipped the stone above his head. Frustrated by the wasted effort, Michael resolved to make a break for it, regardless of whether or not it put him at risk.

Bullets kicked up tufts of snow at Taggart's feet as he sprinted in the direction of the house. It was with mingled relief and pain that he slammed his shoulder into the house's brick siding, out of the sniper's line of fire. Nursing a throbbing arm, Michael stepped toward the front door, lifting his gaze toward the upper floors. The Russian's rifle was gone.

Boards had been nailed across the front entrance, and none of them yielded when Taggart did his utmost to pull each one free. Upon closer inspection, it appeared that this was true of the windows as well. It occurred to him that the sniper needed a point of entry for himself, so it stood to reason that at least one entrance remained unobstructed.

To the left of the house was a detached garage which seemed to offer better cover than anything else on the property, so Taggart made his way over to it. As it turned out, there was a gap of only a few feet between the two structures, so he slid through with his back feeling the uneven, sometimes sharp edges of the bricks that made up the house's exterior. This opening gave way to the back of the house where a lone door stood, this one free from any boards.

Taggart tried to open it, and, upon finding it locked, fired a shot directly below the handle where the locking mechanism was sure to be. Pausing only to take a steadying breath, Michael kicked the exact same section, and the door swung inward with a sickening lurch.

This entrance gave way to what appeared to be a pantry; canned food lined the walls, bottles of various content were scattered here and there, and the room gave off a distinct impression of disuse that most pantries seemed to have. In fact, the room would have had all of the workings of a bomb shelter if it hadn't been any larger than a cubicle (and aboveground, for that matter).

In addition, everything was covered by a thick layer of dust, indicating that the safe house wasn't exactly used for day-to-day living. This included the floor, which was strewn with filth, save for a set of footprints that were so clear there was no doubt that they had been made recently.

A second door stood opposite the first, and Taggart opened it with the greatest caution, leveling his pistol at the room ahead as he did so. His heart was pounding in his ears as he turned to face the area, but it appeared to be completely empty. There was no mistaking the function of this room – it was a kitchen, plain and simple. The same layer of dust rested on this section of the house, and the footprints continued through it and past a swinging door in the left-hand wall.

Michael stepped past a rusting sink and a table with a checkerboard tablecloth, being careful to make his movements as silent as he could. His head swiveled in all directions, ready to pick up any real or perceived sign of movement.

This door pushed inward to reveal a long, narrow hallway with footprints leading straight ahead and around a corner at the end of the hall. The prints reminded Taggart vaguely of clichéd clues left for fictional detectives. Shaking off this thought, he proceeded with caution past each door that branched off of the corridor. Even though there was no indication that any of these rooms had been entered, Michael was unwilling to risk being ambushed by someone who might be hiding somewhere without leaving any noticeable trace. This precaution ended up proving unnecessary, as he reached the other end of the hall without incident. Taggart didn't care; it was worth the extra time spent.

He was then presented with a chicane of sorts, hooking around to reveal what must have been the house's parlor. It mirrored the rest of the house's look of dustiness and disuse. Sure enough, the door was at the opposite wall, and the glass border around it was partially blocked by boards on the other side. This caused the light that filtered through to be hazy and scattered, casting eclectic shadows over the entryway. Taggart was keen to escape this atmosphere, so he mounted the stairs which were built into the wall beside him.

Each footfall sounded to him like a strepitus, while in reality he was being no louder than an uptight librarian. Fortunately for him, there was a layer of carpeting on the stairs which served to muffle his movements even further.

It appeared that the sniper had either chosen to remain motionless or was taking similar precautions, because the second story was equally silent.

Another hallway revealed itself, this one far shorter than the first. The footsteps resumed their course where the carpet ended, leading to a room to the left. Taggart pressed on, unconsciously tightening his grip on his pistol until his knuckles were white. Scanning the area as he passed, Michael approached the open doorway. His breath quickened along with his pace, and it wasn't long before he was beside the doorframe. Taggart took another breath to steel his nerves. He checked his pistol to ensure that it had enough rounds. It did. He counted three... two... one... Michael stepped into the doorway, leveling his pistol in front of him, awaited the sickening sound of a shot being fired at him and was met with...

Nothing.

Taggart collapsed against the doorframe, his hands shaking from the adrenaline that had built up in his system. Before him was the window that the sniper had been using as a nest, and, sure enough, it was cracked open slightly with a rifle propped against the wall beside it. No second glance was necessary to verify Taggart's earlier assertion – it was, in fact, an H&K 416 assault rifle.

Pistol still drawn, Michael approached it with caution and found several magazines strewn around the weapon, most of them empty. He picked up the ones that weren't, including the one in the rifle itself, and turned to face the scene below.

The car he had taken from Moscow was still resting on

its roof by the side of the road. Tracks and holes littered the layer of snow on the ground where he had sprinted as bullets whizzed past. The atmosphere around the house had become an entirely different one now, an almost unnatural stillness replacing loudness and frenzy. A chilling breeze made its way through the cracked window, and Taggart slammed it shut, aware of the great deal of noise that this caused.

He whirled to face the doorway behind him, expecting a shadowy figure to appear because of the clamor that he had triggered, but the hall remained empty. Holding his pistol aloft, Taggart lowered his gaze to the footprints in front of him, trying to discern the sniper's from his own. It seemed as if the attacker had left the same way he had come in, only diverting toward the opposite end of the hallway when Michael had been on the bottom floor. He took a breath to steady himself, watching the vapor from it rise in front of him before fading into nothingness.

It was with a great deal of caution that he moved to follow these prints, but it wasn't long before they ended abruptly, as if the sniper had been met with the rapture. Michael looked to his sides and saw only the faded expanse of floral wallpaper. It was upon looking above his head that he noticed what he was looking for – not the rapture, but the outline of an attic access door and a string hanging from it.

The door made only a minimal amount of noise as he creaked it back open, but even this was ear-splitting to Taggart. He could only hang onto silent hope that the sniper wouldn't be able to track his movements. It was with great care that he pulled the attic's access door cord and mounted the ladder contained within. It seemed as if it might collapse without warning. Balancing on each rung, he kept his weapon aimed above his head, waiting for a sudden ambush.

None came.

Taggart reached the top uncontested and was confronted with what appeared to be a completely empty storage space. Boxes, disused furniture, even a moth-eaten bed had taken residence there, but there were no other people to be seen. Even the footprints had died out; it seemed as if the sniper had taken to covering his tracks.

Opposite the entrance and beyond a ruined sofa was an object covered with a white canvas, the exact nature of which was indiscernible. Pistol aimed in its direction, Michael crept toward it until he was within arm's reach of the covering. Taking a furtive glance over each shoulder before doing so, he pulled the canvas off in one swift motion, revealing the surface of a cracked, faded mirror.

He was about to turn away from this and back to his pursuit of the sniper, but something stopped Taggart short. Even he wasn't entirely sure what caused this. Maybe it was simple fascination about the ornate, hand-carved nature of the mirror and the haunting filter it put on the objects reflected on its surface. Far more likely than this was the shock and surprise at the reflection itself.

Staring back at Taggart was a version of himself which he had never even remotely seen. His face had become sallow and gaunt. This was paired with the impression that he was carrying some sort of immense burden on his back – a once firm posture had been reduced to a slumped one which could be anything but healthy. The most disturbing change, however, was the look in his eyes, or, rather, the lack of one. He was staring back at himself with a vacant expression, free of warmth or emotion, and this scared him. Even more than the immediate danger that he was in, this lack of emotion frightened Taggart to the point of trembling. Even after blinking repeatedly in an attempt to diffuse the dead look in his eyes, the emotionless appearance remained. It was not unlike shell-shocked soldiers undergoing a "thousand-yard stare," and this scared him. This was something that he was readily willing to admit to himself, and the intensity of it was undeniable. It frightened him.

A throbbing sensation had begun in his head, filling his ears and drowning out both sound and thought. As Taggart gazed into the mirror, the intensity of this feeling multiplied. Fear had manifested itself in strange ways for Michael in the past, but nothing to this point had been so severe. The familiar sensation of fading focus presented itself once more. Conscious thought began to slip away, and it was all that Taggart could do to avoid sinking to his knees. Fear disappeared and was replaced with an insatiable anger, and even he knew that there was no cause for such a feeling.

In addition, his senses had been heightened to a dramatic degree. He could hear distinctly every movement of every insect flying and scurrying through the attic, he knew what boxes were on the verge of toppling over due to poor stacking, and he could instantly discern the audible click-clack of a pistol being readied to fire.

He didn't need the mirror to know what was behind him, and its faded surface wouldn't have revealed much anyway. Without the slightest pause, Taggart dove to his left and behind the sofa, narrowly avoiding the shards of glass which flew in all directions, not to mention the bullet that made a clean hole through the back of the mirror, where Michael's head had cast its image mere moments ago.

"What of the hunting, hunter bold?"

The voice echoed around the attic, joining the fading-but-still-present sound from the gunshot. The words were tinged with a thin Russian inflection, and each word was clear and crisp – the speech of one who is quite confident and in no particular hurry. He spoke this in a non-questioning manner, rather as if reciting something before a long-awaited audience. It left Taggart with a sense of deep unease.

"Brother, the watch was long and cold!"

Taggart heard each word clearly, but he made sense of only a few phrases. His focus was on the location of the sniper's voice, but this was exceedingly difficult to place. It seemed to be constantly on the move.

"What of the quarry ye went to kill?"

Taggart was mystified. He recognized the verse from Rudyard Kipling, but... *why?* He couldn't escape the feeling that he was playing a game which was designed by Daniil. If Michael's intuition served him, the game had been rigged against him from the start.

"Brother, he creeps in the jungle still!"

Taggart was on the move, circling around several stacks of boxes which were marked in Russian. If he wasn't mistaken, the label read *'Dining Room.'* He held the rifle magazines together in his pocket, doing his utmost to prevent them from *clacking* against each other and revealing his position.

"Where is the power that made your pride?"

Continuing to circle the attic, Taggart found himself behind an upturned table, and he took care to reveal as little of himself as possible as he looked out from behind it. Directly ahead was the sniper, crouched behind a pile of refuse. For a moment that seemed to be frozen in time, their eyes locked. There was no surprise on the face of the hunter. There was no fear. He merely smiled, seeming to be overjoyed at finally having his prey in sight.

Three bullets splintered through the table as Taggart threw himself to the ground. He could feel the air rush past him, and it was with great difficulty that he raised his pistol and waited for the sound of the hunter's voice.

"Brother, it ebbs from my flank and side."

The voice rang out as clear as ever, and Taggart closed his eyes in an attempt to detect its location. Using muscle memory rather than any real, rational thought, Michael raised his pistol and fired it twice into the surface of the table. This was met with a groan and the sound of a body and a weapon dropping to the floor.

Still wary and still fueled by his inexplicably heightened senses, Taggart cast a wary glance around his cover and saw the sniper on his back, his hand still groping for his pistol, which was well within reach. Taggart regained his feet and hustled over, kicking the sidearm away from the hunter and underneath the bed. He let his focus snap from that to the man himself, who was already making a motion which seemed odd from the outset.

His hand had emerged from his pocket and was cupped in front of his mouth. Realization came over Taggart, who lost no time in grabbing that hand and yanking it away. It was empty. He used both hands to pry the sniper's mouth open, who had clamped it tight. When it wouldn't yield, Michael sent a sharp blow to the man's gut, making him gasp and leaving his mouth wide open. Unwilling to waste this opportunity, Taggart shoved his hand into the hunter's mouth, and almost instantly felt his fingers being bitten. This was with the ferocity of a German shepherd, but Taggart persisted, feeling around until he felt what he was looking for – a small, smooth capsule. He gripped it, then kneed the sniper in the same place, releasing his fingers which were now starting to bleed and bore teeth marks which came dangerously close to revealing bone.

With his other hand, Taggart examined the pill, and if his intuition served him, he knew it to be a cyanide capsule. He threw it in the direction of the discarded pistol and wiped his injured hand on his shirt before shaking it to mitigate the pain.

The sniper glared up at him, unable to move with a bullet in his leg alongside a matching one in his chest.

"I am lung-shot. I'm dead anyway."

The voice was strained, as if he was fighting for each word.

"Then you won't mind clearing up a few things for me," Taggart said, trying to ignore the pulsing in his right hand. The sniper appeared to be reluctant to say the least, so he added, "You're dying in this attic, one way or another. I can make that a whole lot easier or a whole lot harder. Give me something."

"Like I said, I'm dead. There's nothing more that you can do to me now. Go home. Leave me in peace."

Taggart wasn't fond of delivering pain because of how much he himself had endured, but his patience and energy were short, and this was made no better by the state of his hand. He rose to his feet and pressed his boot against the wound in the hunter's chest, steadily applying more and more pressure. At first, the man made no reaction, but it wasn't long before his eyes were bulging and it seemed that he could withstand no more. He lifted a hand and waved it feebly as a sign of submission.

"Kenthill," he said, wincing with the effort of the word.

"What?" Taggart said, leaning closer as the dying man's voice dropped in volume.

"Kenthill Mansions. North… North Point district. Hong Kong. That's where the weapon is going. That's where the buyers are."

Taggart kept his eyes fixed on the hunter's. "Is that all you can give me?"

It was clear that the man was fading fast, but he managed to rasp out one final word.

"Triads."

Unable to hide his surprise, Taggart started. "The crime syndicate? They want the Affliction? Answer!"

The sniper simply stared at him, eyes beginning to close.

The coldness that had been present in them for so long was diminishing, if only slightly. There was no warmth to be found there, but Daniil's gaze had definitely softened. "End it. Please. The pain is… impossible."

Taggart raised his pistol, aimed, and then paused. "Did you kill a man named David before coming here?"

"Your associate in Moscow? The one in the bar? Yes. Yes, I believe so."

Michael lowered his pistol, holstered it, and then stared down at the man. He opened the pockets of the hunter's jacked and found a key chain with a car key on it and a walkie-talkie which seemed to be almost military-grade.

Taggart again reached for his pistol, but he stopped short, hit by a sudden thought.

"Where is the haste that ye hurry by?" he asked maintaining a cold gaze in Daniil's direction.

Sputtering as he spoke, the adversary replied, "Brother, I go to my lair to die."

With that, Michael turned on his heel and went back through the attic's trapdoor, leaving the hunter to bleed out.

Taggart snapped to attention in alarm as Daniil's walkie-talkie crackled to life. He turned a knob on the top of the device and could make out several hurried Russian phrases.

"We are on your street now. Wait for us there, we'll take care of this. Backup on the way."

Michael dropped the walkie-talkie back onto the hunter's body and clambered back through the attic's trapdoor. He returned to the sniper's original hide and again looked down into the front yard. Sure enough, two SUVs sporting tinted windows pulled up alongside the upturned car, and almost a dozen masked men spilled out of them.

The H&K 416 still rested on the windowsill, so Taggart shouldered it, loaded a magazine, and took aim. His first shot connected, sending one of the attackers to his knees, clutching his chest. Michael continued to shoot, and it was at this point that the professionalism of these reinforcements became apparent. They moved in a loose formation, making targeting multiple people in quick succession almost impossible, and they made their way forward with militaristic precision and swiftness. Taggart had emptied two magazines and started on a third when, quite suddenly, the rifle refused to fire. He ducked beneath the window and examined the weapon, seeing a shell casing protruding from the side. Knowing that each second he wasted here meant more time for the reinforcements to close in on him, Michael pulled the weapon's charging handle several times before the casing finally snapped free, landing on the dusty wood floor with heat vapor rising from it.

Taggart had already returned his focus to the front yard, which he found to be empty and unnaturally quiet. Only the sound of his heavy breathing and of a dog barking far away could be heard. He had downed only three opponents before all the rest were out of sight and presumably at the back door already.

Tossing aside the rifle and drawing his pistol, Taggart

made his way back to the hallway, wishing he had had the presence of mind to lock one of the doors on his way in. He moved to the stairwell in a hurry, still careful to avoid making too much noise. Footsteps pounded on the floor below, letting him know that the reinforcements were closing in and making a thorough sweep of the house.

Having arrived at the top of the stairs, Taggart looked around wildly for a place to hide. Nowhere seemed to provide viable cover, so he opted to hide in plain sight. Parallel to the top step was a dividing wall which would be invisible to anyone coming upstairs, provided that they didn't turn their head or catch something in their periphery.

Taggart flattened himself against this wall and reloaded his pistol, even though the previous magazine was only half-empty. Shortly afterward, footsteps could be heard on the staircase. No voices accompanied them, the attackers continuing to show their professionalism. Michael readied his pistol, not knowing if he could take on all of them, even with the element of surprise. He doubted it.

The reinforcements filed past Taggart, pausing a few paces in front of him. He froze with his weapon leveled at the back of one of their heads, his breath caught in his throat. Even though it was an irrationality, one thought kept running itself through Michael's head: *They know I'm here somewhere.*

He half-expected all of them to turn around as one and open fire, cutting him down like an overzealous firing squad. The only sound was that of the Russians' heavy breathing. Opposite Taggart, one of the men held up a signal of two crooked fingers, and the rest of the squad filed in behind him and moved to clear the rooms on the top floor.

His pistol still aimed in their direction, Taggart backpedaled down the stairs, only turning around once he could no longer see anyone on the top floor. Hoping that the footsteps of the Russians would mask his own, Michael sprinted back into the kitchen, through the pantry, and back into the snow. Breathing had not become easier once he was outside, however, and it was with staggered gasps that he made his way to the garage beside the house. Taggart pulled its door open and was met with a jet-black Lincoln Continental. He took the Russian's keys from his pocket and unlocked the car, hoping that it would start.

The car certainly made its best effort to do so, but all it could manage was a strained whirring sound. Taggart turned the key again, knowing that the noise that he was making couldn't go unnoticed by the reinforcements upstairs. He pressed in the clutch and tried again, this time getting more of a positive reaction from the engine. It sputtered to life, giving a reassuring growl when Taggart pressed down the gas pedal.

The Lincoln peeled out of the driveway, passing corpses, shell casings, and the shell of Michael's old car alike as he shifted into second gear. Shots were fired in his direction from the upstairs window, possibly even the one which he and the sniper had both used previously. None of the rounds connected, however, as he was already around the corner and headed for the highway. He was on his way to the Latvian border, where extraction by helicopter awaited him. He'd made it. He was finally leaving Russia. Taggart felt that if he ever had to revisit the country in his lifetime, it would be too soon.

Letter Found in the Personal Effects of Michael Taggart, Written 30 October 1999

Dear Michael,

I've held on for this long, sweetheart, because I love the man you are. The man I know you are. Right now, you're someone else entirely, and I don't even get to see you much at all anymore! I can't sit through months and months of wondering if you're still alive and not hearing a word from you! It's something I can't take, Michael. I love you, but we're fading farther and farther apart, and that's something we really can't afford to do. I can't afford to, at least. It's tearing me apart, and I have to focus on my own wellbeing too, instead of centering all of my focus on trying to strengthen us. I know that this might sound conceited or selfish, but, when it comes down to it, I have to come first in my life. If I don't focus on myself, I'll have nothing left; I'll go crazy. I know that this isn't what you want to hear, and I know that you're fighting, too, but... I think we should just separate for a while. It won't be permanent, but my mind just can't take this much strain anymore. I really do hope you understand that I love you and want what's best for you, and I think that this choice is in the best interest of both of us. I don't know when this will end, or even if it will, but I'll be thinking about you, Michael. You're still so important to me, but I just can't come to terms with how foreign our relationship has become to both of us. We'll talk as soon as you're back.

Love always,
Cathy

Along the Border of the Russian Federation; 24 February, 2016: 1:26 A.M.

The A116 road was flanked on either side by trees, and that was about it. Michael had engaged cruise control once traffic had thinned out, and it had remained active for quite some time before he reached a sign reading 'Latvijas Republika' and bearing what must have been the Latvian coat of arms. Taggart counted 1.5 miles on the car's odometer, then he pulled over into a field on the left hand side of the road. Abandoning the Lincoln, he jogged to the silhouette of a helicopter that was waiting for him about fifty feet away, grateful for the chance to stretch his legs. He stepped into the craft and watched as it ascended above the treetops. Russia and Latvia faded from view as he gained altitude.

He had something to go on – an address. Michael had no doubt that his next destination would be Hong Kong, which would undoubtedly be quite a change from Russia. He would be trading cold weather and cold people for a city in which he could go practically unnoticed, and that suited him just fine.

INTERLUDE

Taggart Residence - 21 November 1999

"I… I understand that what you do is important to you, Michael. And I had never intended to be someone who spoke out against the ambitions of someone close to them. I never intended to pull you away from something that gives you meaning. It's just that I can't watch you tear yourself apart over and over again, leaving me to pick up the pieces.

"It doesn't make things easier knowing that you may not be home on any given day. Michael, I don't even know if you'll be *alive* on any given day. It's more than I can take."

Cathy had started to tear up at this point, and her voice faltered more and more as she spoke. Michael moved to put a comforting arm around her, but she pushed him away and even backed up a few paces. She shook her head, tears now running down her cheeks in earnest. He backed away as well, anguished yet not surprised that his touch would be so repulsive to his wife.

"No, Michael. No. You can't fix it this time. You can't tell me that 'everything's going to be okay' or that 'we'll figure this out.' I've let you hold me in your arms and convince me that our relationship is fine when we both know that it isn't. We might not be willing to admit it to each other or even ourselves sometimes, but it's true. Tell me honestly that you think we can make this work anymore, Michael. I know you can't."

He closed his eyes and ran a hand through his hair, trying to summon what fight was still left in him. "Please, Cathy. I'm trying everything-"

"See? You really can't. I would apologize for cutting you off, but I know you, and I know what you were going to say. You're doing everything you can to balance our marriage with what you do. I understand that, sweetheart, but *it isn't working*. It's not.

"I'm not saying that you didn't try. Anyone who would even think that is ridiculous. But... sometimes trying our hardest won't be enough. Some things won't work, no matter how hard you try to force them to. I know that you don't want to acknowledge it, and neither do I, but we won't work. We as a couple, I mean.

"It hurts me so much every time you leave, and it hurts worse every time you come back. When you leave, I don't know what to do with myself. It just shows me how dependent on you I am, and it really has been a toxic thing. I should be able to function without the help of anyone else, and I need to focus on being happy with myself. If I'm constantly worrying about you, wherever you might be, it feels like I'm the only one left in our marriage.

"I know how much it hurts you to hear this, sweetheart, and please know that it hurts me, too. I know that you don't believe me and that you probably don't see how I could still feel pain about this and do it anyway, but we need to spend some time apart. How long, I don't know. You won't like this, either, but there's a good chance that it'll be permanent. I just can't go on feeling unloved. I'm sorry."

Michael was looking at her with fear and desperation in his eyes. "I never, ever meant to make you feel unloved, Cathy. Never. I'm so sorry that I did. I can't begin..."

"I know, sweetie, I know." It seemed as if his panic had made her more calm, as if their emotions were weights balancing a scale. "It's not you, it's not me. It's just that it was never meant to be. I never intended to sound like a bad country song, but that really is it. We've done everything we can, and it's just time for us to quit pretending."

Michael didn't know what to think or how to feel, so he only nodded. He wasn't nodding in agreement; rather, he was using the only expression he could muster. All things considered, he would probably agree with her judgment in the long run, so feigning assent at this moment would suffice.

From years of being around him, Cathy seemed to sense this, pulled up a chair across from him, and sat down. He had gone back to burying his head in his hands, so she gently took each of his wrists and lowered them until their hands were interlinked. His head remained down.

"Michael, I'm not going to ask anything more of you after this. Would you please look into my eyes?"

In a motion which was now incredibly difficult, he gripped her hands more tightly and raised his head. Eyes stinging with the few tears that would come, he took a deep breath and looked into her eyes.

In a barely audible whisper, she said, "I will always love you. Period. Even if our marriage is gone, even if we end up not speaking for years, *I will love you.* You are an unforgettable person, and you have made every effort to treat me well. That is something amazing, and you'll always be a part of my life. I hope that's more meaningful than 'we can still be friends.' Even though we can, you'll always mean more than that to me. Always."

Trembling now, Michael nodded in earnest, hoping that she knew how much he appreciated those words. Even so, the effort of keeping his head up was proving too much to bear, and his chin returned to his chest a moment later. Her words were tender, well-meaning, and necessary — but this didn't stop them from cutting him like so many knives.

The pair sat in overwhelmed silence for the next few minutes. Memories of their relationship flooded Michael's mind, a vignette of so many happy memories that had met such a dismal ending.

Their hands remained clasped, but the grip slackened over time, at last resulting in them sliding apart entirely. Michael's eyes were closed, but he could hear his wife taking a deep breath and rising to her feet.

Michael started to lift his head again, but he already knew what he would see - Cathy walking from the room and closing the door behind her. This would make the room much darker, and the only light that would remain would come from his desk lamp.

Instead of raising his eyes to see all of this happen, he closed them and let grief and frustration take over. In fact, these were only two of the many emotions tearing his mind apart. He was exhausted from fighting to hold on to Cathy, he was aggravated with her for giving up on them, and he was even more aggravated with himself for failing to accept that she had justifiable reasons for leaving.

It was all tiresome, but it was a weariness which refused to let his brain shut down. Because of this, Michael sat in the dark with his head buried in his hands for quite some time. Tears wouldn't come, only the feeling of them being formed at the corners of his eyes. He wanted to cry out in anguish, but something intangible kept him from doing so. It was an unfamiliar feeling, but it was one which would become quite accustomed to over the next few years.

One thought which would not leave Taggart's mind was that he could have done more. Not only that, he was convinced that he *should* have done more. He had known at least some of the emotional turmoil that his wife had been going through over the past few years, and he had tried to help her through those times, but he couldn't escape the fact that he could have done something else about it. He could have left Interpol and the Sentinels as soon as he had enough money saved up to live a stable life with Cathy. He could have come home and brought the wonderful news that he wouldn't have to be gone anymore. They could have led happier lives, leaving behind the grim realities which his work had brought.

As he sat in his study, anguished and exhausted, a question occurred to him which would reappear many times throughout the rest of his life.

Why am I still doing what I do?

Taggart figured that this must be a question that everyone asks themselves at one point or another, but it had special relevance to him. After all, the vast majority of people didn't fly overseas with a gun and a sensitive mission in order to collect their paycheck.

It wasn't as if he was paid particularly well, either. Working for an agency which didn't officially exist made its members expendable and their pay sub-standard. Their standard of living had never been a vocalized issue in the Taggart household, but it was one of those issues that managed to create tension nonetheless.

Taggart was never fond of walking away from a bad situation without finding *some* lesson or bit of happiness from it, but this was a special case. Divorce proceedings, when they're not desired by both of the spouses, aren't exactly full of practical lessons or silver linings. The only thing that immediately came to his mind was that he would only have to support one person from here on out, but that only widened the hole left in him.

There has to be something, anything, *that I can take away from this. Hell. Maybe I've just fucked up beyond repair this time. The one person who I care so much about, the person who I needed to care about me... she's gone. I feel empty now. That's something I'll have to get used to over time, but I'd really rather not. God, I don't believe in you, but do me a favor here. Ha. Somehow I doubt it works like that. I just can't do this anymore-*

No. I can't fall back into this cycle. I've always done this, but I can't let myself get addicted to grief again. If I fall into that again, there's no way I'm getting out. Alright, Mike. You're wondering why you should keep going, and maybe that just isn't up to you. Maybe you should make your own life worth living. You want self-worth? Do something to make yourself worth a damn.

Wow. So now I'm talking to myself in third person? I must be going crazy. Well, if I am, there's no sense in going halfway. How long it'll take me to snap is the big question. Alright, that's it - I need to sleep. That won't magically fix everything, but it's a start.

PART TWO

A CAPTIVE AUDIENCE

"The prisoner, having reached the depth of his depression, gradually reawakens to the life around him. He licks himself and his wounded pride, opens his eyes, and finds that far away on the horizon there is still a ray of sunlight left.

-- P.H. Newman

"Battle not with monsters, lest ye become a monster, and if you gaze into the abyss, the abyss gazes also into you."

-- Friedrich Nietzsche

After-action report for Michael Faust Taggart (Section A – Russia, 2016)

- Overview: It has been determined that individuals operating out of the Kremlin have developed weapons for use against unarmed targets, with at least one of these persons showing symptoms of the Affliction.

- Goals & Objectives: Ascertain the degree of threat presented by Russian radicals who may have sensitive information regarding the Affliction (Supplementary: Meet with Sentinel contact who possesses additional intel.)

- Analysis of Outcomes: Contact met without issue, intelligence gained from meeting, two Afflicted suspects and numerous associates killed, malicious intent discovered (Read: Plans to sell weaponized Affliction to Triads), rendezvous in China identified.

- Analysis of Sentinel's Performance: Taggart has accomplished all assigned tasks in a largely professional manner, if at times reckless. Adviser assents that he acted as well as any agent could in each given situation, aside from the loss of sensitive information.

- Summary: The investigation into the Russian situation has uncovered a more far-reaching scheme than anyone at Interpol had expected. Further action in this manner is mandatory, and it is advised that Sentinel Taggart should be the agent to pursue this lead, due to his extended experience with and exposure to those suffering from and relating to the Affliction.

- Recommendations: As stated, Michael Taggart is recommended to follow up on the Russian/Chinese affair. In addition, it has come to the attention of his handlers that his mental state has reverted to that of a person suffering from severe anxiety and possibly clinical depression. It is not yet known whether this will cause an interference with his performance in the field, but this will be monitored closely over the course of the following months.

A Commercial Motorboat off the Coast of Hong Kong, China: March 18, 2016

It was raining. Colonel Kate Grant sat across from Taggart in a boat which looked like it might start sinking at any moment. The waters were calm that day, and this seemed to be the only reason that they were able to stay afloat. Grant was carrying a stern expression which betrayed quite a bit of concern as well. Taggart was looking at the skyline in the distance, wishing he could be away from the Colonel. Her presence had once been a comforting and reassuring one, but it had turned into a source of frustration. She had been one of the people who was in charge of dictating his every move, and Michael couldn't help but feel a sense of annoyance at this. Even bringing up this feeling would have been futile because of her staunch sense of duty, so he kept his mouth shut.

It was because of this that Taggart refused to speak first, leaving an uncomfortable silence on the voyage toward Hong Kong. As they approached the shore, Colonel Grant had no choice but to speak up.

"I know you're familiar with your assignment, so I'll keep this recap brief. You're to make contact with our agent already in the field. Her name is Wang Fang, and she's posing as a transsexual prostitute working out of the Wan Chai district of Hong Kong. Your phrase is 'Taking a new step, uttering a new word, is what people fear most.' Once you say that, she'll respond with, 'Peace comes from within. Do not seek it without.'"

Taggart raised his eyebrows at the oddly philosophical phrases, but he remained silent.

"She has information regarding your 'friends' from Moscow and their weapons exchange. You'll find her on the roof of a brothel called 'The Last Resort.' It has signs posted in English as well as in Cantonese, so it shouldn't be too hard to find." She handed Taggart two photographs, one of the contact and the other of the establishment. Without looking up at her, Michael took the photos and studied the first one intently. It bore the image of a woman with an attractive face, along with the sharpest brow-and-jawline that he had seen in quite some time. Pocketing the photographs, he slowly raised his head to meet Grant's eyes. She paused, as if waiting for a comment, but Michael only looked at her expectantly.

"In addition," she said, confused at his silence, "your overarching objective here is to identify the key players in this situation. There's a stash of supplies that were left in the city by your contact. There should be several covert listening devices, your pistol, and a disassembled rifle in a briefcase, along with some other hardware. It's located in a storage facility near Wing Tai Road and has a combination lock which can be opened with the digits '505.' The box itself is number seventeen. Don't take any action until you have authorization. Interpol was reluctant to send us out here in the first place. We're already violating dozens of protocols by coming in here unannounced, so the situation needs to be handled as delicately as possible. In all likelihood, we'll be cutting a deal with the Triads to get this weapon out of their hands."

"Why?" Taggart asked, looking at her in confusion. "Putting more funds in the hands of China's biggest criminal organization… this would just have the same effect as letting them have the weapon."

Grant shook her head. "It's in the hands of Interpol now, Taggart. They know what will have the fewest political ramifications and what will be best in the long run."

"What if those two things are different? I know that our superiors will choose the path that leaves them in the least trouble, but what if that means an increase in crime in this region? Maybe they just need to accept that people need help, and by *people*, I mean the ones who are being put into immediate danger. No matter what the consequences would be for Interpol's political standing, even if it were disbanded completely, this weapon needs to be destroyed. And that doesn't mean buying it off of criminals and locking it up in a facility, leaving the Triads to build a bigger criminal empire off of bribes from us. It doesn't make sense."

Colonel Grant stiffened, growing red behind the ears. "Taggart, this isn't up to you, and it's not your place or even mine to make these decisions. You've been good so far about following orders, and that's just what our agency needs." Michael looked at her with disdain before narrowing his eyes and turning to look at the city in front of him.

"Are you ready?" she asked. Taggart gave a barely perceptible nod, not lifting his eyes from the skyline. "Good. Before I run through this mission's parameters again, you should know that Interpol has you on a strict psychiatric watch. One sign of mental instability, and they'll pull the plug on this operation and take you back in."

Michael dragged his gaze over to her and nodded slowly. "I know."

Grant looked at him in genuine surprise, her sense of concern gone for the moment. "How could you know? I wasn't even supposed to disclose this to you in the first place."

"It's not too hard to guess, Kate. I know that none of my evaluations have come back in a positive light. Not the mental evaluations, at least. You all think I'm losing my mind; I get it. It was only a matter of time until I got put on some sort of watch like this. To be honest, I thought you all had started this when I was back in Moscow."

Colonel Grant sighed, and this time it was her turn to avert her eyes. "I don't know what to tell you, Taggart. Even you have said that you're feeling worse by the day. We're not trying to victimize you here; we just want to help."

Michael looked mildly offended at this but chose to not speak yet.

"Just keep your nose clean, Michael. It's not my place or yours to organize these things. We're both small gears in a big machine with our own purpose. The least we can do is accept that the other, more significant ones are doing things properly."

"Why, though? Why should we just expect them to know what's going on? They're so detached — it doesn't make any sense."

Grant sighed, quickly becoming annoyed. "Taggart, listen to me. Do your job. I do my job organizing these assignments, and do you think that makes it any easier for me to send you out to what could possibly be your death? Have enough respect for me to do your job."

Michael shook his head, visibly weary. "You're not understanding. I'm not sure why not, but you're not understanding me. The hierarchy that we live in… it doesn't make sense to begin with. It's something that I don't -"

"Listen to me," Grand was fuming now, her voice full of quiet frustration. She enunciated each word individually, and each one carried a great deal of intensity. "Do. Your. God. Damned. Job. Do it. I don't want to hear any reason or fabricated piece of shit moral quandary you've made up to get out of this. You have a commitment to me and the rest of our agents to do your job, so stop trying to shirk your responsibilities and do what you're ordered to do. Like it or not, *that is an order!*"

Taggart wasn't entirely sure why he snapped at just this moment, and why he hadn't snapped before, but all of his latent emotions came forward. He wasn't prepared to restrain them this time.

"You know what I don't understand?" he said without preamble, standing up in the boat and almost capsizing it. Grant gripped the edge of the craft in alarm and looked up at him with a new expression – *fear*. His presence had always been one of quiet obedience, and this shift was both a radical and alarming one.

"I really don't understand why it's the people sitting in desks that they haven't left for years who are the ones who send people into their schemes without the slightest regard for how we feel." He jabbed his finger at his chest, desperation filling his eyes.

Colonel Grant had snapped out of her own fury and was too stunned for words. She seemed to be edging away from Taggart, making herself as small as possible. Michael realized this and his expression momentarily softened, but his frustration continued to pull at his consciousness. The familiar sensation of his focus narrowing returned, along with the accompanying loss of reason and rationality. He hated it. The feelings he couldn't control, the complete unease which took hold of him – he couldn't stand it.

"I'm done. I'm done taking all of this onto my shoulders without getting a single word in of my own. Nobody in their right mind would work like this, and maybe that's why Interpol has been able to have me under their thumb for this long – I must not be in my right mind. I'm a liability. Do you really expect that I can go out and kill the people you tell me to kill on a daily basis? Do you expect that it won't have any impact on me? That I can do all of this and be okay with myself? Okay with everything I've done? Well, you can rest assured that I'm not okay with any of it. I'm done." Taggart paused for a moment, trembling from emotion. When he continued, his voice was level but still teeming with frustration.

"I had often thought that no human being deserves

to be truly hated. I believed that all the way up until this point, in fact. You and Interpol proved me wrong in more ways than I can count. I used to think, sure, I can't stand that, or I loathe this, but hate – that is a word that should solely be reserved for all of you. Never before has someone been such a foul excuse for a human being and been a part of such a foul, damaging group. No one has been more unconscious of common sense and basic emotion. But you all, you have lost both of those and have taken out your ineptitude on myself and everyone who has the misfortune of being in your presence, and that is something that I can easily hate.

"I hate Interpol for roping me into something that destroyed my mind. I hate the Sentinels for choosing to fund terrorists instead of being patient and dismantling them without throwing me in danger. I hate you for refusing to see that we're both being manipulated. Last, and most of all, I hate myself for staying around for so long."

With that, Taggart cast one final glare at Colonel Grant before flinging himself off of the boat and into the rough waters surrounding Hong Kong.

Numbness spread through Michael Taggart's body with the speed of a rumor spreading through a grade school classroom. His breathing was strained, but the fiery sensation in his mind had begun to ebb away for the moment.

Each stroke that he made through the water left Grant and the small boat farther and farther behind, and Michael was mildly surprised that she hadn't set off after him. Dwelling on this wasn't much of an option, however, as thoughts of hypothermia and frostbite began to dominate his thoughts. Because of this, Taggart doubled his pace, the rain beating down on his head doing nothing to help things along.

His mind turned from thoughts of freezing to ones of confusion and exhaustion. Michael had suspected that his dealings with Grant and Interpol wouldn't last forever, but he hadn't foreseen such a sudden and complete departure. As his arms cut through the tide and his legs kicked him forward, Taggart held onto the hope that his actions were for the best. In fact, he did his utmost to convince himself that he couldn't *possibly* be in the wrong – negativity had always drained his mental and physical energy, and this was far from an opportune time for that to happen.

There was no reason in going back and making things right with her. Hell no, not anymore. His mind had been made up, and there was no point in looking back. What was left at this point was going forward and finding people like himself – sick, alone, and desperate.

He knew that person could be found in Emelia Kotova, but he hadn't the faintest idea of where she was. She had said that she would stay in touch, but this had been promised quite some time ago, and maybe her offer had expired. Taggart clung to the idea that she was still out there, using that thought to propel him forward through the tide. The intrusive, craning necks of Grant and Interpol were gone, and it left him feeling both relieved and secluded. The thought occurred to him that over the next several hours, he would be alone in the world, no one knowing where he was or what he was doing, no one following him around, no one to hold him up or force him down. This isolation made Taggart at ease, yet very, very small.

Graffiti Sprayed on the Side of a Building in Hong Kong's Wan Chai District

"God have mercy on my soul. Nobody else will."

Hong Kong, China: Wan Chai District, March 18, 2016

As soon as he reached the water's edge and flung himself on the hard concrete of a shipping yard, Taggart lay where he was for quite some time, shivering and letting rain pool around him. There were no passersby to wonder why a middle-aged American man was coughing and sputtering – the area was vacant.

Michael would have been content with lying in that spot for a few hours, or maybe even a few days. Regardless, he eventually managed to regain his feet and turn to face the city in front of him. It took several moments for his eyes to adjust to the many neon, flashing lights beyond the shipping yard. Once the blurriness had subsided, Taggart was met with the seediest area that he had ever laid eyes upon.

Through the fine mist that the rain created, Michael saw a stretch of road flanked by dozens of signs promising "Cheap, clean sex now!" This proposition was echoed on the sidewalks themselves, with women hiding under balconies from the rain, wearing little more than scraps of clothing. They beckoned to passersby in a manner which bypassed seductive and went straight to sexual. The whole place seemed to reek of desperation, and Taggart felt more at ease there than he probably should have.

As Michael walked down the street, no one paid any attention to him, other than the prostitutes who displayed their 'wares' to him and hurled insults at his back when he passed without a second glance. The other people along the way were either too distracted by the women to pay him any mind, or else curled up on the pavement trying to get a bit of sleep.

Several more blocks down, the area improved, if only by a small amount. The working girls still were present at each corner, but more tourists could be seen now, as well as food stalls serving a spectrum of rice, chicken, duck, shrimp, scallops. It seemed that both the vendors and the girls made their living by ushering tired travelers out of the rain and into their company, and the area was booming as a result.

In the midst of all of this was Michael Taggart, who wanted nothing more than to find a warm, dry place to stay and sort out his thoughts. At that moment, he would have even been content to join the gaunt, huddled figures who were using cardboard boxes and other bits of garbage for shelter.

Ultimately, he settled on a cheap motel wedged between a grocery store and a nightclub, with an owner who asked no questions and barely looked at Taggart when he paid for the room's very reasonable charge with his Interpol-issued currency. Where the residence lacked in luxury, it repaid Michael tenfold with anonymity.

Without so much as telling him where his room was, the owner handed Taggart a key with the number *489* etched into its surface. Rather than asking for directions, he took the key in silence and walked up the stairs at the back of the establishment, observing the dim mood lighting and clichéd Chinese wall art which must have been put in place to attract tourists. As far as anyone else in the country knew, that was all that Michael was.

The meager price of the accommodations had initially confused him, but Taggart had written it off as a reflection of the district. Upon opening the door to room 489, however, the real reason became evident. It could hardly be called a "room" at all, its size being less than that of a walk-in closet. It was furnished with a bed featuring moth-eaten sheets, a nightstand which supported a desk lamp, and nothing else. There were no adjoining doors, so Taggart assumed that the bathroom must be down the hall. Trying not to think of the state of *that* area, he shut the door behind him and pulled on a cord which activated a single bulb on the ceiling. Michael had to crouch to avoid running into it, but the lack of amenities didn't bother him. The room had four walls, a bed, and a lock on its door; that was all he needed.

It would have presented a problem if he suffered from claustrophobia, but Taggart found something oddly comforting about being in such an enclosed space. It gave him a sense of control, a sense of security instead of confinement.

In fact, the entire city had presented this feeling so far, and if it weren't for the unstable nature of the district and the fact that he was involved in international espionage, he would have thought of Hong Kong as a pleasant place to spend retirement.

Pushing these thoughts aside, Taggart took off his shoulder bag, propped it against the wall, and sat down on the bed. The events of the past hour were still running through his mind, and he couldn't help but second-guess his tirade against Grant. The more he thought of the repercussions of this action, the more his head felt unbearably sore.

It would have been so much easier to keep my damn fool mouth shut. But I couldn't. Not anymore. This had to happen. It just should have happened at a more opportune time.

Taggart buried his head in his hands, gripping his hair in his fingers and pulling hard, just to feel some sensation of pain that wasn't in his mind. He felt pain and comfort in equal measure, not sure which was which anymore.

What is an opportune time for this to happen? There isn't one. God damn it. I know I need to rest, but what's the point if tomorrow's going to be the same? I just don't feel right and I won't feel right. Can't. But I also can't stay under Grant's thumb anymore. I'm free.

Letting out a rattling breath, Michael raised his head and stared at the wall in front of him.

Then why am I here? Besides the fact that I'm stranded, I could just fly back… Right. No place to go. And I can't abandon what I've been doing. Not now. Not after I've put so much into this already. Pretty sorry excuse for staying, but I've got to. Got to. Come on. Come on, Michael Faust. Come on.

It was clear to him that no sleep would come that night. After staring into the light bulb for a few minutes and letting spots fill his vision, Taggart swung his legs over the edge of the bed and opened his bag. Its contents were sparse, with only spare clothes, toiletries, a notebook, a small medical kit, and a ballpoint pen present. His previous journal had been confiscated by Interpol in order for them to screen its contents for any "dangerous thoughts or behavior," but they had left him with another and requested that he fill it with his thoughts. With too much energy to sleep and too little will to do anything else, Taggart opened the book, uncapped the pen, and began to write.

Personal Journal of Michael Faust Taggart, March 18, 2016

I don't like this one. This notebook, I mean. Too new. Pristine. Empty. Like it's meant to be on a shelf and not be written in. Like it's a book that nosy librarians would watch you take off of the shelf and almost dare you to dog-ear one of the pages. It's been soaked through, but still. It still looks too new. Hopefully after I write in it some more, it'll look more like a journal. Until then, I really don't like it.

So I've left Grant behind. That happened. It still doesn't feel like it happened at all, but it did. I'm only convinced of that because I'm still soaking wet from jumping out of that boat. Just being loaded with expectations and responsibilities that I can't deal with and that tear me apart I can't handle it. I just can't. Even as I write this, I need to pause so many times, just to not get angry. Angry at Interpol, angry at society, angry at myself. Myself, mostly. Being convinced that doing what I'm told will get me far in life… Finally I know that this isn't true. ~~It's the biggest lie.~~ Maybe not the biggest. Maybe not. There are so many that we just take for truth that I don't even know of. I doubt that any of these thoughts will make sense on paper. They make sense in my head, and that just concerns me even more because it might mean I'm losing grasp on what makes sense and what doesn't. What if my version of that is different from everyone else's?

I just want to stop. I just want to stop fighting this imaginary war in my head and this war against the Affliction. At least the one against the Affliction is real. I think it is. I hope it is.

Whatever the case, I need to get out of this. Maybe it won't be for a while, maybe I'll have to deal with the Affliction first, or maybe I'll die in the process, but… I just need to plan on living with some peace in my life. I need to take some time for my own benefit. Some people would write that off as selfish, but that's bullshit. I doubt myself on this a lot, but it's complete bullshit. I've spent so long looking after other people and doing their work for them — none of that would have been done if I wasn't here. And I feel dangerously close to not wanting to be here at all. Alive, I mean, not just in a shoebox of a room in China. That's just another disjointed thought fighting for attention with all of my other disjointed thoughts, but it's there. It's a pretty sad day when I can't even contemplate that because so many other things are going on. And if I contemplated it and decided that I didn't want to live, then none of the other things would matter at all.

I guess that means I want to stay around. I probably would have already resigned myself to suicide and done it if I was really meant to. Who knows? I certainly don't know much right now, so I guess it's up to this city to carry me along. This overflowing dumpster of a city is my guiding light. It's a depressing thought, but I'm not exactly a stranger to depressing thoughts. Hopefully when all of this is over, they'll be less familiar. Hopefully when all of this is over, I'll still be here.

Hong Kong, China: Wan Chai District
Flophouse, March 19, 2016

He had no idea what time it was in his interior room, but when Taggart was at last able to sleep, it was from ten in the morning until eleven o'clock at night.

With no notion of where he was about to go, Taggart stood up, left his belongings, and headed back downstairs and into the heart of Hong Kong. It was just after midnight, so the heart of the city was beating vigorously.

In every direction that he looked, something was happening. Despite the rain, people were filtering through the crowds without umbrellas, seeming to be unaware that they were being soaked. Taggart joined them, and no one took any notice. He had become a faceless part of the city already, and this provided a welcome change which he could easily get used to.

He was free from the prying eyes of Grant and Interpol, and this was a reassuring fact, but Michael couldn't avoid the feeling that he was still operating under their wing. It might have been because this had been a reality for so long, but it is true of any long-term prisoner that freedom is a welcome yet uncomfortable change to them. Taggart was through with being a prisoner.

Regardless, it was only a few minutes before he moved his soaking wet frame through the entrance of a bar. It never occurred to him why he chose this place. He had never been a serious drinker, except at the time of his wife's death. That had long since passed, however, and the most he had consumed in recent memory was the beer back in Moscow. Considering the circumstances, Taggart thought it might have been an unconscious expression of his freedom – Strictly speaking, Sentinels were supposed to stay straight-edge at all times during their assignments. Michael had been given a thorough lecture even for the one beer in Moscow. The experience might have been like that of a sheltered teenager departing for college and getting his hands on all the booze he could handle, and then some.

In any case, Taggart found himself in a high-class restaurant with high, glass windows adorning the far wall, ornate tables lain out in an organized fashion, and a fully-stocked bar lining the left-hand side of the room.

Trying to maintain an air of dignity despite his disheveled state, Michael made his way to the bartender. It was at this point that he realized one critical disadvantage he had – he didn't know a word of Chinese. The operation in Russia had been planned in such a way that he had time to study the basics of the language, but he had been afforded no such luxury for the assignment in Hong Kong.

The barman didn't seem to mind, however, when Taggart put several bills on the table and pointed at a bottle on the wall without a word. The man must have assumed that he was either a tourist or simply a bizarre person – or perhaps both.

Whatever the case, the bills disappeared off of the counter and were replaced by a glass and a bottle of what looked like red wine. Both of these were emptied by Taggart in equal measure until the bartender took them away and informed him in broken English that he could sit at the bar until closing time, but he had reached his limit for the night.

Too tired and disoriented to care, Taggart staggered to his feet. Stumbling over himself, he managed to cross the room and sink into a booth, hit by a sudden wave of paranoia. He had already been trembling, but this intensified until he was hardly able to stay seated. In fact, he was on the verge of standing when what he saw rooted him to the spot.

Michael was sitting in the corner, absently watching the smoke rise from an old man's cigar. The vapor rose in curling, undulating wisps, and it made him shudder for reasons unknown to him.

Through these wisps of smoke, strangers floated into the room with their heads down. There were three of them, and Taggart found all of them to have a threatening presence. They made their way straight toward Michael, all of them dressed in dark coats and clutching what must have been weapons beneath them.

With a yell, he sprang from the booth and lowered his shoulder into the one in the center. Rather than feeling his body connect with another's, Michael tumbled to the ground and felt his head hit something solid, likely a barstool. The bartender called over two gruff-looking types who must have been bouncers, but Taggart was already clambering to his feet and hurrying to get outside. Everything was so much louder now, the pain from this forcing him to plug his ears.

It was at this moment that thoughts began to fill his head, ones which he could neither control nor comprehend. They were thoughts of the questions that could not and would not be answered. They were thoughts of things that he forced from his mind during the darkest sleepless nights. They were the thoughts of color's smell and sound's texture. They were the thoughts of the insane.

As soon as he began to struggle his way through the exit, the walls felt as if they were closing in on him quite rapidly. He felt as if every eye was on him as he was about to be crushed to death, and he wondered why in the world they weren't helping him, or at least panicking for themselves. Fear replaced fatigue in Michael's mind, and he threw himself toward the door, tripping over a chair leg and crawling the last few feet until he was back on the sidewalk. The three strangers were gone, and it was possible that they had never existed at all.

It was here that terror truly took hold. Much like when he was faced with a dangerous or tense situation, his adrenaline spiked, and everything seemed to take on a red tint in his vision. Instead of feeling dizzy or sick, Taggart felt every sense sharpen painfully. Except – something was off this time. Something was different about that street and people on it. This feeling was faint at first, but it grew into a grotesque image, with people's faces morphing into shapes which were so unnatural, it made him recoil in fear. Each person who passed was deformed in a way that made them stumble along their way, some crawling and seeming to grasp at other's legs to drag them along. The worst of all were their faces – if they could be called faces at all.

Where their eyes should have been was a deep gash, extending all the way around their head like some sort of visor. Inside this slit was nothing but darkness, more penetrating than a shadow or even the blackness of the sky above. The rest of their face was blank, save for wrinkles which surrounded noses and mouths that should have been there - but weren't. Each one also had what looked like several red-hot pokers running horizontally through their heads and necks. Every "person" was the same in grotesqueness, and this created a fear which cut off Michael's breath and left him shaking.

In fact, saying that he was jittery didn't nearly do the situation justice. His fear wasn't only the distorted apparitions that were swimming in and out of his consciousness. No, the majority of his fear came from the unknown. If the things in front of him were perceivable to the human eye, then what else was? What else was hiding behind the thin veil that these creatures had cut down that night? Hell if he knew, and he sure as hell didn't want to know. All Taggart could do was hope that this was all a product of his overly imaginative and often grim mind. That too brought worries - all of them regarding his sanity and state of mind - but things outside of one's self are always more dangerous than those occurring within. *Actually,* Michael thought, *No. That's complete garbage. I think. Or maybe I can't even think at all right now.*

Taggart stumbled backwards, backpedaling on all fours and completely forgetting his thoughts from a few seconds ago. One of the unnatural, impaled figures followed him, crawling forward and seeming to stare into his eyes without any eyes of its own. Even so, the face was somehow familiar. It was like a caricature of a deranged grandfather, complete with yellowing teeth and a wrinkled face. The only thing missing were lines on his visage usually created by smiling. This image swam in and out of focus before snapping into a clear representation of David from Moscow. He had a sinister smile on his face, quite unlike anything Taggart had seen from the actual man.

Before Michael could give this any more thought, it morphed once more, this time into a perfect recreation of Cathy. This image drew a stronger reaction than any of the others could, especially since she was looking down at him with a sardonic grin. It was as if she was laughing at him, laughing at his futile attempts to put himself together. She was full of mirth at the fact that he had been trying for more than a decade to move on after her death and failing to do so even a little bit. This was more than Taggart was able to take.

Breathing heavily now, Michael aimed a kick at the thing and missed, but the creature recoiled for a moment, allowing him to scramble to his feet and run. Granted, he was running in the direction of another mass of these creatures, but his fear had been replaced with pure, unfiltered *rage*. This was mixed with a feeling of guilt at having attacked even a façade of his wife. It sickened him even more that he felt a small measure of satisfaction from having done it. It wasn't easy to put this out of his mind, but Taggart did his best to repress these thoughts.

He knew that he couldn't take on all of them. Not at once, anyway. Running forward, Michael lowered his shoulder into a wall of these beings, knocking them to the ground and causing them to panic. The only reaction to this that Taggart had was a faint satisfaction that he was the one causing the fear, and he had already left that group behind and turned a corner into an alleyway.

It was an alleyway for a moment, at least. The walls on either side of him stretched higher and higher until they formed an archway instead of an alley. These barriers closed in on him just as the restaurant's walls had, but there would be no escaping from these. The surface turned from brick into a writhing mass of slime-covered flesh and bone. All of it was pulsing in a threatening manner as it closed in, and Michael could think of nothing else but to fight back.

Still feeling overcome with rage-filled fear, Taggart swung his fist at the disgusting mass, expecting a soft surface but coming into contact with a surface which split his knuckles on impact. The thing was overjoyed; it was *laughing* at him. Laughing at his attempts to fight the inevitable. It was still closing in; there was barely enough room to stand.

Taggart crumpled to the ground and accepted his fate.

Whatever this is, it needs to stop. Alcohol doesn't do that.
Whatever fits of rage I get, combined with alcohol… maybe.

These were Taggart's only thoughts as he lay on the
pavement with his eyes closed, not entirely sure how he
got there. He was sure that something had happened to his
right hand. His knuckles were split open and bleeding, and
it was a wonder that the pain hadn't woken him up earlier.
Grains of brick and mortar were scattered in the wound,
the remains from the "monster" that he had fought.

Something told him that none of this could be the
effects of the alcohol. No drink, no matter the proof or
percentage, could affect someone like this. Again feeling
like a college freshman who had gone overboard with
their drinking and had awoken with a miserable hangover,
Taggart lied to himself and swore that this would never
happen again.

It took quite a while for him to collect himself and
struggle to his feet, but when he did, dizziness took over
and he almost fell straight back to where he started.
Resting one hand on the wall for support, Taggart
stumbled toward the sidewalk and tried to remember the
address of the hotel. If the hotel wasn't a figment of his
imagination, too.

Michael must have looked like a typical early-morning
alcoholic as he stumbled back to his room, as no one
seemed to pay him any mind. This was something for
which he was immensely grateful.

Once he reached the confines of his quarters, Taggart
took his medical kit from its place in his bag and washed

his hand with antibiotics. After that, he wrapped the area with a bandage, making sure that he still had the dexterity to move and possibly shoot. This made him think of his pistol, and he felt an odd sort of longing for it, as if he was naked and alone without it. Some people take comfort in the company of others, and Michael Taggart took comfort in the cold weight of a SIG P226. He shook his head and smiled – no one ever claimed he was normal, and he was glad of this because "normal" seemed to be a pretty low standard to set.

Retrieving the pistol and the rest of his gear from the storage locker would have to be done soon, but Taggart felt that one order of business would prove to be more important – getting in contact with Emelia Kotova. Taggart didn't delude himself into thinking he could stop the Affliction on his own, and she seemed to be better equipped to handle it than he was, even though she had to look after a newborn child.

Michael had memorized the number that she had given to him, and he hoped that his memory served him well as he punched it into his room's phone. Vaguely surprised that this was even included at this hotel, Taggart listened to the ringing telephone for quite some time, switching hands when his right one began to pain him.

It was only when he thought the voicemail message would play that a rustling sound came over the line, followed by a muffled voice, as if the speaker had placed a cloth over the phone's receiver.

"Yes?"

Taggart considered asking for Kotova by name, but

thought better of it. Phones were just about as private as a room with glass walls, and he had no idea with whom he was talking.

"We met in Moscow," he said instead, trying to keep his voice casual. "You had said that you would keep in touch, but I haven't heard anything from you." Taggart waited, but only a thin layer of static could be heard. "When will I be able to see you again?"

The person on the other end of the call paused for a moment, and Michael was becoming more mystified by the minute. He thought that he could hear other voices in the background, but they were quiet and indistinct.

"Meet me on the 8:00 train bound for North Point tomorrow evening. You'll find me in the third compartment from the back."

With that, the line went dead.

Taggart lowered the receiver slowly, puzzled. It was understandable that Kotova would want to conceal her identity, but this left him with no knowledge of whether he had talked to her at all. In any case, he had the distinct feeling that he would need to retrieve his stash of equipment before doing anything else.

It was with heavy strides that Taggart left his apartment, and each step he took was one of determination. He walked as someone would when having some sinister purpose, when, in reality, he had little purpose at all. Acting like he had a concrete purpose would have to be enough until genuine motivation took hold. Taggart could only cling to the hope that this would happen soon.

The storage unit off of Wing Tai Road was little more than a wall of over-sized post office boxes embedded into the wall of an industrial building. Taggart punched *505* into the keypad on box 17. Its door swung outward to reveal a matte-black briefcase which looked too conspicuous and sturdy to be used for regular, civilian purposes.

Taking the case by the handle, he shut the storage container's door with his other hand and looked at his surroundings for a place he could examine the briefcase's contents. Feeling exposed on the sidewalk, Taggart followed the steady flow of pedestrians until he reached a modest-looking restaurant. After heading inside and giving a quick nod to the cashier there, he hurried past rows of tables and booths until he reached two bathroom doors. It thankfully had the universal 'male' and 'female' silhouettes posted on each one, so he pushed open the former and hurried to lock himself inside the lone stall inside.

After lowering the seat, Taggart rested the case on top of the toilet and opened it. Inside it was a disassembled rifle resting on a contoured foam surface and shining in the dim light of the bathroom. Michael recognized it as being an M24, complete with a telescopic sight and a small kit of tools to assemble the weapon. Interpol had spared no expense in acquiring this weapon, and for a moment he felt guilty for taking it after having left their employ. Just for a moment. He had become something of an independent contractor now — there was no desire to work with the sentinels anymore, but the drug-like effect of his work continued to push him forward in his fight against the Affliction.

Also crammed into the case was his pistol, freshly cleaned and oiled, alongside assorted ammunition and magazines for both weapons. A discreet surveillance device was included, and it was a bit smaller than a penny. It came with an earpiece and brief instructions regarding how to operate it.

The last item was tucked into a corner, and it was only present because Taggart had specifically requested it – dozens of Aspirin tablets. Seeing that everything was in order, Taggart closed the case, set it on the floor of the bathroom, and slumped down onto the closed toilet seat.

It was a good feeling to be armed again. It made him feel less vulnerable, less alone. At the same time, he was struck by the sad reality that cold steel provided him more comfort than people of flesh and blood could. Even leaving behind Grant and the Sentinels was a relief in and of itself, but it also meant that he would be left in a state of isolation.

In fact, he carried with him a feeling of deep longing which was not entirely sad. In fact, it brought with it a sense of immeasurable joy, but this was offset by a feeling that something in his life was… missing. For years, he had loved his work and found his skill in it as something to be truly proud of. Each moment, each simple task he completed was a nostalgic memory. Taggart had given a part of himself to the Sentinels, and, each time he thought about what he had done for them, he was simultaneously satisfied with what he had accomplished and quite saddened by the fact that a piece of him was gone and could never be recovered. Michael knew that this part of him was in a good place, but it remained something he would never get back. Because of this emotional conflict, his work wouldn't leave him, and he couldn't bring himself to leave his work.

Even so, he wasn't done. Not remotely. He knew full well that he had the option of leaving behind Kotova and Nikolai and all of the mess caused by the Affliction, but... No. If he was being honest with himself, Taggart really didn't have that option. The draw of doing something directly fulfilling, something which would have an immediate and tangible impact – that draw was too great to resist.

In the back of his mind, Michael also knew that completing this task might lead to a world in which he could live with himself. It would be a world free from the onslaught of stress and violence that had followed him around for too long. He had tried for so long to resist thoughts like this one. In the past, they had only led to high hopes and harsh disappointments when things didn't work out as he intended. Taggart was stuck between hope driving him forward and giving him purpose, and hope putting him into a higher place to fall from.

It was maddening, all of it, and it made him physically ill. The thought occurred to him that he should be leaning over the toilet in case he vomited, but his feeling of nausea had been present for ages. There was no reason to believe that it would make him sick now. Coughing, though, was unavoidable. There was a hollow feeling in his stomach, even though he had been eating well for once, and it was paired with a sensation similar to the one which a person experiences when nervous about a test or performance. As far as he could tell, Taggart had no reason for this anxiety, but then again, he had no explanation for *most* of the things happening in his mind.

He was living in a state where emotions were all dulled, except, it seems, for the pain which comes from one's own mind. The self-destructive pain which forced him further and further away from everyone else. Further from help.

He hated the world and himself at the same time, and it was tearing him apart. Michael knew this full well. It was all that he could do to push himself to his feet, heft the briefcase in his right hand, and struggle his way back through the restaurant and onto the sidewalk.

The only thing that other pedestrians saw that afternoon as Taggart passed by was a vacant man who looked to be troubled and putting on a false, calm demeanor. If any of them had looked into his eyes as they passed, they would have noted how they tended to twitch and looked unfocused, weary. No one did, of course. They were absorbed in their own lives, and he was absorbed in his own thoughts.

It was by memory that he drifted toward the train station, remembering faintly that he had agreed to meet Kotova on a train to North Point. Taggart took three of the Aspirin from the case and dry-swallowed them all at once. The last one lodged itself in his throat, and it left a sickening, bitter taste before it finally passed through.

Michael shuddered from the familiar sensation, but his head was already beginning to feel lighter. After making a mental note to conserve those pills, he jogged through a crosswalk and into a train station. The building seemed to be a miniature copy of Grand Central Station, albeit a great deal cleaner. Everything was moving with a great deal of efficiency, and even the janitors seemed to take pride in their work.

Careful to avoid getting in anyone's way, Taggart hurried to the appropriate train, paid his ticket, and climbed into the vehicle's interior. To someone who was used to ideas of industrial-era passenger trains and creaking, clanking machines, this could hardly be considered a train at all. The interior resembled an airplane cabin, and the compartment was quiet, air-conditioned, and as clean as the rest of the station. For a moment, Michael was able to forget the ongoing battle in his mind and enjoy the culture and technology around him. Hong Kong may have been overflowing with people, but it more than made up for this with their use of space and dedication to getting things done.

The third compartment from the back was close to empty, so it didn't take more than a few seconds for Taggart to spot Emelia Kotova. She was in the back row, dressed in a black topcoat and staring out the window at the rest of the station. As Michael approached, she gave him no more than a quick sidelong glance. If he hadn't been paying attention, it would be impossible to tell if she had noticed him at all.

He took a seat beside her, resting his briefcase at his feet. Still, Kotova made no greeting or acknowledgment. Taggart stared at her for a few moments, waiting, then resigned himself to sitting with his head facing forward and his hands folded in his lap.

It was not until a voice recited the upcoming stops over the intercom in Chinese and English that Kotova returned to reality and looked over at Taggart.

"Glad to see that you're still here. I had my doubts."

"I still have some things to finish. And I know that you do, too." Taggart did a double take, surprised that he had not noticed something earlier. "Wait… where's your son?"

Emelia Kotova's expression was passive, save for her eyes. They betrayed a sense of fear and concern which only mothers can be familiar with. "I had to leave him in a day-care center back in the city. I found the most reputable one I could, but I'm still not quite convinced. I'll be going back to check on him often. Especially since…"

"Since what?" Taggart asked.

"Never mind. For now. It might come up later, though I hope it won't. Anyway, I have been watching the address that your late friend in Moscow had given. From what I've seen, nothing good is going on there. I haven't been able to hear anything directly, but the apartment itself receives at least a dozen visitors per day, most of whom arrive in the early hours of the morning. The owner of the place is a tough-looking type, might be affiliated with the Triads."

"Have you seen our friend Nikolai?"

"I was getting to that, and yes. I have. He's the most frequent visitor by far. The closest I've gotten to listening in on one of these meetings was three days ago. I made my way up to the room and was listening at the door. There were only two voices on the other side – Nikolai and someone I didn't recognize. If I had to guess, it was the room's owner.

"Anyway, they seemed to be discussing philosophy and politics. Not exactly what I expected. Things got pretty heated when Nikolai expressed that he was a Marxist."

"Really?" Taggart asked, raising his eyebrows. "Marxism… how classless."

Kotova paused for a moment and considered this before recognizing the joke and rolling her eyes. "This is too important, Taggart. You need to focus." She resumed her businesslike manner, but Michael noticed the ghost of a grin come across her face.

"Sorry," Taggart said, even though Emelia knew that he wasn't sorry in the slightest.

"Moving on," she continued, "I had to stop listening in because hotel staff came walking through the hallway. I don't think they tipped Nikolai and the other man off, but we should be on our guard anyway."

"What's the plan?" Taggart asked, remaining focused and composed even though his mind and the train were moving at nearly two hundred miles per hour.

"I was hoping that you'd tell me. I've exhausted all of the ideas that I have, and besides, it probably isn't a good idea for me to go back."

Taggart leaned his seat back and closed his eyes, thinking. Far from helping the process, this only served to remind him of how exhausted he was. Several ideas occurred to him, and it was the most simple of these which seemed the most plausible.

"I have a bug in my briefcase," Taggart said, hurrying to explain when Kotova looked confused. "A listening device. To hear conversations from a distance. If I can plant it in that room somehow, we can get a better idea of what's going on."

Emelia Kotova nodded, pondering. "Sensible. Smart. Fair enough, Taggart. I'll stay discreet and watch out for people trying to get into the room after you. The tenant is usually gone during the early evening, so it would be in our best interest to go there straightaway."

Michael nodded. "I agree. It would probably be a good idea for me to hide the rest of my gear, though," he said, indicating his briefcase. "I can't really afford to be searched if I raise any suspicion."

Kotova agreed, and it was at this point that the train slid to a halt in North Point. She resumed her previous unconcerned air, again pretending to be unaware of Taggart's presence. As she walked past him on her way off of the train, Michael could hear a faint whisper.

"Follow me, but keep your distance." Taggart did so, met with an unexpected thought – even the conversation that he had just had with Kotova was enough to give him energy. Interacting with someone who shared his dedication and drive toward a goal was refreshing, to say the least. If nothing else, he had found another positive thing floating in a sea of negatives.

The sun had long since set, replaced by multicolored lights shining down on Hong Kong. Under these lights, Kotova led Taggart through a maze of streets, not looking back once. For a change, Michael was grateful for the opportunity to follow someone without the paranoia of having his cover blown.

Even if they had been walking arm-in-arm, it was unlikely that other pedestrians would have paid them any mind. In any case, they both knew that precautions such as this one would have to be used for the entirety of their time in China.

Not a word was spoken between them, even as she led him into the lobby of an up-scale hotel which seemed to rise miles above the city. Taggart opened his briefcase a fraction of an inch, hastily grabbed the bug and dropped it into his pocket, and handed the case to a bellhop. He gave the confused man several dollars and told him, "Hold this in the lobby please. I'll be back for it."

Kotova, who had been pretending to read a magazine at the other end of the room, continued to lead the way, funneling them into an elevator. A group filed out of the box, after which she and Taggart stepped in. The former jabbed at the *'close door'* button, ensuring that there would be no unwanted guests joining them.

The silence continued on the elevator ride, which lasted the better part of a minute. Taggart's heart rate was increasing, and it was with a great deal of effort that he suppressed the usual semi-conscious state which he encountered in tense situations. This caused his head to twitch to the side several times, causing Kotova to glance at him in concern. She said nothing, however.

The moment the doors slid open, Emelia Kotova exited the elevator, turned left, and made her way to room 878. She stood, as if at attention, opposite the room. Taggart remained as inconspicuous as he could and walked to the door. It had occurred to him that the door would be locked, and, sure enough, it refused to budge when he tried the handle. Using a trick which had gotten him back into his college dorm when he had forgotten his keys, Michael withdrew his wallet from his pocket and looked for a card of some sort. He had forgotten that he had even been carrying it. In fact, and it still bore the effects of having been dragged through the bay. Suffice it to say, water and leather do not make the best combination.

Alongside soaking wet bills and several business cards that Interpol had provided to make his belongings seem more legitimate, Taggart found a temporary identification card bearing the name 'Eric York.' Michael rolled his eyes. Even though *Taggart* wasn't even his real name, he still preferred it. It had a nice feeling. It seemed like that and his gear would be the only things from Interpol which he would be keeping.

Taggart held the card between his thumb and forefinger and proceeded to slide it through the crack between the door and the wall. It took a great deal of effort and cautious glances around the hallway, but the door at last clicked open with only Taggart and Kotova standing in the hallway. He gave one last glance back at her before entering the room and closing the door behind him.

The interior of room 878 was dark, save for the light filtering in from its massive windows. It cast shadows across the entire room, each of them stretched out to an eerie degree. Once his eyes had adjusted to the darkness, Taggart began to scour the area for a place where he could plant the bug. If Nikolai and his associates were intelligent, they would have the room swept before every meeting. If that was the case, he needed a place which would remain hidden from people trained to find it. He also had to be certain that he didn't disturb the furniture in any noticeable way – the room was kept in immaculate condition, as if it hadn't been lived in.

Options were limited, as the contents of the room

included only a bed, a night stand a sectional, a coffee table, a television, and a bathroom area. Since night stand and the bed were close to the couch, Taggart opted to open the face of an alarm clock atop the former and slide the bug inside it. After returning the clock to its original position, he made his way back to the coffee table. Sitting upon it was a laptop, and he felt like he couldn't pass up the opportunity to examine its contents. In fact, the coffee table was the only unkempt part of the room, with empty beer bottles scattered across its surface.

Michael had little time to ponder this, however, because as soon as he had lifted the laptop's lid and seen its screen light up, he heard a shuffling coming from behind the door. His head snapped in that direction, and by instinct he slammed the laptop shut and picked up one of the beer bottles. He smashed the latter on the edge of the coffee table, resorting to the only weapon that was available.

As he turned to check on Kotova, the door burst open in front of him, revealing three muscular, well-dressed Chinese men standing in a pool of light. For a moment, everything was still. The only movement was that of Taggart's hand clenching tighter around the broken bottle.

At the same moment, the stranger on the left and the one on the right charged to either side, grabbing Taggart by the arms. He threw all of his weight to his right, toppling all three of them. Michael was able to roll to his feet before the others, and he faced the remaining attacker and assumed a fighting stance. Rather than waiting for the man to make a move, he feinted right and shifted the bottle to his left hand. As the stranger was recovering from his misstep, Taggart sent the bottle crashing down on the top of his head. Shards of glass rained down alongside the man as he fell into a heap on the floor.

It was clear that Taggart had kept one more thing from Interpol – his close combat training.

As he made to turn and face the other two, however, he felt his arms being pinned together by a pair of strong hands and another pair pressing a rag to his mouth and nose. His arms and legs flailed, and he tried his hardest to pry the hands off of him, but it was only seconds before his body surrendered and Taggart slid into darkness.

United States Army Code of Conduct (Sanction IV)

If I become a prisoner of war, I will keep faith with my fellow prisoners. I will give no information or take part in any action which might be harmful to my comrades. If I am senior, I will take command. If not, I will obey the lawful orders of those appointed over me and will back them up in every way.

North Point, Hong Kong, China: March 19, 2016 – 8:34 P.M.

This must be the closest I'll ever come to being deaf, dumb and blind. Like Tommy. The Pinball Wizard. God, my head aches. I know I haven't been able to get my thoughts straight recently, but this… this is something even worse. I don't know where I am… I'm moving. Argh… I'm definitely moving. My stomach can tell me that much. People breathing… I think. Two people? Their footsteps sound like it.

I think I'm lying down. I think. I'll just try to sit up… Nope. Not going to happen. I can breathe, but I think that's about it. Wait…

I hear other voices! Maybe? Yes, I think so! Cars are here, too. I must be on a sidewalk… Hey! People! Help! Can't you see that I'm being kidnapped! Help!

I know they can't hear me… Shit. Looks like they can't see me, either. Maybe if I vomit, people will smell it and investigate. At this rate, I might…

Okay. Need perspective here. I must be concealed somehow. On a stretcher? That would explain why I'm laying between two people while moving – and why I feel so nauseous. Or that could be from whatever that cloth had on it.

That's right! I was in the hotel room, and I had just planted the bug… Shit, the bug. Did I take the earpiece with me? Do these guys have it? Does it matter? Just need to get up somehow.

Oh… okay, then. Going up. Am I being loaded into a truck, or – yes. That is a car door slamming. For sure.

Argh. This is not much easier on my stomach, guys! I know you can't hear me and wouldn't care if you could, but jeez! Give me a break!

Turning right now, and… yep. I've flipped over. They must have had a sheet over me, because there sure isn't one now. Are they posing as EMTs? Smart. Backhanded, unnecessary, and painful for me, but smart.

Oof! Okay. We've definitely stopped. Okay boys, how much do I owe you for the fare? *Ha. Ha ha. Guys?*

Anyone?

Maybe they left. Maybe I'll come to my senses in a minute and go back to Kotova and go – damn it. They didn't leave. Speaking of Kotova... where is she? Must be in a similar place to me. Maybe right beside me, for all I know.

The sheet's back on now. Thanks guys! I was getting cold over here! *You know, I would sigh if I could right now. Maybe later I can – whoa.* Easy there! Okay... feels like I'm on a boat. Wait! Can I move? My hand is starting to go... come on... Yes! Now I just need to make sure they don't know –

"Hey! He's coming to!"

Damn.

With that, a sharp blow came down on Taggart, shattering his nose and sending him back into unconsciousness.

Unknown Location: March 20, 2016 – 2:29 P.M.

Taggart was vaguely aware of the fact that he was alive. His vision remained blank, but he was now able to move his limbs. This was with great difficulty, however, and he found it preferable to remain still and wait for something to happen. That seemed like all he could manage.

When Michael had thought that his hangover would be the worst feeling he would encounter in China, he had been dead wrong. If he was still in China at all, that is. All Taggart knew was that he was lying prone on a cold, stone floor. That, and he could hear the sound of rushing water outside. He knew that he couldn't be on a boat – he wasn't swaying back and forth, and, besides, what boat has a stone floor?

The coldness of the ground was refreshing against his

cheek, but Michael forced himself to roll onto his back and open his eyes. He was staring up at bricks which seemed to have been shoved together by someone with little idea of how to build things; each one was chipped and crooked. Even though the room was about the size of a jail cell, it gave Taggart the claustrophobic feeling of being buried alive. There were no windows to speak of, and the only apparent access to the rest of the world was a steel door. This was the only part of the room which looked to be well-built and immovable.

There were no footsteps from the other side, no sign that anyone else was nearby. Taggart remembered reading *The Count of Monte Cristo* in high school, and he had never thought that he would share the fate of Edmond Dantès. He had hated that book, but he would have appreciated having it if he was going to be spending a great deal of time in this room.

Overcome by fatigue, Michael crawled to the corner of his prison and leaned against the wall, resting his head on the jagged bricks. One edge stuck out at an odd angle, pushing against his temple, but Taggart didn't care. In truth, it felt more pleasant than trying to keep his head upright.

For quite some time, Taggart had been fighting between the idea of leaving behind his mission and pursuing it to the death. The given circumstances had taken this choice out of his hands, it seemed. He had reached the point of complete and utter ambivalence. There was nothing left, and that was fine by him. There was nothing –

This train of thought was snapped all at once. A scuffling could be heard from the adjacent room, so faint that he probably wouldn't have heard it if it wasn't for the fact that he was leaning against that wall. Taggart cracked one eye open, waiting to see if the sound would return.

After a minute or so, it did. From what he could tell, someone was in a similar position to his on the other side. Sure enough, panicked breathing could soon be heard, and Taggart considered calling out to the person. The only thing holding him back was the concern that his voice would be heard by some third party – the one which put him in the cell in the first place. Because of this, he remained silent and hoped that the other prisoner would do the same.

All the while, he wondered who exactly that other prisoner was. The only person who he could imagine was Kotova, and that made him all the more anxious to find some way of communicating with the other inmate.

Putting those thoughts to the side for the moment, Taggart tried to stand, fell back against the wall, tried again, and slumped down once more. This led him to believe that he had been drugged as well as knocked out, and that thought left him no more confident about the situation.

The confines of his cell appeared to be empty, save for a rotting, wooden chair in the corner and chipped pieces of brick scattered across the floor. Michael did his best to avoid cutting his hands on these pieces as he crawled toward the chair.

He tried to hoist himself onto it, but one of the legs collapsed as soon as he put pressure on it.

It was several hours before the hole began to reveal the other side, and it was apparent that the other prisoner's handiwork had created an opening just above his. A set of hands appeared across from him, and with a combined effort, they created an aperture which was only a bit larger than Taggart's eye. The other person dropped their piece of brick, wiped the grime from their hands, and knelt down to look back at Michael.

He was met with a familiar pale, blue eye, except that it was now creased with lines of fatigue. When a voice came from that side of the wall, it was shaking with bitterness.

"Hello, Taggart."

"Emelia! What happened back there? How'd they get you, too? Are you okay?"

"Jesus, man; calm down. I'm fine. Coming down from something nasty, but I'm fine."

From the tone of her voice, Taggart doubted this very much, but he continued, "Any ideas on getting out of here?"

Kotova remained silent for a moment, her eye turning away from him as if she had heard something from outside of her cell. After a brief pause, she turned back. "A few. Nothing of any substance, though."

"Me either. Unless waiting for these walls to collapse counts as a plan." Taggart chuckled to himself for a moment before realizing that even he couldn't find mirth in the situation.

"Speaking of which," Kotova said, "The people who put us here in the first place probably wouldn't like the fact that we can communicate like this."

"Right," Taggart agreed, looking around for something with which he could cover the hole. "Hang on."

Before long, he had swept a collection of brick and mortar from around the room into the corner.

"This should work," he said as he placed pieces of debris in the space that they had created. It still didn't look like a proper, sturdy wall, but, then again, that seemed to fit the motif of the cells.

"It'll work fine," he could hear Emelia say from the other side. Her voice was muffled, but she didn't have to raise it for him to hear with more clarity. Taggart was glad of this, as it meant that intrusions from their captors would be less likely.

For minutes which felt like hours, there was no sound but the crashing of waves and the labored breathing of the two prisoners. Taggart felt as if the sounds should have been calming to him, but they instead proved to be maddening. He had become so accustomed to noise and activity that the lack of it felt fundamentally wrong. At the very least, there was no rocking sensation of being on a boat. To break the monotony, he turned to face Kotova and said,

"Tell me something, Emelia. When your government and your husband left you out in the cold, why did you decide to keep pursuing the Affliction? Wouldn't it have been easier for you and your child to lie low? It could have been safer, too."

Kotova continued to look straight ahead, and when she spoke, it was almost as if she was addressing herself. "The easiest paths are the ones that have been crossed countless times, and people who travel on them can only discover what everyone else has already found. Cutting through a new, difficult path of your own may not provide the same security, but it gives one the chance to do something which they believe is right. True, it is more dangerous, but the alternative is a death which begins long before you stop breathing."

It was Taggart's turn to let his eyes slide out of focus and contemplate the meaning of this. It was quite some time before he found any words to say. "That's... profound. What's that from?"

On the other side of the wall, Kotova shrugged. "My mind."

This was followed by another period of silence, this one much longer than the first. This time, it was Emelia who decided to speak up.

"What about you, Michael? When you became so frustrated with everything, why didn't you leave your assignment?"

Michael could do nothing but shake his head. "In all honesty, I'm not sure. It may be something similar to your reasoning, just wanting to pursue some form of truth. Some sort of meaning. Or, it could be that I've just lost it altogether. I've been so exhausted by this way of life for so long, it makes me nauseous just thinking about it. To answer your question, the only thing I know for sure right now is that I don't know *anything* for sure.

"All in all, though, I think I just want to rest. I'll find somewhere in the mountains to settle down and give my mind a break. I'll take a car out and drive for hours along windy roads before circling back to my house, where a fire will be waiting for me. That'll give me the warmth and peace I need to really let everything else go. I'll just let go of the rest. Try to not be so high-strung for a change."

Both of them remained motionless after he said this, each one forgetting where they were for a moment and escaping to the mountain retreat which did not yet exist. This was broken when a sudden realization hit Taggart.

"Wait..." he said, concern visible on his face. "Where is your son? Is he safe?"

Kotova was trying to remain passive, but Michael could see the apprehension growing in her eyes. "That knock to your head must have done more damage than I thought. Like I said on the train, I've left Alexey in a day care in Hong Kong. One near the industrial district that I know I can trust. The last thing that I wanted to do was leave him with strangers right now, but... I can only imagine what would be done to him if he was there when we were captured. My only fear is of my ex-husband."

"Why is that?" Taggart asked.

"Because I know what he's capable of. Because I know that he wouldn't hesitate to inflict the same pain on my son that he inflicted on me. The emotional pain will be spared, only because he is too young to understand, but the physical... There is almost no chance that he would survive the same ordeal that I was put through. Since you've bared your soul, I suppose that it's only fair that I do the same.

"We had been married for six years when he started

becoming violent. I didn't see it coming at all before then. Hell, we were married so young that I didn't see anything at the time. We met while he was on a furlough back in '99. All of the girls were obsessing over the army boys and how strong and brave they were… except for me. I couldn't have cared less. That is, until he walked up to me and introduced himself with the three most damaging words that he could have said - *you are beautiful.* Of course, I was over the moon at this, being young and stupid like I happened to be. We married two years later, when I was seventeen. We even had to obtain a special license to marry so soon, but… I was in love. Or what I thought was love. In any case, I haven't gone around claiming to know what love is since leaving him.

"He was, like most of our country's troops, sent out to fight in the Second Chechen war. I wanted nothing more than to have him back in my arms, and it seemed for some time that he felt the same way. As the years stretched on without him there, he fell out of touch with me and seemed to fall in love with that damn war. He relished in it. None of the notes that he sent back to me contained any hint that he might be missing me, let alone peace and safety. He was hypnotized by the excitement that war provided him. If he had been killed in a hole somewhere for that unworthy cause, he would have done it with a smile on his face.

"As it turns out, it would have been better if he *had* died in the war. When he returned, he had changed. That might even be too mild of a term for what happened to him. The handsome, fresh army recruit who I married had become someone else. He was vile and cruel. This wasn't directed toward me, at least not at first. I noticed how he behaved toward people who had been our friends. I say 'had been,' because all of them distanced themselves from us before long. I honestly can't say that I blame them.

"Then…" she paused, her voice shuddering as she pronounced the last word. "Then he turned his aggression on me. It started with — you've probably guessed — drinking. I know about the stereotypes of Russians being perpetually drunk and obsessed with vodka, everyone does. But he took that concept and made it a lifestyle.

"On the nights when he decided to come home, he was so far from sober that I started locking myself in our spare room and covering my ears. I started convincing myself that this was just a temporary phase, pretending that everything was okay. When we both signed on with the Security Service, I thought that it might bring some sort of balance into our lives. It took me so long to realize that I was lying to myself. By that point, he combined his drunken rage with his rage left over from the war. What came out of that were bruises that I lied about to friends, fear for my life, desperation, and guilt.

"Guilt was there because that's what a manipulative person gives out in droves. That son of a bitch convinced me that I was the cause of his 'suffering,' the reason that he was so angry. He accused me of not being there for him, even though I had done everything I could. Apparently that wasn't enough. Even when I tried to alert someone at the Service about his behavior, I was ignored. Things like this should never go unnoticed, but a combination of misogyny and my ex-husband's military experience made the issue get swept under the rug.

"That wasn't even the most harmful thing. The

traditional views of marriage hurt me in a way that nothing can heal. I've been told so often of the sanctity and wonderful nature of being in such a union, but nobody had ever thought to let me know that if I'm being hurt, I should distance myself from the cause of that pain. Nobody ever thought to tell me that I should be the most important person in my life. Yes, I should love others and be there for them, but if I don't look out for myself, then there will be no 'me' in the first place.

"I may have been a fool for staying with him, but I will not let *anyone* convince me that this was my fault. I won't be guilted into believing that I deserved those bruises, scars, and two broken bones. I finally have enough self-respect to take care of my basic needs first. What it took to wake me up was a night that I try to forget, but know I never will. He had been away for a week, and in the meantime, I was working so many hours that I didn't know that the landlord was fully prepared to remove me from my home. On the last day before we would be evicted, my ex-husband decided to come back. He was drunk out of his mind again, but I still tried to explain the situation. As soon as I started expressing that I was unhappy with how he had been treating me, he shut down and refused to listen to anything else.

"Well, I still had these issues to deal with, so I continued. I talked for a few minutes, but it was like having a conversation with a brick wall. When I asked what he was going to do to help get us out of our financial situation, all he did was look up at me and say… he commented on how long it had been since we had had sex. Of all things, he brought *that* up. I told him that there were a million reasons for that, and then he started saying that this was why we were so badly off. Suggesting that if I had *'acted more intimately,'* he would have stayed home, and we would be a proper family."

There was a long pause after she said this. When Emelia continued, her voice was shaking in sadness and anger. "He said something along the lines of *'well, we can fix that right now,'* and he started walking toward me with a look in his eye that no person should ever have. I backed into the kitchen, fumbled on the counter, and picked up a knife that was laying there. When I raised it, he only laughed. He didn't have to say anything. We both knew that I wouldn't be able to defend myself with it. Then… he took me." Tears had begun to roll down her cheeks, and it was a wonder that she could continue to talk so evenly. "He took me out of anger and possessiveness, not knowing that the consequence would be Alexey. As he was doing it, he laughed. It was a cold laugh without any humor, but I knew what it meant. He knew. He knew that I didn't have anywhere to go.

"Soon, I was put on another assignment, and I left that house for the last time. Even if it means my death, I will not go inside that godforsaken house again. Then, soon into the assignment, it was discovered that I was pregnant. My career and my husband had left me behind, and all that I have left is Alexey. The man I used to love so much told me - not asked, told me - to have an abortion. By this point in my pregnancy, it was illegal to do that, and he knew that. I refused.

You might think that I'm crazy for wanting to keep a child conceived by such dysfunctional parents in such horrible circumstances, but believe me when I say that I made the right decision. Rather than explaining reasoning

177

that you won't relate to, I'll just sum it up by saying that you aren't a mother, and you never will be. The bond between a mother and her child will always be different from the one with the father. As far as I can see, the mother's connection is always stronger. Always more valid. The man may drop off some of his seed and help the woman with payments and such, a luxury that I wasn't given. No surprise there.

"But carrying another living being inside you… being directly responsible for another life in what you eat and even how you're able to move… It's so vastly different from what a man will ever experience. Don't get me wrong, I would have had an abortion if I was still in the first trimester and wasn't able to care for him, but neither of those were the case. I had a government position giving me financial stability for a while, and I also almost had a child. It was still a fetus at the time, but *soon*. I respect that it is a woman's choice of what she does with her body, and this just happened to be the choice for me. Whether my ex-husband liked that or not.

"If the only thing I do in life from this point out is teach my son to love and respect and to be an honorable man, then I'll have done my part. I'll be content with my life then. Like I told my husband when he tried to force me to abort Alexey - 'I'm going to raise this child no matter who tries to stop me, and I'm going to make sure he's not a complete fuck-up like his father.' Until that point comes, I need to keep him safe. I need to get out of this place and know that he is safe.

"I haven't trusted a soul since that man. Whether it's stubbornness or poor adjustment on my part, I won't. I can't afford to have that life again. And you may still wonder why I decided to have Alexey after all. Well, I don't blame you for that, because I wonder the same thing sometimes. I think it was the last thing I ever heard from my ex-husband, once he discovered that I was pregnant. *'I won't have any child of yours taking my name and defiling it.'*

"Ha. As if the child or I would take the name of the man who made our lives hell. I'm bringing Alexey as far away as I can, and the Affliction is the only thing keeping me from running away with him. As soon as I can be done with this, I'm gone. I've had enough."

Having not expected this answer in the slightest, Taggart was struck dumb. "I… I'm not sure what to say. I would say 'I'm sorry,' but it feels like those would be the most shallow words of comfort in the world right now."

Kotova almost laughed, but it ended up being nothing more than a quick breath through her nose indicating ironic amusement. "Yeah. From what I've observed, he's already in Hong Kong, posing as a factory worker in an electronics plant. Something like that. I have a few choice words for him the next time I see him. None of them are very appropriate for public consumption." She sighed and leaned back onto the wall. "I just know that if I ever get out of here, the first thing that I'm going to do is find my son. He's not leaving my side until all of this is over."

"I agree," Taggart said, "Aside from where you said 'if' we get out. It seems more like a matter of 'when.'" Kotova made a noise indicating skepticism. "No; I'm serious. Provided that whoever captured us isn't too organized, we should have a chance at some point. Either that, or I'm kidding myself, but it seems like I won't last a day in here if I took any other mindset."

Kotova nodded but offered no further comment.

"Since it's not like we're going anywhere, I'll offer a story of my own. It's not so life-changing, but it feels pretty relevant right now." He turned his head and looked through the hole, wondering if he should go on. Kotova didn't appear to be bothered by the idea, so he began, "I don't mean to be starting a contest of dysfunctional families, but my story is along some of the same lines as yours. I get your feeling of not being able to let go of someone, even when you need to. They're family. Nothing can really change that, even if we want it to." Kotova gave a shuddering breath, but when Taggart stopped speaking for a while, she only waited for him to continue.

"Well, my dad's family is one which I try not to think about. Every family seems to have an odd one out, and that was my dad. He was the only one with any sense. That might come off as pretty biased, but looking at the rest of them... yeah. It's a wonder that he turned out how he did.

Most of them died out pretty quickly when I was pretty young, so I was shielded from most of what they had done. That is, except for my uncle. Uncle Jeff. He was one of those people who just looked at death and laughed at it. Cancer and two heart attacks weren't enough to do it, and I wasn't able to believe it when I heard that he finally had passed.

"He and my dad were the two youngest siblings in their family, but they were still the farthest apart. Hell, they never even mentioned that fact, but it wasn't like it was hard to tell. It's like my uncle was born at a time when everyone else had their own things to do and couldn't be bothered with him. I have no doubt that that's the reason things turned out like they did.

"When everything really went wrong was when I was… wow, I must have been about thirteen or fourteen at the time. Uncle Jeff wasn't a heavy drinker, but that was pretty much the only thing that he didn't indulge in. If anything could be smoked, snorted or shot up, he was all over it. It wasn't surprising to anyone when he ended up in prison for narcotics possession. It might have surprised him, but I don't think he was conscious enough to notice much.

"Then came his time behind bars, which ended up being a good time for my family and a terrible time for my uncle. He was put through the process of cutting off all his addictions at once. It was so sudden and difficult of a change, I heard that he tried to sue the prison for mistreatment of an inmate. Funny enough, nobody wanted to take the case of a convict who was arguing that he should get his drugs back.

"He served his time, which was extended a few times for different infractions while he was inside. When he got out, though, no one would hire him, and I can't say I blame them. He also had no place to stay, and my dad was the only option he had left. You wouldn't believe how pissed my mom was. She might have known the most about Uncle Jeff's addictions. I'm not really sure how, but she was always aware of what he was doing. In fact, she eventually refused to attend family reunions if he would be going to them as well. One of my oldest memories of this was her talking about his 'special salt shakers.' Cocaine probably wasn't the worst of it, either.

"Well, when he moved in, we were still in a one-story, two-bedroom house, and we had the less-than-ideal system of having my uncle sleep on the bottom bunk of my bunk bed." Taggart paused, shivering at the thought of what had happened. "It's weird… I had suppressed this for so long, it feels even worse bringing it back to the surface.

"In any case, this arrangement didn't last very long, but it still lasted longer than it should have. I guess that he was still adjusting to being drug-free, because he was a mess the entire time. The only time my parents ever saw him during the first few weeks was when he had to go down the hall to use the bathroom. Even at meal times, he took supplies for cereal and locked himself in my room. That room was such a constant mess, and my parents didn't even once assume that I was the one who caused this. Well, they were right. Uncle Jeff just wasn't able to take care of himself, and I think that was one of the things that pushed him over the edge.

"When he went over the edge, though… there was no doubt of when that happened. It was one night that my dad made him eat dinner with us as a 'family.' Well, that went over well for the first few minutes. As soon as my mom asked what he was doing to find work, he stood up, kicked his chair back, and stormed off. We could all hear my door slamming, and there's probably still a dent where he drove my baseball bat through the wall.

"After that, everything went silent. For a reason that I still don't understand, my dad went back to another dinner conversation as if nothing had happened. If we had addressed what was going on, it probably would have prevented what happened next.

"It was that same night. I walked into my room as quietly as I could, not wanting to wake him up if he was

sleeping. He was - or so I thought. As soon as I was in bed
and fading between waking and sleeping, I felt a hand grab
my arm. I had had nightmares about monsters doing the
same thing when I was a lot younger, and I was so dazed
at the time that I thought that was what was happening.
That is, until I was pulled from the top bunk and went
tumbling to the ground. I landed on my head, and that
didn't help with the disoriented feeling. The next thing I
know, Uncle Jeff is punching the living daylights out of
me. It just wouldn't stop; it's a wonder that I wasn't too
disfigured after that. I think I might have screamed out,
but it's possible that I wasn't even able to. This went on for
weeks. Pretending that I had gotten into fights at school to
hide what he'd done. The randomness of it made things so
much worse. I would climb into bed wondering whether
or not I would be beaten that night. It made even days
when he didn't do anything unbearable. So many times,
I was pulled out of sleep with the same rush of fear and
anxiousness when he threw me onto the ground.

Something caught my parents' attention one night,
though, because my dad came in a few seconds later and
tackled him. I think he asked my mom to call the police.
I specifically remember how calm Jeff seemed in the
situation, and that only made me feel more uneasy. My dad
had him pinned down, even though the sick, twisted guy
wasn't even struggling at all. He was just looking straight at
me with a *hungry* look in his eyes. I'll never get rid of that
image completely.

"And then... well, he was thrown back into prison,
this one more high-security. His name became worse than
profanity in my house, and any mention of him was shut
down before it even started.

"I was never told what happened to him directly, but I overheard my parents talking about it when he died. From what I could tell, he had killed another inmate and then himself after only two days. The guards were trying to restrain him when he had a shiv in his hand. He held it out at them so that they'd keep their distance, and then he turned it on himself. According to the reports from the prison, he was whispering my name the entire time. He wasn't talking to anyone at all, just whispering my name with an unfocused look in his eyes. My parents were right to try and hide this from me, but I believe that everything happens for a reason.

"I don't like going through bad situations without learning something from it. Or at least trying to. Even though I was barely a teenager at the time, I remember that I was able to convince myself that everything was okay. Through the nightmares and moments of waking fear I had, I knew that everything was okay. School was the biggest challenge for me, especially in terms of staying positive. I started writing in the corner of each notebook page while I was taking notes. As soon as I started a fresh page, I wrote the question 'What's going to be okay, Michael?' When I had filled that page and was ready to move on to another, I wrote one word at the bottom: 'Everything.'

Forcing myself to acknowledge this was the only way that I recovered. My mind has never been the same, despite the medications that have been thrown at me. And the more I told myself that everything was okay, the more it started to be true. Since then, I've been convinced that perspective is one of the most important parts of a person's life. A positive or negative perspective can shape days and weeks, and the decisions that are made during those times. A positive perspective is like the body's own placebo pill, especially when it would be easier to look at the negative.

"I'm probably telling you something that you already know, but I've found that it never hurts to be reminded of it. Hell, I need to remind myself of it more often than not. I guess what I'm trying to get at is that this wasn't meant to add a depressing story to another one. It's that bad experiences can destroy people, but truly great people take those negative times and use them to form themselves into better people. I'm not claiming to be a great person, but I'm trying. I'm trying really hard to be."

Kotova, who had been staring straight ahead in contemplation, turned to look at Taggart through the hole in the wall. Though he could only see one of her eyes, he thought he could see a sense of appreciation in her gaze. Michael gave a small nod and formed as strong of a smile as he could. It must have come across as pretty comical, because he was met with muffled chuckling from Emelia. At this, he smiled even more broadly, and it actually looked natural this time.

This was cut short by a sharp gasp of pain from the other side of the wall. Taggart, who had been reclining against the wall, sat bolt upright in alarm. "Emelia? What is it?"

There was no immediate response, only a few groans and profanities uttered in Russian. "Don't bother yourself about it," she said through gritted teeth. "People seem to forget that women have something to deal with once every month, whether they're in a Chinese prison or not.

I'll spare you any more about it; men tend to run away like squeamish children when topics like this come up."

Taggart's heart was still racing with alarm, but it had slowed a little with the knowledge that there was no immediate danger. Relaxing his posture, he said, "Don't worry about it. I've never really been bothered. After all, I'm not the one who has to go through it, so there isn't much room for me to complain."

On the other side of the wall, Kotova raised her eyebrows. "Honestly, I didn't expect that. Maybe I've just been in the wrong company, or maybe you're just strange, Taggart. Hell, it could be both. In any case, I'm impressed." Taggart only shrugged, and Emelia continued, "I've taught myself to reserve judgments about people, but you're something different, Taggart."

"I'm just doing my best," he said with a great deal of weariness. Emelia

"I should probably try to sleep this off, if I can," Kotova said after giving a drawn-out yawn. She was still trembling from whatever chemicals were running through her system.

"Yeah. Me, too."

With that unceremonious goodbye, each of them found a spot on the stone floor which would become their bed for the rest of the foreseeable future. It wasn't the best place that Taggart had slept, but he realized with some bitterness that it wasn't nearly the worst. That would have been his own bed after what had happened. Later on, when his uncle was long gone, he had slept only on the couch in the living room, and his parents didn't try to stop him even once.

Life in Taggart's cell became no easier over time, and this was due, in large part, to the silence that hung over the place. Only the waves and the sound of footsteps in the hall could be heard, and it was maddening. This was broken up only by the conversations he had with Kotova, and those were whispered for fear of the guards.

One such conversation arose after about a week in captivity, at a point where both had resigned themselves to their fate. Kotova had removed the loose brick in the wall to communicate with him, and she was the first to speak.

"What's your stance on cats?"

"What?" asked Taggart, bemused and almost laughing.

"I don't know; I figured I might as well say something. This place is driving me crazy."

"Hm. I really never thought that much about cats… I mean, I had one back in Pennsylvania, where I was born. Never liked it that much, but it died when I was nine. The only thing that I really remember about it was that it killed a snake and brought it into my parents' house. Looked so pleased with itself for bringing in such a catch, and it looked so confused when my mom screamed when she saw it. I was pretty excited, so I ended up keeping the snake skin in my room for a while. Well, my mom wasn't too pleased with me or the cat when she found it. I guess I'm pretty indifferent on cats, but mine gave me a few memories."

Kotova gave a weary chuckle. "Yeah, my experience was

about the same. Where everyone stereotypes us Russians as owning polar bears and such, you'd be amazed at how many cats there are. The rest of my family never wanted any pets, but there were so many cats on the streets of Kursk, I could pretty much choose whichever I wanted. It only took me a few days to distinguish a dozen or so of them, based on their colors and markings. Then, I gave them names and wandered around with them. I was never very social with other people, and you don't strike me as someone who is, either. Hell, I don't think anyone in our line of work is very social. It comes with the territory, as you Americans say.

"Anyway, my friends were the strays. The strays and my books. I carried three or four wherever I went, even if I had no intention of reading any of them. They gave me comfort. I took names from famous book characters when I was a child — Lev, Elena, Alexei." She sighed. "Alexei. I gave that name to my son for the same reason. Because of the man in Dostoevsky's book. I gave him a name of someone honest and virtuous, in the hope that he will be the same.

"It really scares me, you know. I've had to put on a brave, fierce face, mostly because I won't be taken seriously if I don't. It's one of the worst realities I have to face, but it's here to stay, probably for good. But it really does scare me. I've been put in a position that pretty much guarantees my failure. I mean, come on. Single mothers are apt to complain, and they have good reason to do so, but being a single mother on the run from *at least* one criminal organization? Yeah, it's hard to not be bitter.

"I'm sorry. I didn't mean to take a conversation about cats down such a deep route. It just… it just happens sometimes, you know?"

Taggart nodded. "I've had that happen more times than I can count, believe me. I've never been much for small talk, to be honest. It's always been hard for me to be around people who talk without really saying anything, if that makes any sense.

Emelia smiled. "It makes quite a bit of sense, really. There's a Russian idiom that I've always liked. It translates to something like 'throwing words into the wind.' Real, earnest conversation is vastly underrated now. I really can't stand people who are afraid of discussing things that matter. They act as if you are crazy for being earnest, and it's infuriating. Instead, they dilute your mind with useless things. It's not really talking at all, it's filling silence with garbage.

"I know that you're of the same mind, and I don't want to take over the conversation completely, so I'd like to hear what's on your mind, Taggart. It's always refreshing to hear someone speak instead of just *talk*."

Michael, having forgotten about his grim surroundings for a moment, was energized by the presence of a like mind. After thinking for a moment about what he would like to mention, he said, "Well, something that's been on my mind for quite some time is a question that I don't think I'll ever be able to answer. I don't think anyone will. *What if I hadn't gotten into this in the first place?*"

I know we touched on this a bit the other day, and I know that drowning yourself in 'what-ifs' is a toxic thing to do, but this thought just stays with me. It eats away at my mind until I can't think anymore. Then, all I can do is sleep. I sleep until I can think again, then these thoughts drag me back down. The thoughts re-create themselves, and they'll never leave.

He was breathing hard at this point, and his words began to come out at a rapid pace. Kotova had no words to offer, and she had already thought that he wouldn't be able to continue when Taggart resumed his litany. His voice had steadied a little bit, but some shakiness was still very much present.

"I just don't know. At this point, I can't be happy with my choice to join the Sentinels in the first place. I can't help but regret my involvement in such backwards operations and activities. It's just… what if I had stayed back in Pennsylvania with my wife and done something *normal.* Something that would have provided a steady income, given me a consistent schedule, and probably bored me to death.

"Come to think of it though, that might have driven me crazy faster than this job has. I don't know; I'm just all mixed up. The only thing that I can say with absolute certainty is that I don't know anything with absolute certainty."

Kotova laughed. It was a light and emotion-filled laugh at first, but it soon faded into the corners of her cell. This was followed by a sigh and a long pause. Several times, she began to say something before reconsidering it and remaining silent. It was only after several minutes that she said, "I say, fuck it. No, really. Fuck it all. You don't have a reason to be tied to Interpol anymore, especially if they're forcing you to do things that you don't want to do. Remember, I'm no stranger to abusive relationships, and this doesn't just apply to 'romantic' ones."

Taggart raised his eyebrows and half-smiled. "Actually… I already cut ties with them. Just as soon as I got into Hong Kong."

With an impressed smile, Kotova said, "Good for you! The person being abused always seems to be the last one to know it, and you're one of the few who managed to see things for what they are and get out."

Michael shrugged. "I wouldn't want to put that up against your experiences, though. You went through more real abuse than I did, and that must have been a lot harder than my split with the Sentinels."

"I don't know about that, really. I'm not going to use my past as a crutch, and I'm not willing to downplay it as anything minor, either. Either way, you were impacted by what they were having you do, right? And they were putting you in dangerous positions against your will?" When Taggart nodded to both of these questions, she continued, "I thought so. And that's just as abusive as my ex or any son of a bitch like him. It's not your fault that you were trapped by them. Just like it's not my fault that I was in the position I had been in."

Where nothing in his own mind could give Taggart comfort, Kotova had done so over the course of about a minute. His mind felt lighter, and he was almost dizzy with relief.

"Thank you," he said finally, looking over at her through the hole in the wall.

She looked perplexed. "For what?"

"For giving me perspective I couldn't give myself. On that same subject, I want you to know that you're not a bad person for how you feel."

"What do you mean?"

"The look in your eyes, the way your voice changes when you talk about your ex-husband... please stop me if I'm wrong, but I think some part of you still loves him." Kotova didn't object to this statement, she only lowered her gaze. "Everyone hears from others that you should get out of an abusive relationship if you can. Everyone tells you to take care of yourself and get as much distance as you can from that person. What they probably neglected to mention is that you'll still be in love with them. No matter what they've done.

"I'm not blaming you for it, by any means. And I know that I'm not really an authority on situations like yours. It's just... my experiences with wanting to run back to Interpol and how you still feel about your ex... I might be completely off-base here, but if I'm not, then I want you to know that at least one person understands how you feel. At least part of how you feel. I should probably stop now, just so I don't end up putting my foot in my mouth. That is, if I haven't done that already."

Kotova was at a loss for words and simply shook her head vigorously. There were no tears, but her eyes were brimming with emotion. Most of it was too abstract and complex for anyone but her to understand, but Taggart could see quite a bit of gratitude in them as well. Relieved, he put out his hand to offer a reassuring gesture. Rather, he started to do this until realizing that there was a wall between them. With the emotional closeness that they were sharing, it was easier to forget physical barriers.

For quite some time, both of them sat back and allowed emotion and exhaustion to wash over their minds. Mental exhaustion brought its strange effect over Taggart and Kotova — neither of them felt capable of saying or doing anything more, but their weariness wasn't a negative one. Far from it, they felt content. This, in and of itself, was a new and welcome sensation.

There was no vocal sentiment of 'goodnight.' It wasn't necessary. As the two misfits drifted off, the emotions and thoughts exchanged were enough to fill the place of countless words.

Days passed in the prison without incident, but according to the prisoners, it could have been weeks or even months. With nothing better to do, the pair continued to talk about whatever they could think of. They often amused themselves by wondering how one topic could lead to another, such as how a discussion of culture and food somehow transitioned into one about ridiculous misconceptions about life that they had had as children.

Overall, however, they made their best effort to avoid topics which had the potential to turn somber. Motivation was already hard to come by, and neither Taggart nor Kotova had the desire to worsen the situation.

Such conversations weren't always avoidable, and it was one which arose from the most mundane of sources.

Sleep came easily, and Michael was met with erratic

dreams, disjointed and frantic. He was alongside a back road, with cars roaring past and their lights blinding him. He knew that he had to cross, but the constant flow of traffic held him back. All of the vehicles were bumper to bumper, going too fast to tell one from another. Throwing caution to the wind, Taggart launched himself into the chaos.

Bracing for impact, Taggart shut his eyes and grimaced. He felt the rush of wind approaching, felt the light glare against his closed eyelids, and then there was a sound so severe that it couldn't have been in a dream at all.

Wincing as he opened his eyes, Michael was met with the sight of a lanky, Chinese man who was opening the cell door and banging on it with a wooden club as he did so. If the noise was intended to disorient and annoy Taggart, it did its job well. The aching, strained feeling in his bones had just begun to subside, but this unexpected visitor brought those back up to the surface.

Whoever this visitor was, he apparently had no desire to speak, as he crossed the room in three strides, glaring from behind thick glasses and grabbing Taggart's arm with a surprisingly firm grip. His breath smelled of fish and contempt, if contempt could have a scent.

Only half-conscious of what was happening, Michael was dragged out of the cell and along a cave-like corridor. The stranger proceeded to club the back of Taggart's head as they went, and the latter quickly found that these beatings became less severe as he began to walk of his own accord.

Moments later, the pair arrived in a windowless room

which was lit with blinding lights which would have been at home in a construction site of some sort. Even when Taggart shut his eyes, they burned into his retina and made him feel no more at ease.

Taggart couldn't see what was going on, but he felt as if he was being thrown in a chair and bound to it with something too painful to be rope. Oddly enough, only his legs were lashed to the chair. His hands were free to move and swing at his captors, but he knew better than to try.

When his eyes had focused, Taggart raised them to look at the man in front of him – only now there were two. The thin man was joined by one who looked as if he could be a wrestler of some sort. By most standards, he would have been considered overweight, but this weight came from muscles which were covered in scars and tattoos. It seemed like he wore those with a sense of pride, as they were both on prominent display.

The man with glasses nodded to his associate, who stepped forward and grabbed both of Taggart's wrists. It felt as if they would break at any moment, and trying to pull them free only made things worse.

As this was happening, the other captor came into view, looking down with his brow furrowed. Without meeting Taggart's eye, he asked, "Which hand is used to pull the trigger?"

The voice was thick with a Chinese accent, but this didn't hide the venom behind the words. Michael felt himself recoil at this question, not even sure where it was leading him. In lieu of an answer, he decided to lie and point his left index finger into the air. The strongman pulled that hand higher into the air.

"That question was a test, Michael Taggart, agent of Interpol and founding member of the 'Sentinel' splinter group. Yes, we know quite a bit about you, including the fact that you attacked two of my associates with a broken bottle in your *right* hand. One of those associates is clutching that hand at this very moment, and he's quite eager to return the favor.

"Let's start with the little finger for his lack of trustworthiness, I think," he said to his friend, who released Taggart's left hand and slammed his right onto a table beside them. Until this moment, he had no idea that it was standing there.

Without a word, the man produced a ball-peen hammer from his pocket and held it aloft. Before Michael could brace himself for what was about to happen, the hammer was sent crashing into the center of his little finger.

White-hot pain. Nothing else existed. Agony. The sound of bone being crushed added to this, making Taggart scream until his lungs wouldn't take any more. Every profanity in the book flashed through his mind, and he wanted nothing more than to wave his hand in the air in an attempt to ease the pain. The strongman made sure that this wasn't possible, however, and Michael was left to writhe in the chair and let the anguish run its course. That course felt like it would last for quite some time.

At any other moment, Taggart would have agreed with the concept that pain is only temporary, but this was a separate case. This pain felt eternal; this pain took hold of all nerves and wouldn't let go.

Taggart's thrashing became so intense that the strongman lost hold of him, and Michael came crashing to the floor with the chair on top of him. The captors both worked to make it upright again, and the one with glasses needn't have bothered – the other had things well in control.

Even though he had little conscious sense left, Michael could tell that he was being put upright, and his hand was again forced onto the table. At the same time, it seemed as if the lights surrounding him had become even brighter.

His entire body had stiffened and his eyes were squinted shut, but Taggart could hear someone speaking to him from across the room. He threw his head back and let the words roll past.

"Now that you're aware of the consequences for lying to us, it is time to start the *actual* questions we had prepared. Don't fool yourself during this – we have no reason to keep you alive, no one who's waiting for us to deliver you to them. You're in charge of giving us a reason to care. We're putting you in charge of the most important thing to you right now – whether you live or die."

Taggart swung his head downward so that it was hanging limply, pressed against his chest. His torturer was wrong. Life and death weren't the most important to him – they hadn't been for quite some time. He felt ambivalence toward both of them, in fact. His only thoughts revolved around defiance. When a person has been torn away from their own desires and ideals for so long, defiance tends to be the only thing left. It was with this attitude that he addressed the next question, which the captor seemed eager to deliver.

"Even though my associates and I are aware of your dealings in Russia, we have not been able to see why you are cooperating with their government. Now, to save your trigger finger from being snapped like a twig, be so kind as to tell us what is behind this alliance between an American Interpol agent and a Russian Federal Security Service operator."

Looking up through mostly-closed eyes, Taggart remained silent. He was careful to avoid moving his hand, especially since the pain had lessened for the moment. The strongman's breath on the back of his neck made him feel no more at ease, but Michael remained as still and resolute as he could.

"Nothing?" the man asked. "I'll give you a chance to reconsider, just this once. I'll have you know that your friend Kotova is imprisoned here as well, and she'll undergo this same process if you don't comply. You can prevent your death *and* hers in just a few words. Either that, or you can bask in your selfish silence and sacrifice yourself for a cause which you don't believe in."

These were the first words to hit Taggart severely, and it took a long time for him to process them. He knew he was being goaded, and he knew that he was being coerced, but he couldn't ignore the truth in the interrogator's words. How the man knew of his conflicting thoughts, Michael couldn't be sure. It must have been more apparent than he had thought. Nonetheless, every instinct fought against giving them any information. Whether it was because of his training or because of his defiant tendencies, he had no idea. Whatever the case, he lowered his head once more, waiting for whatever might come.

What did come was another sharp blow to his hand,
but he had been waiting for this one. The shock was still
present, but he had time to clench his teeth and wait for
the hammer's impact. It arrived with a vengeance. Taggart
could feel his bones snap before the pain had time to sink
in.

He screamed at the top of his lungs, and tears began to
form at the corners of his eyes from the exertion. Heavy
panting came next, and all that he could manage was a
soft groan. His left hand was clenched so tightly that his
wedding band was beginning to cut into his skin.

Anguish and desperation fought for control of his
consciousness, but neither one was winning. Taggart could
feel his mind shutting down, losing its grip on him. The
interrogator must have been aware of this, because he
grabbed Taggart's jaw and yanked it upward so that they
were face to face.

"I'll try asking something else," he said with venom in
his voice, "since you're being so shy."

With his vision blurred and almost no concept of
where he was, Michael fought to stay conscious and alert.
He could tell that someone was speaking to him, and it
wasn't hard to guess what he was saying.

Without waiting for the question, Taggart lifted his
mangled hand and slowly extended his middle finger
before placing it on the table for the strongman. It was the
other kidnapper, however, who grabbed the hammer and
delivered the next blow. Not willing to stop there, the man
continued hammering in a frenzy, breaking Taggart's other
two fingers and further damaging the rest. The man with

glasses was becoming more erratic, so much so that the strongman had to pull him back. If he hadn't, it was likely that the beating would have gone on until both had lost consciousness.

Unconsciousness. The sweet release from the stress and misery that life will often bring. This was Taggart's only wish, and he wished that it would come swiftly. He knew that his two "friends" would do nothing to help this along, so he fought against his pain and managed to stand up. Before either captor could react, he threw himself to the ground, making sure that his head took the brunt of the impact. This dazed him and amplified his pain, but he was still cognizant for the moment. Vaguely aware that people were trying to pull him back, Taggart continued to slam his head onto the cold, stone floor. Before long, he had faded completely. Only one thought was present in his mind at that moment – *Whatever is keeping me going, I hope it stops. I won't stop by myself. I can't.*

Location and Date Unknown

"Taggart! Come on, Taggart! Well… shit."

Bits and pieces of brick were landing on Michael's face, and he had only a faint idea of what was happening. Some of the pieces trailed across his lips and landed in his mouth, but he was far from able to do anything about it. Still, a voice was calling to him, sounding as if it was coming from underwater.

"Wake up! We don't have time for this; wake up! Just don't be dead, okay?"

He twitched, faintly aware that his right hand and head were sore, feeling disconnected from the rest of his body.

Only partially able to control his motions, Taggart turned his head and spit out the shards of brick. Kotova must have noticed this, because her voice then called out to him with increased energy.

"Come on. You still there? Hello? Take it easy. They told me what they had done to you, and they made sure to let me know that they're coming back to do the same to me.

"...Taggart?"

Michael was too far gone to be reached, proceeding to roll onto his stomach and lose consciousness once more. He never remembered the events of those few minutes, and they were lost to all but Kotova.

It was several hours before Taggart was able to regain his senses once more, and this time he was met with no falling brick or voices calling to him. Aching and soreness were still present, but, as far as he could tell, he was alone.

He could hear waves crashing against something nearby as he stirred from his 'sleep.' In a harsh lesson that he would re-learn many times over the next few months, Michael tried to push himself up using both hands. The right one sent a surge of pain through his body, and he fell back to the ground, clutching it and doing his best not to yell from the agony.

After some of his strength had returned, Taggart tried once more to regain his feet, this time with his right hand pressed against his chest. The movement was nauseating, and he had to take a moment to level himself out.

As he did this, he pressed the chunks of brick away

from the hole through which he had spoken with Kotova earlier, and he was alarmed and confused only emptiness on the other side. There were no signs of struggle that he could see, and, whether it was by choice or not, Taggart knew that she was gone.

He felt abandoned. Even though Emelia had made no promise to stay, and it was no doubt better for her if she had escaped, Taggart felt as if she should have helped. He couldn't help but feel a sense of bitterness, and this was only offset when he took the time to think the matter through – she wasn't responsible for his wellbeing. None of their encounters had indicated that. It might have been nothing more than his sense of camaraderie with her that made him feel so alone.

David's words about isolation came back to him, and Michael felt a burst of anger toward his old friend.

He had the nerve to say that I'm not as alone as I think I am. Right. Now he's dead and I've ended up here. Great god damned advice, you idiot. I really think you're right. I'm not alone at all. Sure.

The only thing that was able to cool his anger was the memory of David's confident, knowledgeable manner. It pained Michael to admit it, but he couldn't bring himself to forsake the man. Taggart couldn't reject the fact that he valued his friend's wisdom; discrediting it was tantamount to sacrilege.

It was just about impossible to escape the sensation of loneliness that he was going through, but Taggart pulled his mind together for just long enough to realize that he felt lonely; this didn't necessarily make him a person who was alone.

His mind returned to Emelia and how she had just left without a word. Without helping. He tried to be angry about this as well, but there was never an agreement between them to help the other escape. She had presumably found a window of escape and taken it. He couldn't blame her for that, but his mind was doing a pretty good job of placing blame at the moment.

After all, her goals differed from his, and he wasn't even completely sure what her goals were in the first place. Besides the fact that she was searching for an end to the Affliction and an end to her ex-husband, she had never made clear what she wanted. Taggart reflected that their partnership had been a brief and loose one, and he wondered whether he had the right to feel alone at all. A part of him even wanted to seek her out and see if he could help, but he probably needed more help than she did at this point. After all, placing importance on others rather than one's self is a commonly held virtue, but sometimes that just isn't a possibility.

Not knowing what to think, Michael abandoned this issue for the moment and focused on assessing the damage done to his body. The fingers on his right hand were, of course, still broken, and the pain from that hadn't begun to abate in the slightest. His head felt no better, and he felt as if he might pass out at any moment. The cell swam in and out of focus, but his mind was beginning to return to him. It was a slow process, to be sure, but it was happening.

He might have lost all sense of time, but Taggart still had most of his senses – as far as he could tell. It was because he didn't want to lose these that he forced himself to his feet and proceeded to dart to the other end of his cell. This took only two strides, and he was forced to stop his momentum with his left hand, but it was something. For muscles which had remained still and confined for such a long time, it was quite a strain. Michael knew that staying active and mobile would serve him if he would ever be released, so it was a strain which he welcomed.

With his pace improving by the second, Taggart continued to dash back and forth. The exercise made him feel more alert, more alive. There was no doubt that his captors wanted to make him feel the opposite way, and his defiance made Michael smile through his pain. The idea that he was pushing back against something instead of letting it crush him was a liberation of sorts. He craved it and hungered for it until defiance became as necessary as the scraps of food and drops of water his captors slid through the cell once a day.

This went on for days, with his exercise regimen becoming more strenuous and intensive by the day. It seemed as if the interrogators had forgotten about his existence, or else had given up hope of gaining any information from him.

In truth, the thing that Taggart missed the most about the outside world was music. It hadn't been a major part of his life for quite some time, but the inability to access it at all made him feel isolated. The last music that he had listened to had been months ago, sitting alongside David at the theatre.

Maybe music would be something he could pursue when finished with this mess, something that could make his emotions more manageable. With his attention occupied with other things, he had had precious little time to listen to anything but the world around him. Paranoia had held him back from this as well – Taggart had no desire to be caught off-guard because he was hearing Peter Gabriel or Chicago, rather than footsteps creeping toward him.

My wife really did love Chicago, he thought absently, twisting the wedding band around his finger like he often did. *God, I miss her. We weren't always the happiest couple in the world, but we still had something special. Some of the happiest times in my life. And I threw that away to end up in a Chinese prison. If this is still China.*

He also wished that he had the agency-provided notebook back in his hands. Writing in it had been a relief, the only way that he could find to organize his thoughts. At least, he had organized them as well as he could – as well as a blind person could sort laundry into whites and colors.

Even still, it was markedly better than letting his thoughts wander while in captivity. It wasn't long before he came to the conclusion that being left alone with only one's thoughts was more dangerous than most people think.

It came to a point where Taggart would have preferred more interactions with his captors, if only for a break in the monotony. Such a day refused to come for quite some time. Whether this was days or weeks, Michael didn't know. His only concept of time was varying levels of fatigue. He had read somewhere that without sunlight, the human body reverts to a non-24-hour sleep cycle, so even that wasn't an ideal indicator. The confined, isolated state of his cell made it seem as if minutes were hours, and he had no doubt that this was intentional.

It was after god-knows-how-many days of waiting that Taggart's meals became more infrequent. At first, this was reduced from one meal per day to one every other day. They soon stopped altogether, leaving Michael lightheaded and fatigued at any given moment. This marked the point where he considered escape to be the only option which wouldn't end in a slow death. It is true that a failed attempt would almost certainly result in a death, but, with luck, that one would be swift.

Executing this escape was a different matter entirely, but this fact didn't dissuade Taggart from forming several different plans in his head. Each one revolved around luck and timing, and each one seemed to have little likelihood of success.

The result of his brainstorming was a ploy taken from random thoughts which Michael had had during his time in captivity. The parallel that he had drawn to *The Count of Monte Cristo* had captured his mind, and the idea of a fake death began to appeal to him. If he managed to pull this off without suspicion, he would be able to move in anonymity once more. If he was presumed dead, he would cease to be on his enemies' minds, and that was a reality he could easily live with.

The plan itself was a straightforward one, due to the fact that Taggart saw this as leaving less room for error. He was willing to rely on himself, but anticipating the actions of deranged and sadistic gang members was another matter. His idea involved making loud noises beside his cell door, ideally attracting someone to investigate his condition. When they would open the door, he would continue shouting for a brief time before collapsing to the ground in a feigned state of death. Michael knew if he decided to run at that point, the only thing that would happen would be a series of rifle shots fired into his back.

Instead of that, Taggart planned on letting his captors dispose of his body as they saw fit, most likely by casting him into the water surrounding the prison. This would likely involve tying something heavy to him in order to prevent his body from floating, but Michael had thought of this eventuality as well. In his pocket, he had placed a particularly sharp piece of brick. It would serve to free him from whatever bindings his enemies might place on him. Hopefully.

Michael knew that he hadn't covered every single eventuality, every single variable which might disrupt his escape. It would have been impossible to have such clairvoyance, especially in his state.

Prior planning prevents piss-poor performance.

This phrase had been drilled into his mind so many times, it had begun to lose meaning. For some reason, it stuck in his mind at this moment. There must have been some detail or error in judgment that he had missed, but... he was through with waiting. Through with dwelling on the uncertainty of what would or would not happen to him. He had been doing that for so long already, and to release himself from that mindset was as liberating as his escape might be.

Before he had intended on putting his escape plan into action, Taggart was forced to go through with it. Instead of false yells of hunger and pain alerting a guard, he was struck with ones which were quite real. Why they decided to hit when they did, as well as so suddenly, he had no idea, but the pain in his gut had reached the point of agony. Even crying out was a painful process, as his throat was almost entirely dried out. The pain sent soreness to his temples as well, adding a migraine to his collection of symptoms.

With one hand clutching at his stomach, Taggart crawled to the door of his cell and beat his fist against it before collapsing – with everything else happening, he had forgotten his mangled hand. This brought even more anguished cries, and he was already writhing on the floor by the time someone opened the door and stood above him. He could hear them say something, but the words were garbled and indistinct. The newcomer then proceeded to kick Michael in the ribs with a boot that felt like it had a steel tip.

Despite this, Taggart did his utmost to not cry out and instead tried to let his body go slack. A few moans escaped his lips, but he was soon able to feign unresponsiveness. His face had tensed from the effort of holding back such pain, as well as the process of making his breathing as shallow as he could.

Come on, come on… I can't hold this for much longer.

Taggart was waiting to be dragged or carried out of the cell, but neither of these things happened. Instead, the figure towering above him hurried away from the scene. This left Michael the chance to let out his pain and catch his breath. The door had been left open, and this left him with a way out, but… No. The man would be back. Besides, getting lost was a possibility which he wasn't willing to accept.

From his position on the ground, Taggart was able to take a look at what lay beyond his cell. The view was less than stellar – it was composed of a dirt-walled hallway which was supported by wooden arches which looked less than sturdy. The hall generated images of a mineshaft in his mind, and Michael wondered idly if he was underground.

This was cut short, however, as the first man had returned along with another. Taggart snapped his eyes shut and assumed his death-like state once more. He could hear the men speaking in Chinese before they decided to drag Michael out of his cell and down the hall. The thought struck him that he hadn't thought to pick up a piece of brick to free himself with later.

Instead, he let his hands drag across the floor. Without having to open his eyes, he could tell that there were rocks strewn here and there on the floor. They began to cut into his hands, and this went on until he dug his fingers into the dirt, picking up a flat, sharp stone which must have only been about four inches long. Taggart pressed it into his palm, hoping that his captors wouldn't notice a clenched fist on a presumably dead man.

They had dragged him out of the hallway and outside, the sunlight noticeable even through Taggart's closed eyes. The sound of waves crashing against something had become much stronger, and he could almost taste the salt in the air. He would have been able to breathe much more easily than he had been in the cell, but that wasn't an option at the moment. The captors seemed to be under the impression that he was dead, and Taggart had no desire to change this.

He was dragged for several more minutes, until the group had reached a point where Taggart could feel a fine mist of water splashing against his face. Michael had no idea how many people were watching over him, but he could pick out the footfalls of only two people. Two against one hardly seemed fair to Taggart - that didn't leave his opponents with much of a chance.

Expecting something to be tied around his legs or neck, Michael was surprised when he was dropped on his back and a boot was pushed onto his chest. This was followed by the sound of a rifle being made ready to fire.

Well, shit. I should have known that they would want to make sure that the job was finished.

Before the executioner had time to fire a shot, however, Taggart had opened his eyes and brought his left hand up, wielding the sharp stone. He made contact with the man's cheek, causing him to drop his weapon and fall backwards. Michael kicked the rifle into the water that surrounded them, where it bobbed briefly before sinking.

The other guard hadn't taken the time to arm himself, but he lunged toward Michael nonetheless, knocking him off-balance. Taggart managed to steady himself and lift the stone as if it was a knife, but this was only a pretense. In a sudden, violent movement, he hurled the rock at his attacker. This gave him the few seconds he needed to turn and dive into the turbulent waters.

Thrashing his arms around himself, Taggart was only able to keep his head above water before the current pulled him under. Fighting his way back to the surface was a nearly impossible ordeal, especially since he was swallowing more water with each passing second. When he was able to reach the air again, Michael could only cough and sputter, leaving him with little time to catch his breath.

There was a good chance that the kidnappers had followed him, but Taggart didn't even have the presence of mind to be concerned about this. His instinct for survival had kicked in, and he managed to ignore the immense pain in his hand as he continued to fight his way to the surface of the water.

Each time he emerged from the waves, Taggart made an attempt at getting his bearings, finding some clue as to where he was. The only thing that presented itself was the skyline of a city, and this was too far away for him to swim in this condition.

Taggart was fading in and out of consciousness before long, and the only thought in his mind was the hope that he didn't wake up back in the confines of a cell. If he woke up at all, that is. Exhaustion had overcome his muscles, and the movements of his arms and legs became more dull and lethargic. He didn't see any light at the end of a long tunnel or heavenly figures beckoning to him. No, the only thing that Taggart could see as he sank back into the depths was darkness.

Something was beeping. It was a slow, almost rhythmic sound, but it pierced into Taggart's mind like so many darts. He felt dizzy as well, and he had the curious feeling that he was perpetually falling through the air. As his senses and self-awareness returned, the dull ache in his hand did as well. Taggart tried to pop his knuckles to relieve some of the soreness, but something was holding his fingers in place. He could move them up and down, but bending them at all wasn't an option.

That's probably for the best. Trying to crack the knuckles would just break my fingers even more.

Taggart had no idea where he was, but he was able to tell that he wasn't with his kidnappers anymore. For one thing, the room that he was in was comfortably warm – nothing at all like his cell had been. He was also propped up in what felt like a bed, with splints securing the fingers of his broken hand. Either he wasn't with the kidnappers, or they had had an *extreme* change of heart. Michael laughed at the thought of this, but his grin turned into a grimace when this brought an aching feeling to his chest.

As far as he could tell, Michael was alone. Only the constant beeping sound was with him, and he was content to lie where he was until the end of time. The rhythm of that sound turned from being piercing to making Taggart feel calmer, more at ease. It was as if his inhibitions had abandoned him, leaving room for thoughts of all kinds to flood his mind.

So this is it. I knew it would happen eventually, but I had no idea of when. I really am at a point where I don't care if I get up again. Ever. I don't know why I'm to that point, but I've made it.

Maybe it's because I've been doing the same shit for years without even considering why I was doing it. Just thinking that I was doing my part to help society along. Not realizing what I myself wanted. What I want is… Well, now that it's come to this, I can't even decide on that. I can't decide on the most important thing in my life. No one can say I didn't try. Maybe I didn't try hard enough, but I tried.

Given that I have all the time in the world to think about this now, I might as well keep going. Now that it's too late to achieve whatever goal I have in mind, I can start creating a goal. Jesus. Has my mind really gone this far? Or has it not gone far at all because I recognize what sounds crazy to me and what doesn't? I could do without the irrational thoughts in the first place, though.

But a goal for my entire life... to put a thesis statement on Taggart's life essay...

More than anything, I guess that I just want freedom of mind. Freedom to find happiness how I see fit. I'm kind of kicking myself now. I had so much time to realize this, and it was so obvious. Obvious in hindsight, I guess. I don't want to be reduced to the level of an emotional teenager, but I just want to be happy. That's all I want. I think that this is true of everyone, but why is it so hard to do? I don't even know if my own happiness is up to me, but I do know that it should be. If I ever am able to get up, that should be my first priority.

That is, unless the weaponized Affliction forces itself to be my first priority. I hate putting myself on the back-burner, but it makes sense that I ensure that I have some of myself left first. That even depends on how long I've been gone. If I've been away for months, or even weeks, the whole issue might have died down. Or, more likely, it boiled over.

On some level, I don't want to know at all. Even still, I feel obligated to see this through. I probably shouldn't feel that way, but... What a waste of life I'd be if I didn't finish what I started here. Time to wake yourself up, Taggart. Maybe wake some other people up to the Affliction along the way.

Time to wake up and smell the embers.

Medicine Prescribed to Michael Faust Taggart (Information released in 2023)

Seroquel: 75mg tablet, three times daily (Managing possible psychosis)

Adderall: 80mg tablet, once daily (Managing extreme fatigue and lack of focus)

Xanax: 1.5mg tablet, once daily (Managing severe anxiety)

Doctor's Note - It is recommended that Taggart be given as many dosages as possible during each re-fill, due to the nature of his work (in which additional medicine might not be readily available)

Matilda International Hospital: Mt. Kellet Road, Hong Kong, China

March 23, 2016 - 12:30 P.M.

Fading in and out of sleep for several days, the only constant in Taggart's life was the beeping sound, and it showed no signs of stopping. The aching in his hand hadn't become less severe, but it had become... different, somehow. Whatever had been holding his fingers in place was gone, replaced by a feeling of stiffness unlike anything he had felt before. Bending each of his fingers only resulted in sharp pains, so Michael did his best to calm his now-trembling hand and left it alone.

Taggart opened his eyes, expecting to be met with blinding, florescent lights and shiny, gleaming surfaces. Instead, he found himself in a room which was painted crimson and was almost pitch-dark. The only light that he could see was filtering through a set of blinds, letting only a little bit of the outside world reach him.

The door to his room had been cracked open, and Michael could see the shapes of people passing by. None of them paid him any mind, but he couldn't blame them — it was likely that he had been unconscious for quite some time.

Deciding that it would be useless to try calling out to the people, Taggart resorted to a call button which was located within arm's reach. Pressing it made no sound in his room, but it must have alerted someone nonetheless — moments later, a woman in a white coat pushed the door open and looked down at Michael. She had a svelte figure and a face which was pretty, albeit sunken and almost ghostlike.

"Mr. Taggart!" she said with a light Chinese accent, surprised to see him awake. "You have been away from us for quite some time. Pardon the indiscretion of my colleagues, but they had a betting pool going to see how long you it would take for you to regain consciousness. Looks like Dr. Chen knew what he was talking about."

Michael looked up at her, his mind still not completely in place. "What's happened to me? And where am I? I know this must be a hospital of some sort, but, beyond that... I have no idea."

"We're in the south of Hong Kong, sir. My name is Dr. Wu, and you're quite safe now. Quite unlike when you were found. During my time in the medical field, I've seen people in all different states of suffering, and you're among the most resilient, even in unconsciousness. It appears that your mind was functioning on a higher level than most people's. You even turned your head to the side to let water to drain from your mouth and nose. It's impressive that you knew to do that at all, let alone managing it while not cognizant."

She paused, but Taggart was still looking at her with such concern that she pressed on more quickly. "A fisherman brought you in from Aberdeen Harbor; apparently you were unconscious and floating away from one of Hong Kong's outlying islands.

"You had also sustained some injuries and trauma, but you were in no danger as soon as the seawater was removed from your lungs."

` Again, Taggart adopted an expression of alarm. "I understand the nature of your work, doctor, but… I know that you're aware that my injuries are of a certain nature… That is to say that they're… You already know that someone did this to me, right?" The doctor only nodded, her expression blank. "You see, the nature of my work makes it so that I can't afford to draw too much attention from the authorities."

"I see," said Dr. Wu. Her face was now set in a hard scowl which made Michael's stomach drop. She turned on her heel and began to hurry out of the room.

"Wait!" Taggart tried to shout, but the strain on his voice brought on even more coughing, and he was forced to double back into his bed. Among his wheezing, he heard, to his shock and confusion, the sound of muffled laughter.

Dr. Wu had turned around, partially covering a grin with her hand. "I'm sorry, Mr. Taggart," she said between laughs. "But I just had to leave you worrying for a moment. There is nothing to worry about; everything has been taken care of in that regard." Seeing his still-aghast expression, she continued, "After all, sir, I figured that you of all people need some humor in your life."

Michael cracked a smile, and, even though he said nothing, they both knew that she was right.

"But how can everything be taken care of?" he asked. "Surely the police would like to know that a man was severely beaten and cast into the bay!"

It was Dr. Wu's turn to smile. "While this would usually be true, your superiors saw fit to make a generous… ah… *contribution* to each of the major medical centers in Hong Kong. It seems that they expected you to be in one sooner or later."

It took Taggart a moment to register what she meant by "superiors" — Grant and Interpol had become long-gone memories already. Even so, he felt a pang of guilt for taking advantage of their work when he had already parted ways with them. This thought lasted only a moment, however, as Taggart realized that he wouldn't be in need of medical assistance at all if it hadn't been for them.

"In any case, I'm glad that you haven't given me up to the police. I'd still rather not discuss the nature of my work, if that's okay."

"Of course, sir," Dr. Wu said, turning to leave. "I'll let you get some rest now."

"Wait!" Taggart said. The doctor rotated to face him once more. "I'd like to know how long I'll be in here, how long it will take for my hand to heal. I really need to leave as soon as I can." Michael had swung his legs over the side of the bed and was preparing to step onto the floor when Dr. Wu held up a hand to stop him.

"It'll likely be several months before your hand is functional again. After pinning your fingers, opening them, and inserting screws, it will require quite a bit of physical therapy before they can be used as before. In fact, it was fortunate that we could salvage all of them. The damage was… extensive."

Dr. Wu informed him that the screws in his fingers would have to be in place for four weeks at the least, and he should refrain from any "strenuous activity." Taggart merely grinned at the irony of this.

Not likely, doc. Not at all.

Taggart rested his head in his hands, taking care to be gentle with them. Even though he had been "sleeping" for days, fatigue still managed to come washing over him. The added knowledge of his condition did nothing to help this, and it was as if he had traded one prison for another. While it was true that he was no longer being held captive, the sense of immobility and helplessness remained. Solace, if it would ever come to him, would not be gained in the confines of a small, stuffy room.

The doctor excused herself to let Taggart rest, but he did nothing of the sort. Though his body begged for respite, his brain refused to shut down.

Great. Just great. Even though my mind is unraveling more and more by the second, it won't just let me be for a few hours. Please.

This request had gone unanswered so many times in the past, Taggart wasn't the slightest bit surprised when the same pattern occurred during his brief stay at the hospital. This lasted only two days, and, despite the medical staff's suggestions, he left as soon as he felt able to walk. Michael had always been a self-proclaimed stubborn person, and that much would remain unchanged.

The clothes that he had been wearing had been damaged beyond repair, and he didn't feel inclined to walk the streets of China in a hospital gown. Interpol hadn't thought to leave a set of clothing at each hospital, so Taggart was left with a set of modest, plain clothing that the doctors provided. He was dressed head to toe in white garments. It made him stand out quite a bit, but it would do to protect his modesty until he could access something more innocuous.

His first order of business, after leaving the hospital, was the retrieval of his briefcase from the hotel where he and Kotova had been captured. After that, the only thought on Taggart's mind was that of Emelia's son. It could be argued that he had no real obligation to either of them, but he felt that ignoring the situation would be downright cruel on his part. Also, if Kotova's ex-husband was as unstable as she had described him, time was of the essence. Michael hoped that she had already been able to free herself and handle the situation, but he was more than willing to do what he needed to help.

As overwhelmed as he was by the prospect of putting someone else's safety in front of his own, Taggart felt no hesitation in rushing to Alexey's aid. It occurred to him at this moment that self-sacrifice wasn't the main problem — perhaps it was others taking the liberty of sacrificing his life and limb.

He found a great deal of comfort in this, a welcome improvement from his mindset several minutes prior. Michael had always seen his duty as something which got in the way of personal happiness, but he realized that he could find happiness in anything he did — as long as it was of his own accord.

The words of encouragement and sentiment that he and Emelia had shared in the prison kept returning to him, and they felt more and more relevant each time they resurfaced. Taggart made a mental note to write them in his journal, if he was ever able to retrieve it. In the meantime, he walked in the direction of the hotel, watching hundreds of others pass by, oblivious to the danger which was looming over them.

Personal Journal of Michael Faust Taggart (No Date Provided)

Even though I know it isn't the case, I feel like these entries have been like something you would find in an eighth grader's most angst-ridden journals. Reading back over what I've written has never been fun for me, but… Jesus. In the moment, it's hard to see exactly how worn down my mind is, but now I can see it, and scares me. I won't lie. It really does scare me. For once, I won't even lie to myself about this. Not knowing what to do and not feeling safe in my own mind — those are the worst two things I've ever felt, and they've hit me hard at the same time. I… I feel like I've been so melodramatic, but, at the same time… I know that haven't. Somehow I know that my reaction is normal. The situation I'm in isn't normal. Fuck no, not in the slightest. I accept that. But my reaction is the same as anyone's would be if they were in my place. Just trying to hold on to the idea that I can someday feel better seems like all I have left.

I've had to talk to so many "professionals" about how I'm so lucky to be who I am and to have what I have. I'm sick of it. I know their intentions must be good (I hope so, at least), but I feel so shamed when they use that argument. Like I should feel guilty that my mind is unraveling itself. I understand *that I'm fortunate to be who I am. I guess. On the outside, at least. But what all of these therapists and psychologists and psychiatrists and practitioners don't seem to understand is that happiness just can't be found sometimes. I had thought that this would be common knowledge, but it doesn't seem like it.*

I'm going through another ink cartridge on my pen, and my hand is cramping like hell, but writing in this book kills time, and I still can't stand to see a journal that looks like it's in perfect condition. Heh. I'll let myself use the horrible metaphor connecting that idea to myself — I don't see much value in myself either, unless I've been worn down by constant use. Sure, it might tear the book apart and do the same to me, but at least it's being used. But at the same time, that's how I felt... used. *I still think it was meeting Kotova that opened my eyes. She'd been abandoned by people she had relied on, and she had had enough of it and left. I didn't realize it for so long, but I think I was abandoned, too. Not in the same way, or as badly, but it's still there.*

I just looked up from writing this for a few seconds, and I have no idea what I was talking about. Even re-reading the first section, it seems foreign to me. It looks like my style of writing but... Jesus, I need sleep. That won't happen while my mind is overflowing like it is right now, but maybe after I get a few pages down in this book, I can work on that.

This whole book is full of random tangents, so I guess it works for me to just start another one.

Not being able to decide anything for myself, or even think for myself... That's a mark of an abusive relationship. I hate the fact that I dwell on things like this. My most recent psychiatrist told me that that's one of the more destructive things that I tend to do. For once – I'm inclined to agree with her.

I just want to feel okay with myself. At peace, I guess. I would give the world for just a little bit of that feeling.

In the meantime, can we make it a felony for people to say the phrase "It gets better"?

That would help. Not much, but it would help.

Hong Kong, China (North Point) - March 25, 2016

The bellhop looked startled when he saw Taggart again, but he was still able to provide him with his briefcase. It was intact and looked as if it hadn't been disturbed, so Michael was content. He made to retrieve his wallet to tip the man, only to find that he must have lost it during the past few weeks.

After making a quick apology to the bellhop, he hurried out of the lobby and back onto the ever-busy streets of China. Taggart had been running on fumes since he had left the hospital, and they would have to carry him to the other side of the city. Without money for bus fare, walking would have to suffice.

His hospital garments were drawing quite a few strange looks from passersby, and this reassured Michael that a change of clothes should be high on his list of priorities. Despite the attention he was getting, none of it seemed to be hostile. Bearing this in mind and hoping that it would continue to be the case, Taggart pressed on.

Walking the streets of Hong Kong had almost

become a hobby for Michael in the days before he had been captured, each block brimming with loud and vibrant life. Even if some of that life was desperate, the city's atmosphere was one of perseverance regardless of one's circumstances. This was a mantra which Taggart could identify with, and it was one of the few things that made him feel at ease.

The roads and sidewalks rolled by, and Michael was propelled by his instinct to keep moving forward. Ordinarily, this would have been the only thing keeping him from wasting away, but he had been endowed with a sense of purpose. He was working in the best interest of someone else, with no intention of personal gain.

Well, I think I proved that I can't take care of myself right now. I might as well try to take care of someone else. I only hope that each step I take is a step closer to something fulfilling. Something that will allow me to live with myself. I've served others for the wrong reasons before, but now I might be able to be of some help and still live with myself afterward. I'll have a clear conscience. An honest heart. I don't have that yet, but it's something to work toward.

Night was falling over the city, and this was when the sun was replaced by thousands of neon suns of all colors. Even staring at this artificial sun might have been enough to make a person blind.

To the concern of Taggart, the lights became more sparse as he entered the eastern part of the city. Gripping his briefcase tighter with his functional hand, Michael did his utmost to remember what Kotova had told him.

Day care in the industrial district... Her ex operating out of a factory which might be nearby. Shit. That doesn't bode well at all. I've got to hurry. I've been locked up for who-knows-how-long, and I don't want to waste another second with Alexey out there alone.

He broke into a jog, and this soon became a flat-out sprint. Cursing himself for the time that he wasted by walking, Taggart arrived at a day care and propped himself against its window. As he was trying to steady himself, he noticed a lone, elderly woman inside the building. She was in the process of turning out the lights and hanging a 'closed' sign on the door when he burst inside. The woman was startled by his entrance, but her expression softened as he began to speak.

"Excuse me, ma'am," he said between gasps, "but is a small Russian child in your care? Not even a year old, goes by the name of Alexey?"

"Yes, in fact. He was. In all honesty, I wish you were his father. The man who picked him up earlier had no sense of manners at all."

Taggart's breath halted altogether. "His... father?"

She nodded. "Yes. He came by not five minutes ago, burst into my business and demanded that he have the poor child. I didn't like the look of that man, but he had proof that it was his son, so I had to let them go. It's a shame, too. His mother was so polite when she checked that poor boy in. When she didn't come back to pick him up at the end of the day and wouldn't answer the phone at the number she gave me, I didn't see any other choice but to watch over him myself. He's a sweet child, and it was a joy to have him here. That is, up until a few minutes ago."

"Please," Michael gasped, knowing that he didn't have much time, "do you have any idea where they went? Even a general direction would help. Anything."

"The boy's father said something about a 'take your child to work day.' Sounded like a bad lie to me, so I asked where this was. That's when he called me a nosy slope and stormed out! He was such a sallow-looking man, too! Thick, black hair that looks like it's resistant to shampoo; muscled, mangled arms with military tattoos... I try to reserve judgment about my clients, but he is a type I try to avoid.

"Well, I naturally kept an eye out and saw where he went. It's the electronics manufacturing plant down on that corner." She pointed with a pudgy finger at a decrepit-looking building. "Listen, I hope you're that woman's lover or something. Or you'll become her lover and take her and the boy away from him. You've got manners and respect. That's a lot more than that *pinko* can say of himself. Who are you, anyway?"

"I'll tell you if I see you again, but first I must have a word and maybe a few fists with a certain Russian."

With that, Taggart turned and sprinted in the direction of the factory. As he was leaving, Michael was almost certain that he heard the woman whisper, *"hit him once for me, American!"*

A cab skidded to a halt mere feet from Taggart, the driver blaring his horn the entire time. Michael was too focused on the task at hand to pay this any mind. A familiar sensation was taking hold once more — the same red filter clouded his vision, and the same feeling of rage took over. The only thing he noticed was a net hanging outside of the building where an awning might be.

A suicide net. Looks like working conditions here are... a bit *less than ideal.*

Security was lax at the factory, and in this case, that meant that there was no security to speak of. The front doors were unlocked and he crashed them open with only a little effort. Beyond them was the first floor of the factory, where assembly lines were organized in neat rows. Not a single worker looked up as he ran by, each of them wearing the same dead eyes that he himself had acquired.

Seeing no sign of the father or the boy on the first floor, Taggart found a set of stairs at the back of the room and climbed them to the second story. The same sight awaited him there, and it was only a few moments before he was on the third. This level was bypassed as well, being only a carbon copy of the first two. Michael was vaguely aware that this could be a metaphor for something, but he was trapped in his rage-filled state and could barely register this.

The fourth floor contained a massive room of cubicles, but Taggart didn't even bother investigating this one. Whether it was logic, intuition, or simple madness, something had taken over him and led him to the fifth and final floor.

In this area, there was another maze of cubicles with more automaton-like workers. Taggart could hear the sound of papers being shuffled around, but there was something else, as well — it was less distinct, but Taggart could pick up the steady *thump-thump* of someone's running feet.

Taggart gave chase, even though he had little idea of where his quarry was. The adrenaline coursing through his veins was all-consuming, and this left his vision blurry, his movements rapid, and his conscious mind to make his quarry the only other person in the world.

Before long, he was in the thick of the maze with all sense of direction lost. Each corner was a flat, gray carbon-copy of the next one. The running footsteps continued, but there was no way of determining where they were coming from. Hoping that his intuitive sense would lead him in the right direction, Taggart cut across the room until he reached the far corner of the room.

It was there that he was met with his worst fear, presented to him in an alarming, physical form. A man was standing before a window, his hands carrying a small bundle of cloth. He was dressed in the same uniform as the rest of the workers, but it was clear that he didn't belong.

This was confirmed beyond doubt when he extended his arms through the window, seemingly preparing to drop the bundle to the street below. Without thought or hesitation, Taggart dashed toward the man, making contact in a flying tackle which brought all thee of them to the ground. The baby started to cry, and, as Taggart and Kotova's ex-husband regained their feet, a crowd of workers had gathered around them.

Taggart, trying to steady himself, set his briefcase on the floor and dropped into a fighting stance. Kotova's ex-husband, who had left Alexey on the floor, did the same. This time, Michael was filled with a rage that didn't come from some unexplained, obscure source. In that moment, his anger rushed from his mind in massive waves. Every sense that was still working in his mind turned to pure loathing for the man in front of him, a man who was prepared to take the life of his own son — an infant.

The other man said nothing and merely glared at Taggart through narrow, beady eyes. These eyes had seen so much wrongdoing, a great deal of it caused by the person himself. Even though he had never met Michael, he carried the same look of hatred toward him that he did toward his son.

Because of the things that Emelia had told him, Michael was able to look back with equal venom. He had to wonder how someone could be capable of so much senseless violence, capable of delivering so much pain —

Shit. That's me. I'm the same. I've killed so many people… Jesus, too many. Just because I was told to. The only difference is that I'm not capable of doing that anymore. Not for much longer, even. That's why my mind is escaping me so quickly. It can't cope. I can't cope.

As these thoughts were running through his mind, he and the other man had begun to circle each other, dropped into fighting stances.

No. This is not the place or the time. But I know that this isn't me. I don't think it is. I'm trying to make things easier. If not for myself, then for someone else. I'm not at the level of the people I'm fighting against. I'm not. I hope.

Taggart wished that he could be satisfied with this, but thoughts of his periodic, uncontrollable anger continued to surface in his mind. Then again, it was *uncontrollable.*

Kotova's ex-husband refused to make the first advance, so Michael stutter-stepped toward him, drew a flinching reaction from his opponent, and followed this with a swift jab from his left hand. He was forced to keep his right tucked behind his back, lest it be further maimed during the fight. At this point, he was down to one fist and two feet.

It was clear from the start that Kotova's ex was trained in similar techniques to those that Taggart had learned. He recovered in time to block the incoming punch, moving to the side and circling Michael once more. The bout continued in a similar manner a few more times, and in each instance, Taggart's opponent evaded the attack and continued to pace in a circle. The only reason that Taggart could imagine his opponent was doing this was to tire him out, and, though he tried not to show it, the tactic was working.

Doing his best to hide his awareness of his adversary's plan, Michael continued in the same pattern until he had circled back around to his briefcase. Scooping it from the ground with his good hand, he swung it toward Kotova's ex in one swift movement. The man, clearly caught off guard, escaped the attack by blocking it with his arm. This seemed to enrage him even more, but he continued his evasive strategy.

Like competitors in a game of chess, the two utilized strategies which were familiar to both, and it was only when they varied from conventional tactics that any progress was made. One such move was Taggart's curious decision to drop to his knees and lift Alexey into his free arm. The baby, who had been crying until this point, looked up at him in wide-eyed wonder.

In response, Kotova's ex-husband made a grab for Michael's briefcase, hoping to catch his foe off-guard. The pair slammed into the window in the corner of the room, forming a spiderweb-looking crack on its surface. As soon as Taggart threw his weight against it once more, the crack expanded to cover the entire window, which stretched from the floor to the ceiling. After this, he pivoted so that his opponent's back was to the window.

Kotova's ex once more grabbed at the briefcase, but this time, Taggart *let* him take it. The man stumbled backwards from this momentum, and Michael took this chance to deliver a sharp kick to his gut. This time, the glass shattered completely, leaving the man with the briefcase to teeter on the edge of the building, creating a brief, calm pause from the fighting which had been going on. The only movements were everyone's breathing and the wind buffeting against Kotova's ex-husband.

What followed was anything but serene. Taggart held Alexey more tightly and delivered one final kick, sending the nameless man tumbling backwards, end over end. Michael looked over the edge in time to see his feet make contact with the suicide net below, but there was no salvation to be found there. Its outer edge caught his feet, causing one final spiral before he hit the pavement. The sound that this made was muffled from four stories above, but it was sickening nonetheless.

Wind now whipping through the opened office, Taggart stepped back from the edge and turned to leave. The throng of spectators parted to let him pass, everyone appearing to fear for their own safety.

Back on the ground, Michael found that an even larger group had gathered, and the piercing wail of sirens could be heard approaching. Ignoring these factors, he walked over to where his fallen enemy had come to rest and did something that he would never understand but felt was necessary. He closed the man's eyes and folded his arms across his chest.

Alexey hadn't made a sound since they had been on the top floor. Taggart tucked the boy more securely into a cradled position, then picked up his briefcase from the street and slid its handle over his maimed hand and onto his wrist. At this point, the sirens had stopped, and police officers were busy clearing the scene and investigating the area. Michael was walking away and paid no mind to this until one of them clapped a hand on his shoulder.

"American?" he shouted, pulling Taggart around so that he was facing him. When the latter nodded, he said, "Okay, in English then. Do you know what happened here? Was he pushed out?"

Taggart only shrugged and shook his head in feigned confusion. Seeming to be content with this, the policeman turned his attention in the other direction. Michael hurried to move in the other direction, into the shadows. As all of this was happening, a few members of the crowd were pointing their fingers at Taggart and yelling something in Chinese. This caught the attention of the policeman, who cursed at himself for not detaining the suspect on the spot. As he turned to apprehend Michael once more, however, he and Alexey were gone.

The police would later bill the man's death as a suicide, and this wasn't as far from the truth as it might have seemed. In reality, he had likely been dead inside since he had returned from active duty. Taggart had only helped to complete the process. Try as he might to move on, however, Michael continued to look back on this incident with remorse. The long list of misdeeds committed by the man helped to balance it out, and he had saved a life in the process, but… A feeling was still there. A feeling that both lives could have been preserved somehow. One of the lives could have been changed afterward.

These thoughts chased each other through Taggart's mind as he continued his trek out of the area. The whole ordeal made him sick to his stomach, and he wouldn't have wished his condition on anyone.

No single person deserves this. Nobody. I just need to learn that life isn't about getting what you deserve. Life is just making plans and adapting when those plans don't work. I thought I could handle that. I still might be able to. But god damn it, I just need some rest! Please!

Not knowing what else to do, Michael tightened his grip on the now-sleeping Alexey and pressed on.

———

Alone, hunted by terrorists, and carrying an infant through the streets of Hong Kong was never a combination of circumstances that Taggart had ever imagined, but he accepted the situation all the same. Even under strain and duress, it was as if his mind had been programmed to push everything to the wayside other than a single, insatiable objective.

He was, however, unable to continue walking so many miles at a time. A combination of fatigue and age seemed to have caught up with him, and it was because of this that he stopped on the sidewalk of a busy intersection and held out his hand. In preparation for the mission, he had picked up a few Chinese phrases which he thought might come in handy. He just hoped that this would pay off.

Sure enough, a blue sedan came to a stop at the intersection, and the driver rolled down his window. As soon as he saw the baby in Taggart's arms, he seemed to be more secure speaking to a complete stranger.

"Da-bian-che?" He said slowly, trying to remember if that was the correct phrase for a hitchhiker. It must have been, because the driver smiled warmly and beckoned him into the front seat. Taggart nodded his thanks and said the name of the street adjacent to the brothel. He didn't want to create a bad impression and possibly lose his chance at a ride.

The driver gave a thumbs up, and that was the last communication between them until they had reached their destination. All the while, Alexey remained silent. He seemed content to stare up at Taggart with the wonder that only small children seem to possess.

Taggart's eyes were almost closed, and he was all but asleep when they pulled up outside of a service station near the brothel. Taggart clasped his hands together in a thank-you gesture, and the driver did the same as Michael stepped out of the car. With that and a quick wave, he and Alexey were once more on their own.

Feeling more than a little bit out of place, Taggart carried the child down the block and into the establishment known as "The Last Resort." As soon as he had stepped inside, a frail, old man approached him and asked very brusquely what he wanted. When he revealed that he wished to have a word with Wang Fang, he bristled.

"If this child is hers, I am not responsible. Please go away."

Taggart did his best to assure the man that this wasn't related to the child, and, even though he remained skeptical, the man led him up a flight of stairs and to a small room on the second floor. There stood a woman who must have been in her mid-20s, dressed in the same revealing attire as the other ladies in the building. She was standing in the middle of a comfortably-furnished room, set off with red mood lighting and a dressing screen in the corner.

The old man nodded to Fang, stepped out of the room, and closed the door behind him. It was then that Taggart realized that over the past few weeks, he had lost all concept of what his code phrase was. Wang Fang folded her arms and raised her eyebrows at him, waiting.

"Er... Taking a new step... is what people fear the most?"

She gave a light shrug. "Close enough, I guess. 'Happiness is found within, do not seek it without.'

"I honestly didn't think that you'd be coming. Besides you arriving much later than I expected, I was also given word that you had gone silent on communications. We all thought you were dead."

Taggart sighed and nodded. "As far as they know, I am dead. I should level with you, because I need your help."

"I'm guessing that it has something to do with the baby that you're holding. Somehow I doubt that you started this assignment with a child."

"Right on both counts. Interpol and I had some… Let's just call them 'fundamental disagreements.' I hesitate to say this in case it would mean that you'd refuse to help, but I've parted ways with them. I can't justify living someone else's life for them. I acknowledge that I'm not in a great bargaining position, but I really do need help."

Fang studied him, mouth drawn in a thin line. "It just so happens that you're in luck. I'm not exactly content with Interpol's treatment of me, either. It's an issue of insensitivity, putting me undercover as a prostitute. I don't know if it was intentional, but they should know how terrible that looks and feels for me. They're pushing a stereotype of transsexual people only existing in this line of work, and that's something that I can't stand for. They've made sure that I don't have to have sex with any of the customers, but the principle is the same. It wouldn't be tolerated anywhere else, so why should an international agency based around justice tolerate it? Go ahead. Hey, I might need a favor of my own someday. From one mistreated person to another, what do you need?"

Taggart's expression was grave from hearing this news, and he was a bit more subdued as he went into detail about his situation.

"This baby is the son of another operative. Another mistreated one, in fact. Is there any way that you could look after him for a while? I'm sorry, I can't even determine how long that will be or if I'll be able to return at all, but I just need to know that he's safe. That's the most important thing right now, his security."

Wang Fang pulled a chair from the corner of the room, sat down, and motioned for Taggart to hand the child to her. Apprehensive about handing over such an important bundle, he did it with the utmost care.

The gentleness with which she cradled Alexey in her arms made him feel at ease; it was as if being such a caretaker was in her nature. She laughed to herself while looking into his eyes.

"Well, I guess that decides it. I can't say no now - I'm already attached."

Taggart smiled back, but there was a strain in it that he couldn't seem to avoid. Maybe after all was said and done, that would disappear. Maybe.

Wang Fang looked up from Alexey and said, "I might as well give you the information that I was assigned to give in the first place. The main person that you need to focus on is the Russian called Nikolai. As far as Interpol can tell, he holds the most information about it and its use as a weapon. Believe it or not, he has actually asked to meet with you personally. Every so often, letters are dropped into our agents' rooms and post office boxes. Each one is based around getting in contact with you. He has an alarming knowledge about the Sentinels, so you should use caution. I know that you would even if I hadn't told you to, but it's still something to keep in mind.

"I'll defer to you on this - should I answer his letter? Nikolai has a permanently reserved room at a hotel here in North Point. It's a pretty fancy affair. He has insisted upon that specific meeting place, but he has left the day and time of the meeting open-ended. If you wanted a chance to take him out, there probably won't be a better chance than this."

She returned her attention to Alexey and gave Michael some time to ponder this. The thought of putting himself in so much danger wasn't an appealing one, especially after his time in captivity. Even so, the prospect of meeting Nikolai face-to-face could prove to be exactly what he needed to put an end to the Affliction crisis.

After a long pause, he relented. "Alright. It's probably going to happen one way or another, so it might as well be on semi-equal terms. I'll just need to rest, and... yeah, it would probably be a good idea for me to find some better clothes for the occasion."

Michael had almost forgotten that he was still wearing his hospital-provided garments, and they were neither comfortable nor well-fitting. In addition to this, it was unlikely that he would be permitted to enter the meeting place in such attire.

In a move that surprised him, Fang stood up, walked to the closet behind her, and produced a freshly-pressed suit on a hanger and a pair of wingtip shoes.

"Interpol thought that you would feel this way, so they took the liberty of sending this along." She handed the package to Taggart and returned to her chair. "They were working with pretty old measurements, but if you haven't grown much in the past year, you should be fine."

Taggart thanked her and requested that the meeting be scheduled for eight o'clock of the next day. Fang assured him that this wouldn't be a problem, and he gave one last look toward Alexey before bidding them both goodbye and exiting the room. He passed the same old man on the way out, but he now was resting his head on the front desk, mumbling in his sleep.

It was with a heavy head and a heavier heart that Taggart stepped back onto the streets that had fast become his home. No matter where he slept, every path led back to the streets of Hong Kong. When he had first arrived in the city, Michael had considered living in the city as soon as he could let go of everything else. Like it had done to so much else, however, this mission had given the place a negative feeling that he couldn't quite place.

With his clothes draped over his arm, Taggart made his way back to the tiny room that he had rented upon arriving in Hong Kong. The owner of the place wasn't thrilled to hear that he had lost his key and hadn't paid for all of the days he had "stayed" there, but he gave him a spare key and let him in nonetheless. In return, Michael retrieved his backpack from his quarters and paid the man one and a half times what he owed from the cash that was still there.

This seemed to satisfy the landlord, who finally left him in peace. With no energy left to do anything else, Michael collapsed across his bed. To an outside observer, it would have been comical to see him sprawled on such a tiny surface with his legs hanging over the edge, but to him, it was a paradise. The only things bothering him were the ache in his right hand and the matching soreness that he felt against his temples.

These were easily overlooked in favor of a night's sleep on his terms - no hospitals, no prisons, only a room of his own. This dreamless sleep was a welcome one, and it lasted until two in the afternoon of the next day. Seeing this time displayed on the room's clock-radio didn't bother him. In fact, it was his intention to acquire as much rest as he could before his meeting with Nikolai. If ever there was a time when he had to be of sound mind and body, it would be then. Sound body could more or less be accomplished. The other was a different matter entirely.

To occupy the time before he had to leave, Taggart rummaged through his pack and withdrew a pack of Aspirin and his journal. He pocketed the first of these things, found a pen on the bedside table, and began to write.

Personal Journal of Michael Taggart (No Date Provided)

Well, I'm back to this journal, and it still looks brand new. Like a book that hasn't been used or a life that hasn't been lived. Hopefully I can fix that soon.

Anyway, it's good to be back. Writing this. Gives me a chance to sort out my thoughts. Actually, not really. They're not sorted at all. It's a chance to get them out on paper, that's it. It works, I guess. Not as well as it could, but it's something.

Even though so much has happened recently, and I had thought of so much to say, here I am without any idea of what to write. So much of what I saw once I was captured, I don't want to relive. Not in the slightest. None of the emotions or sights or sounds…nothing. The only worthwhile experience in that hellhole was talking with Emelia. It makes me feel a lot more sympathy for her after hearing her situation. Is that bad of me? I don't know. I hope not. I don't mean to say that's the only reason I feel that we work well on this assignment together, but it does make me feel better. Better to know that someon is t

Jeez. What just happened? I think I fell asleep trying to write. That's not a good sign. I'm not sure it's a sign on anything, but it can't be good. I think I was trying to say that it helps to know that someone can come through something worse than I've ever endured and come out on the other side. Not only did she make it through, but she's still fighting for something. We need more people like that. Hopefully I'm one.

Outside the Regal Dragon Hotel (Hong Kong, China): March 26, 2016 - 7:42 P.M.

He didn't know why or how, but Taggart felt as if his senses had been amplified. It wasn't in the typical rage-filled manner that he had grown so accustomed to, either. This time, it seemed like every subtle movement or imperceptible sound was able to reach him.

This hyper-awareness hit him all at once, and its arrival was both startling and overwhelming. Things were moving so quickly, and there was so much to keep track of. For instance, Taggart's eyes were drawn to the security guards who were watching over the metal detector. Each of the four of them was wearing finely-pressed uniforms and were observing the crowds with close scrutiny. They gave an impression of extreme professionalism, and it seemed to Taggart that getting a weapon past them would require mistake-free planning.

Prior planning prevents piss poor performance. C'mon, Taggart. Let's do this.

He was standing in front of a first-rate hotel, the place where Nikolai had arranged their meeting. At first glance, it looked as if the people entering the hotel were random and unpredictable, but, after a few minutes, a pattern began to emerge. Wait staff and additional security personnel were moving freely through the area, as were men and women sporting tuxedos and ball gowns, respectively. They stood out from the rest not only in appearance, but also in the condescension present in their expressions. Classist undertones were present throughout Taggart's entire experience, but nowhere else was it so distinct.

Some of the ones fortunate enough to gain entrance to the hotel remained outside for the time being, flaunting their affluence to each other and those below them. Michael stepped forward and became a part of the 'social elite.'

It was fortunate that he knew no one at the event, as this spared him from having to make small talk in a language which he couldn't begin to understand. Instead, he was able to get by with a broad smile and the polite waving of his hand. While this part of his mind was maintaining an inconspicuous social presence, the other was searching for any chance that he might have of smuggling his pistol inside. The weapon was resting in his holster, and Taggart could only hope that it didn't look as conspicuous as it felt.

The crowd stayed as a single unit for the most part, but there was one man in particular who flitted in and out of the group. He was disappearing and reappearing in roughly two-minute increments, and this soon caught the attention of Taggart. The reason for his absences soon became clear — the green shade of his face and his intermittent coughing suggested that he was leaving the crowd to vomit, or at least to deal with his condition. This idea was reinforced by the state of his tuxedo, which had small, sickly-green splotches near its pockets.

What interested Taggart more, however, was the man's briefcase. There was nothing special about the case itself; it was nothing more than a leather box with a matching handle. Instead of seeing this alone, Michael saw the potential that it carried.

As the stranger departed from the crowd once more, Taggart followed at a cautious distance. He was led into a poorly lit alleyway, where the sick man had dropped his briefcase and was coughing and retching into a dumpster against the far wall. Even though he doubted very much that he would be discovered, Taggart crept forward, unholstered his pistol, and ensured that its safety was engaged.

With the businessman continuing to be sick several feet away, Michael released the clasps of the briefcase as quietly as he could. Inside, he found only a sheaf of papers. Because there was plenty of free space inside, Taggart slid his pistol into the case and secured it so that it wouldn't rattle around and alert the man.

Heart pounding and paranoia working overtime, Taggart kept his eyes on the man's back, willing him to not turn around. He secured the clasps of the briefcase once more. The faint *snap* caused by this was enough to send the hapless individual spinning to face Michael, but the latter was already on his feet and several steps away from the case.

For a moment, the two could only stare at each other. There was no obvious reason that either one should have been suspicious, but there was a tenseness in the air nonetheless.

If Taggart had waited for a solution to present itself, he would have been waiting for quite some time. Rather, Taggart took the initiative and approached the sickly man.

Not knowing any words that he might understand, Taggart merely withdrew the pack of Aspirin from his pocket and held it out to him.

The look of confusion on the stranger's face turned to one of relief and appreciation. Given the situation, he didn't hesitate to accept medicine from a stranger. After he dry-swallowed two of the capsules, the two waited for them to have an effect.

Wiping sweat from his brow, the stranger straightened up, picked up his briefcase, and gave a thankful nod to Taggart before heading toward the hotel. The latter nodded back with a bit of sadness, knowing that the man was walking from one misfortune into another.

His eyes followed the poor victim as he hurried to the front doors and through the metal detector. As expected, it gave a sharp series of beeping noises which permeated through the area. Every eye was on the man and the security guards around him. Looking bemused, he handed his briefcase to one of them and walked through again. This time, there was silence from the machine. The case was passed through once more to confirm that it was, in fact, setting off the alarm. Sure enough, it once more set off the sharp, piercing noise.

The guards moved in closer to the man, demanding that he hand over his belongings. The stranger was quick to comply, still looking confused as to why he was in this predicament. It took only a few seconds for one of the uniformed men to rifle through the briefcase and produce Taggart's pistol. There was an almost comical look of shock on the faces of the sick man, the guards, and the surrounding party-goers. In fact, only Taggart's expression remained neutral.

He did his best to look aghast as the man was carted away by security, and the weapon was carried inside by one of the security personnel. Two guards remained, and Taggart took this opportunity to approach them and submit his own, empty briefcase for inspection. The process came and went without incident, and it was only a few brief moments before Taggart was granted access to the lobby of the hotel.

Even from the first few seconds of seeing the location, Michael could see that Nikolai had chosen this location for its affluence and class. This contrasted starkly with the grassroots meeting place of the abandoned hospital in Moscow, and it occurred to Taggart that his adversary wanted to create an impression of overwhelming wealth and power. Michael felt it necessary to keep in mind that this was a hollow illusion.

The first order of business, however, would be retrieving his pistol. Taggart assumed that the guard had taken it to a security room somewhere inside the hotel, and he set to investigating the bottom floor. How he would retrieve the weapon without being detected was an issue for when he arrived.

Rather, it would have been an issue if he had found the room at all. Only a few moments after he had passed the security checkpoint, two men appeared on either side of him. It was clear that neither of them was of Chinese descent, and they each towered above Michael by at least a foot.

They said nothing, one instead opting to rip the briefcase out of Taggart's hand in a calm yet firm movement. The other shoved him forward and nodded to indicate that he should start walking. It played into their hands that Michael wanted to remain as inconspicuous as he could, since that seemed to be their goal as well. They led him on a winding route through the hotel, bypassing most of the party-goers and coming to a stop in front of a closed set of double doors.

It was at this point that the strongmen pushed Taggart back and one of them stepped inside. Michael was only able to catch a quick glimpse of what lay beyond - a ballroom of some sort - before the other man folded his arms and stepped in front of the opening. The two stood in tense, uncomfortable silence for a minute or so before the other returned. As soon as he was back, he nodded to his partner. Then, they pushed open the doors to allow Taggart entry before slamming them shut behind him. A faint *click* could be heard, leaving him with one less avenue of escape.

The room itself exemplified the rest of the hotel in its radiance. Blinding light was coming from a variety of chandeliers hanging from the ceiling, with the largest one resting over the center of the room. The walls bore intricate designs of different cultural symbols, such as a fleur-de-lis and a five-pointed star on opposite walls. Each one contained details too intricate to notice without closer examination Tables and chairs had been lain out in neat rows across the room, but only a single space was occupied.

Directly under the chandelier sat Nikolai, staring straight ahead and flipping a coin in his right hand. Taggart stepped forward, his eyes beginning to water from the intense lighting. The effect conjured up images of torture and pain during his captivity, and he couldn't help but wonder if that was exactly the point.

Nikolai placed the coin in his breast pocket and motioned for Taggart to sit down. At first, he made no attempt to engage in conversation. Instead, he turned his focus to the meal in front of him, which contained only white rice and a glass of wine. Despite the fact that his greatest opponent was sitting across from him, Nikolai seemed to be perfectly at ease. This was contrasted by his use of chopsticks — his hands were trembling as they had been when Taggart had first seen him in Russia.

He waited patiently for Nikolai, even though the silent tension was beginning to get to him. The thought occurred to him that his opponent was waiting for him to speak first, but this was soon proven to be incorrect. The Russian, not looking up from his meal, addressed Taggart as if he was a normal dinner guest.

"I'm pleased that you decided to come after all. I apologize for the rough nature of my guards, because I've asked you here as a friend. In fact, I have a business proposition which would be of great benefit to us both."

He raised his eyes from his plate and waited for a response. When Michael remained impassive, he continued,

"You see, this world is an old man whose social security checks bounced a long time ago. It is living on the good graces of friends, and we both know that this system will collapse before long. We have the unique opportunity to give this old man health and virility that it never had! We can revive him! Changes must be made, and men like us are the very ones to do so!

"We are entering an era which only respects people who create revolutions and take initiative. We are not unlike each other, Michael. You and I are nothing more than men who have the world's best interests at heart. The only difference is our choice of methods. Don't see me as your enemy. Don't even look at me as a person. To you, I'm only an idea. I'm a vision of a world in which the poor aren't preyed upon by the rich. A world where society is balanced and everyone has the same chance in life."

Taggart remained silent for quite some time, staring into Nikolai's eyes. Michael was captivated by the unblinking stare; it was unlike any he had ever seen.

"When I look at your eyes, all I can see is a lack of focus and a lack of warmth. Funny. That's exactly what I see in your plan to 'revive' the world. You're an idealist, Nikolai. And I mean that in the worst way possible. You assume that your plan will work, and along with that comes the assumption that everyone will have their neighbor's best interests at heart. This has never happened, and I think it's pretty safe to say that it never will. Even if it did become a reality, what would happen to the people themselves?

"From what I've seen and what I've fought through in my life, if someone always puts others more highly than themselves, *they will stop functioning*. Period. Self-sacrifice isn't noble or admirable — it's sickening. It's destructive. If you sacrifice yourself because someone else wants you to, *you are a part of the problem*. The problem that you're trying to perpetuate. And my objection to this isn't based on some selfish mindset, either. Even to help others as well, it's necessary to look after yourself first. People such as yourself criticize things like emergency airplane procedures. You deem it to be the degradation of society when we're told to ensure that we're safe before we help those around us. It isn't selfish. It isn't degrading society. Without the self, there is nothing. Preserving other lives is wonderful — but it won't happen if we put our own wellbeing on the back burner.

"I'm not sure if you're familiar with baseball, but a player is given three chances to succeed before they're out. Chances one and two are already on the table. You have the fact that your precious socialism has never existed as its founders intended. It can't, and it won't. Strike two against you is that the best interest of the public comes second to the survival of one's self. Now, strike three is —"

It was at this point that Nikolai decided to produce a .357 caliber revolver from under the table and place it beside his plate.

"Continue, Mr. Taggart. By all means, continue. Just be aware that you have eroded my will enough already, and if you say anything more that I do not wish to hear, well... You're a smart man. I'm sure you can put the rest together."

"Oh, I won't hesitate to finish what I have to say," Taggart shot back. "That's because, unlike you, I couldn't care less if I die. I'm not afraid of it. If I had every injury that I've inflicted sent back my way, I'd be dead dozens of times over. Shoot me if you want, but I'll have my say."

In actuality, Michael knew that he was lying through his teeth. He was scared shitless. In the past, he had convinced himself that he wasn't afraid of death. Now, without his adrenaline pumping and with death staring at him across the table, he was more afraid of death than he had ever been.

In addition, most people would have had reservations about standing down a delusional, violent man with a loaded gun, but here he was. Trying to prevent these thoughts and worries from impacting his voice, Taggart continued, "The third strike is that sharing wealth *does* give everyone an equal amount of resources, but there is no way that everyone's level of effort will be the same. Instead of relying on the government's support to survive, they'll just get paid for other people's effort. There's no incentive left. Without any real reason to work, that leaves no room for a country to grow."

Nikolai took a deep breath before saying, "I will outline for you what my intentions are. I really do want to establish communication and trust between us, Michael." He clapped his hand on Taggart's shoulder as if he was a father speaking to his young son. The only thing missing was warmth.

"An integral part of my plan, as well as the reason that you are here is the disease which you and those around you call 'The Affliction.' In truth, it was because of me that you know about my weapon. Something a friend of mine concocted in her lab. In one little syringe, there lies the power to create chaos. You have the opportunity to change the dynamic of crowds and even cities and nations! You saw for yourself on that bus in Moscow the power of this serum. I am not a fool, Michael. I know that if I want to enlist your service, I must be honest and transparent with you. Because of that, I think it is time to make you aware of what will be happening as of tonight.

"I am well known in political circles in Russia. This is both a gift and a curse. Since the collapse of the Soviet Union, socialists such as myself have become quite...

unpopular, to say the least. What the Federation fails to realize is how they are creating a state which is almost socialist by themselves - almost. They need one final push. But, because of their denial, telling anyone of importance about this would be counter-productive. I'm forced to be more subtle, and that is where my dealings with the Chinese come in. The crime lords in Hong Kong believe me to be a greedy *gweilo* who is only concerned with making a profit. I have sold them a portion of my storage of the Affliction, and the money is only a bonus.

"You may question my methods, and that is natural for someone of your background. One thing that you must accept is that if someone takes something from someone else without right or permission, he is breaking the law. That is what has happened throughout the twentieth century and continues to happen today. Socialist parties and nations were blackmailed and forced into submission by other groups. Because of this, it is only proper that such deceit is used in re-establishing the prominence of socialism. It is an equal trade, and I have no problem with a peaceful resolution. That is to say, I would react with fairness and peace if my people had been extended the same courtesy.

"The criminal underworld is at war, Michael. Studying the waves and currents which run through Hong Kong, it isn't hard to see that the tide is coming in, and one side will have to wash the other away. I have negotiated a deal to put the serum into the hands of both sides. The chaos that this will cause will be overwhelming for the Chinese people, and the government will be desperate for a solution for the riots and madness that the distributed Affliction will bring.

"This is why the only cure for the disease has been given to the Socialist Democratic Party of Hong Kong. While the rest of the government is busy floundering around and doing nothing for their citizens, the socialists will be revealed as the only ones who are able to cope with difficult situations such as this. They will be lauded as heroes. They will become the predominant governing forces throughout China, and this will not take long to spread through the rest of the East. Eventually, I have no doubt that Russia will follow the example of others when they see that socialism is the most practical concept in the modern world."

Taggart, who had been listening intently, found it difficult to keep an open mind. "I accept that your intentions are good. I think they are, at least. But you're trying to form this new society accepting that it can't come about by natural means. You're creating unrest in the hope that it'll end up creating balance, but eventually humanity will reject it just as they have in the past.

"The more I think about it, the more I'm convinced that this world needs to be changed. It really does. One of those changes, though, is that people need to start ignoring destructive forces like you. We need to be taking steps away from that. I'm not going to claim to know what would be the best at this point, but it's pretty easy to see that what you're doing is the farthest thing from productive.

"Despite what you might think, I don't want to kill you. I'm done with killing people just because of a difference in opinion. I just need you to know that what you're doing makes so little sense; it's hard to listen to it without shaking my head in disbelief. It just won't work."

Nikolai clapped his hands slowly several times in mock applause. "Admirable sentiments. I know that you are only saying that because you were forced to meet me unarmed. I also know that you will continue to interfere with my plans if you are allowed to leave here. Every hero throughout history has needed a villain to contest with; every good must have evil to banish. Otherwise, how would goodness exist? Where you've gone wrong, Michael, is your assumption that you stand for something good."

With his other hand still resting on the table, Nikolai picked up his revolver and made it ready to fire. The subtle *click* that resulted from this was enough to make Taggart shake with anxiety. Nikolai was trembling as well, but it was doubtful that this was from fear of any kind - the man always seemed to be this way.

As Nikolai raised the weapon so that it was pointing directly between Taggart's eyes, the latter said, "So, about that coin of yours... what's it for? Are you going to flip it to see if I'm allowed to live or something?"

Nikolai gave a sardonic grin. "No. It's only here as a keepsake of mine from 1917 - the greatest of years. And apparently it is also a device for you to prolong your life, it seems. Whatever side it lands on is irrelevant to you. You'll be dead no matter the outcome."

With that, he rested his finger on the trigger and prepared to fire. Taggart saw the trigger being pressed down for only a moment before he closed his eyes. There was no moment of his life flashing before his eyes or profound thought about the finality of life. There was only his breath catching in his throat and the sickening sound of the trigger being pulled in.

As he heard this, Taggart flinched so violently that it looked as if he was trying to jump out of his chair. This must have had a comical effect, because Nikolai had begun to laugh in earnest. "Oh, Michael. If you weren't so counter-productive to my plans, I'd keep you around just for amusement. As it is, I will still have to kill you, but at least we both had a good laugh out of it!"

Taggart looked up at him through skeptical eyes. *Sure.* Both *of us are laughing.* He knew that he had to stall for time. Even if he didn't have a plan at that moment, a few extra minutes could be what he needed to figure out a way to escape the room alive. Only one phrase came into his mind, so he voiced it without hesitation.

"What's your stance on cats?"

Nikolai, who had been reaching for his weapon, stopped short and stared at Michael, incredulous. "Excuse me?"

"You know, *cats.* The four-legged furry things that sleep a lot? Surely you're familiar with them."

"Of course I know what cats are," Nikolai said, trying to pretend that he wasn't getting impatient. "I only fail to realize why you're talking about them right now. Right now, at such an important juncture of your life. The moment that could very well be the last you ever experience."

Taggart shrugged. "Honestly, I don't know, either. Maybe I've gone crazier than I'm willing to admit. Maybe I'm trying to prolong my life for a few more moments. You know what, it's probably the second one. But while we're on the subject, I'd just like to say that I find more to admire in such a simple creature than I find in you."

"You do realize that this makes me *more* inclined to shoot you now, don't you? You just admitted that you're stalling, and you've just insulted me." Nikolai was visibly fuming, much to Taggart's satisfaction.

Michael shrugged again and gave a half-grin. "Well, you could do that. The way I see it, though, is that you valued me enough to take an interest in what I do. You valued me enough to invite me here to receive your sales pitch for your socialist scheme. If I'm worth that much in your eyes, I doubt that a man as smart as you will end my life before I've said my fill. If you want to, then, by all means, go ahead, but I really don't think you will."

Nikolai withdrew his hand from the revolver, instead placing it on the table, palm-down. "Alright. I see that you're trying to appeal to my senses with flattery, and that won't work. I assure you, that is something that won't work. What has convinced me is your logic. I do value your intelligence, Michael. I do, in fact, value it so highly that I will let you finish your treatise on… er… *cats.*"

"Thank you," Taggart said, not convinced that his flattery had failed entirely. "Now, as I was saying, I value a lot about how cats operate. They do what they need to do, and most civil cats only lash out if they're given a good reason. You've turned into one of those cats that wants something and has decided to claw your way towards it without any regard for the consequences. Jesus, even the cats try to be subtle about it. They creep around in the night, waiting to pounce on their prey. They take things slowly and usually are able to get what they want, at least for a time." Taggart couldn't make sense of what he was saying or where this metaphor was leading, but he continued nonetheless.

"The difference here is that you've left subtlety behind. Well, I should correct myself there. You've *mostly* left it behind. This pretense of spreading socialism to China… like I said, it just proves that you aren't convinced of your own beliefs. Some small part of you knows that a legitimate, worthy form of government should come about through natural means. It should come about by people agreeing that it has merit and adopting it. The problem is that your plan doesn't have any merit at all, and you know it. You're trying to convince yourself otherwise, but you know it.

"Also, have you ever noticed how cats spend most of their time alone? I mean, they hang around people, sure, but they never really want to be at the center of things. Let me guess, you see yourself as a loner. Nikolai, the kid who always sat by himself and stewed about how misunderstood he was. You like to think of yourself as a person who doesn't need anyone else. Sure other people can have their uses, but are they ever really necessary?

"Now, you might be saying to yourself, *'Nikolai! How does he know all of this about you?'* Well, that's an easy one. I've been in the same position. In fact, I was up until a few seconds ago. I've been making all of this up as I go along, but this is… this is amazing! I've realized something while talking to you.

"You feel lonely in this world, you feel that no one else can relate. I did too, but that's just it. If I feel this way and you feel this way, that probably means other people do, too!

"I had an old friend who told me about this, and I always wondered what the hell he was talking about. It's just so logical and concise. Aren't you excited, Nick?"

Taggart was in a daze; he was lightheaded and his words were coming out of his mouth before he could fully process them. Nikolai, on the other hand, was growing visibly impatient.

"Get to the point, if there is one. I'm starting to doubt that there is, especially since you admitted to improvising these vapid thoughts."

"My point is that if so many people feel alone, that means that they aren't alone at all. That feeling is one that we all share in common, and that means it's just in my mind that I feel isolated. It's up to me to change that, not anyone else! It's up to you to do that for yourself, too! Breaking down the barriers that we put up... that's the only way to stay sane. It really is. It just makes me envy the people who never put up those barriers in the first place. I didn't before, but I feel sympathy for you now. I really do.

"You were right in telling me to not see you as an enemy, but it's wrong to just see you as an ideal. You're a living, breathing person sitting in front of me, wondering what will happen to him. Come on, Nikolai. You have humanity, just acknowledge it. You're not some villain from a bad comic book whose entire life is spent making diabolical plans and manipulating people. You have some of the same sensibilities and ideas that I do. I really don't have the right to say who is more human, but you just might be more so than I am."

Nikolai made no comment, and his eye was now twitching with impatience. The man's hand hadn't yet strayed to his revolver, however, so Michael pressed on.

"I really think it'll go over your head, but I might as well try to express the rest of my thoughts. To summarize for you, this leaves you as a lonesome, feral cat begging for a treat from your master. The master, in this case, is the Russian government, and the treat is that radical change you want. If they were going to give that treat to anyone, they would have done it by now. They tried before, and the treat poisoned the Russian people. You're trying to bring it back, and it'll just do the same thing again. It's -"

Nikolai cut him short by slamming his fist on the table. It landed on his plate and upended it, but he pretended not to notice. "I am tired of your labored garbage. You're only moving us in circles, and I have no more patience for it. In fact, it makes me doubt my first impression of you — it looks as if you weren't worth my time in the first place." His voice was shaking with suppressed anger. When he continued, it was in a quiet, falsely calm manner. "I will stand by what I said. My instincts don't often betray me, and I will still do my best to see you as an equal.

"When it comes down to associating with equals," Nikolai said as he loaded a single round into his revolver, "it can not be said of me that I am unfair. I will offer you one more opportunity, out of the kindness of my heart. Remember how similar our goals are, Michael. If you can find it in yourself to come around, we'll be the best of friends. We are even so close to brothers that I could even call you 'Mikhail.' Work for me, brother, and we can see that the world is given the justice that it deserves."

Still recovering from the past few moments, Taggart

straightened himself until he was looking down at Nikolai from across the table. Even this change in stature gave confidence and strength to his voice.

"I am not your brother, and I am even less of your friend. There is no chance of me coming to see the logic in a man who is about to kill someone in the name of fairness to humanity. Even more, I am through living my life for other people. The only self-sacrifice that I'll make to you is my death so that I won't live an empty life in service to someone who I don't even begin to agree with. So, go on. Do it."

What happened in the next few moments occurred so quickly, it took quite a while for everything to register in Taggart's mind. Nikolai's face was contorted with rage, and he readied and aimed his weapon with the speed of a gunslinger from the Old West. Pulling back its hammer once more, he clenched his teeth and pressed the weapon to Taggart's forehead.

This time, Michael left his eyes open. He wasn't sure why he felt compelled to do so, but it felt necessary to look Nikolai in his eyes to remove any doubt of his conviction.

Before his enemy had the chance to deliver the final blow, a muted sound came through the room. Then another. No louder than a whisper, the sounds caused Nikolai's arm to go limp and drop his revolver on the table. Taggart was greeted by the sight of his adversary slumped back in his chair, penny-sized holes in his forehead and neck. Each one was covered in overly dark blood, which was characteristic of those suffering from the Affliction.

Standing above the dead Russian, still-smoking pistol in hand, was Emelia Kotova. She carried a look of intense anger with her which made Taggart almost as anxious as Nikolai had. She was wearing a white smock that the cooks and waiters of the hotel had, but hers was now stained with red. The resulting effect made her look like an overzealous butcher, albeit with a pistol instead of a meat cleaver.

She let out a deep breath, then held out the pistol to Taggart, and it was only then that he realized that it was his. Too adrenaline-filled to form anything more coherent, Michael said, "Emelia... when? Where were... how? Just how?"

Waiting for a moment so that he could collect himself, Kotova leaned against the table for support and said, "I would love to tell you everything, but we are in a pretty incriminating spot right now, and now that I've finished digging you out of a hole, I've got to keep looking for my son. You owe me one, Taggart."

She made to walk back through the swinging doors at the opposite end of the room, which presumably led to the kitchen. She only stopped when Taggart called out for her to wait. She only half-turned, and it was clear that she wanted to spend as little time there as she could.

"I don't think I owe you anymore," he said, his voice barely carrying across the ballroom. She raised an eyebrow and waited for him to continue. "Your son is safe. I've dealt with your ex-husband, and your son is with a friend. Someone I trust. He's okay."

Even Kotova was unable to hide her reaction to this, surprise and relief washing over her face. In contrast to her states of anger and worry, this was a natural, heartening response. Her excitement began to grow, but she was able to suppress this enough to stay in control of the situation. Her breath picked up, and her energy seemed to have restored itself from this news. With renewed strength, she beckoned Taggart to follow her through the kitchen.

They walked past a staff of alarmed and confused cooks, behaving as if there was nothing out of the ordinary happening. Emerging in an alley behind the hotel, the pair sat down to rest on a set of upturned crates. Taggart then asked the first of a long line of questions.

"How did you manage that? Finding my gun and arriving at the right time, I mean. I can't imagine better timing, and it doesn't seem like you were there by chance."

Kotova gave a half-smile. "You weren't the only one invited to a meeting with Nikolai. I chose to pose as a waitress at the hotel instead of meeting him face-to-face. I had even added a dash of sodium cyanide to his meal, but the man insisted on having something else at the last minute. It was a bit of life-saving intuition, I guess. Well, life saving for a little while. To think, I had been given that cyanide to use on myself in case I was captured...

"After you started talking with him, one of the big security men pushed off a job on me; he wanted me to bring a briefcase to the contraband locker. I have to admit that I was curious what contraband anyone would want to bring into the hotel, and that's when I found your calling card. Then, it was just a matter of concealing it until the right moment. I know that my actions were last-minute. I also have to say that I won't apologize for that, either. You were pressing a great deal of information out of him, and I was trying to hear as much as I could."

Taggart raised his eyebrows and grinned. "Well,

thank you for not letting him finish me off, at least."

"Oh, I was actually planning on it, but the fact that he didn't want my lovingly prepared meal was just too much to handle."

She said this in such a deadpan manner that it took several moments for the sarcasm to fully sink in. When it did, they both broke into a fit of laughter. It wasn't forced or nervous laughter, either. It was that which made their sides ache and made their heads lighter. In short, it was the most welcome thing in the world.

"I've taken the liberty of recovering the earpiece from our listening device while you were still locked away," she said, producing the dime-sized device. "I've been monitoring it while I wasn't busy killing other Russians or pretending to be a waitress, and I've heard something very interesting over it. Would you be interested to know where Nikolai stashed the Affliction?"

Taggart was taken aback. "You've really found out? You're kidding! You've got to be."

She shook her head, enjoying his look of shock. "It should be stashed under the couch in his penthouse. The same couch that you sat on before we were ambushed."

"That's... amazing! I'm impressed that you were able to figure that out; I'm sure that they didn't just outright say where it was."

"No kidding. A lot of their conversations didn't make much sense, but the Russians in there were talking a bit too carelessly. One of them must have bumped into the couch, because another one was furious and asked if he wanted to infect all of them. This caught my attention in a hurry, and I could hear a third voice faintly in the background. It said something about not worrying and that sitting on the couch hadn't set anything off, so nothing could. They started to argue about this, but I stopped listening when that went on for a while. I had what I needed."

"Amazing. Well, thank you for that! We're one step closer from ending this. *Finally* ending this."

They remained where they were for a little while, heartened by the progress that they had made over the past few days. Things had begun to pick up, so neither one felt very bad about taking a short break.

This, like too many happy things in life, was interrupted in a hurry. They were able to hear the faint sound of sirens, causing the pair to spring to their feet and dash away from the hotel. With Taggart leading the way, they were bound for Alexey and a great deal more chaos than the incident with Nikolai had caused.

Hong Kong, China (Streets of North Point): March 27, 2016 - 12:16 A.M.

"Taggart. Taggart!"

Kotova was calling to him as they hurried through the darkening streets.

"Wait!"

Michael slowed his pace, coming to a stop in front of a dark storefront. He bent his knees and rested his hands on them, taking the opportunity to catch his breath. As he did this, Taggart looked up at Emelia and waited for her to continue.

"I can't keep going until I know the details of where Alexey is and what happened. I need to know."

Taggart nodded and held up his index finger, signaling that he needed a few more moments. As soon as his breath had returned to him, he ensured that no one was within earshot and began to tell her what had happened at the daycare and the factory. When he informed her of the death of her ex-husband, Kotova's expression was difficult to read.

She had slumped against the store window and began to slide into a sitting position against it. Emelia then tilted her head back and closed her eyes, breathing quite slowly. When she decided to speak again, it was in the same detached manner that she had used when describing her past experiences while in the prison.

"I wish I could say that this is the ultimate relief and the most liberating thing in the world. I really wish that. In all honesty, I feel exactly as I did when he was alive. I won't say that the world isn't better off without him – it is. I also can't say that you killing that snide little fuck gives me any more peace. To know that people like him are still out there, doing to other women what he did to me… It's revolting. Even killing every abusing scumbag on the planet wouldn't make me content. There would be no men left. Not to say that men like you have done anything as horrible as he had. But you have abused emotions, even if most times it was unintended. It's a part of human nature. But he had a chance to be one of the non-compulsive abusers. One of the normal people who hurt others out of nature and not anger. He had a chance, and it's gone. I would say that I don't mind his passing, but that would be a lie. I don't miss the man who threw me out in the cold. I miss the man that he could have become.

"I try not to see the world in black and white

anymore. I don't even try to analyze the shades of gray in between. No, I try my best to see it in its own, vibrant color. That includes the vivid beauty this world brings, sure. But it also means seeing blood and violence in full detail. It wears me out to look at things this way, but the alternative would be ignoring how things work. That's just not something I'm willing to do."

Taggart said nothing, letting Emelia have peace and quiet to reflect on the situation. He personally could not understand the notion that the man could have been changed so easily, but he also reminded himself that he had not spent years at his side in sickness and in health.

Sighing heavily, Kotova said, "But that's something to mull over later. Right now, I need to know where Alexey is. As soon as possible."

Michael had expected incredulous or angry looks when he informed Emelia that her son was being watched over at a brothel, but she showed neither of these signs. She merely took a deep breath to collect herself, rose to her feet, and told Taggart to lead on.

It struck him as odd that she was so trusting of his choice of caretakers for Alexey, and he thought that this might be the first time that she showed *trust* to him. Especially considering her vocal opinion of the male population, she had accepted his help and honored his decisions. Even though he was a bit confused as to how he had earned this trust, Michael appreciated it and reminded himself to not take it for granted.

The Last Resort: Hong Kong, China - 12:27 A.M.

Ignoring the old man who tried to stop them as they walked through the door, Taggart and Kotova rushed to Wang Fang's second-story room. She opened the door on the first knock, revealing her still carrying little Alexey in her arms.

"I can tell by the look on your face that you're the boy's mother," she said to Emelia, who was looking at her son with overwhelming relief and joy. After handing the child to her, Fang said, "I stopped admitting customers for the past two days. My boss is furious, but I want the child of an operative to have the most normal upbringing possible. I figured that keeping him here while… working… wouldn't be the best choice."

Kotova thanked her profusely for her help, as did Taggart. The latter was on the verge of telling her what happened with Nikolai, but she stopped him short.

"It's probably better that I not know about that. Don't get me wrong, I'm pleased that you're back and in once piece, but I've had enough of the agency's bloodbath. I can see just from how you carry yourself that you've seen death recently. Let's just call it a gift."

The three all sat down on Fang's bed, ready to have a moment's peace after the events of the past few days. This would have to wait, however, as the sound of someone shouting emanated from the hallway. This was followed my multiple screams and quite a bit of yelling. It brought all of them to their feet, and Fang opened the door a fraction and peered outside. There were people running past, all of them seeming to head for the exit. She beckoned the others to join her, and they all watched chaos erupt throughout the brothel. Something was being shouted in Chinese by the old man, and Wang Fang served as a translator for them.

"He's saying something about a terrorist attack," she said, "He's mostly just yelling nonsense, but something is not right. Follow me."

Not wanting to delay by asking for more information, Taggart, Alexey, and Kotova followed her down the hall, against the sea of people who were running out of the building. They made their way up three sets of stairs, each one revealing a floor identical to the next. From the top floor, Fang opened a maintenance closet which also happened to have a wall-mounted ladder in it. At the top was a square hatch leading to the roof, and they climbed through it one by one.

The wind buffeted against them from such a great height, and they all had to struggle to make their way to the edge of the building. This afforded them a view of the intersection below, where it was difficult to tell what was happening.

The "terrorist attack" that the old man had been describing was in full force, and two different mobs of people had begun to fill the streets. Ignoring the traffic, the two groups filtered past cars and every other obstacle until they were facing each other at opposite sides of the intersection.

At that point, all of the yelling, shouting, and screaming that had been filling the air were cut off completely. The only movement from either side was the collective, heavy breathing that they shared. It looked like two armies which had been itching for combat but lost heart upon seeing their enemies. They seemed to be waiting for something, maybe just a small provocation to bring them back into action. Instead of a general calling these "armies" to action, they sprang to life when one single person sprinted to the middle of the intersection and hurled a stone at the other side.

Instead of rushing forward to fight the opposing side, the mobs began to fight amongst themselves, and the two groups soon merged into one. The three onlookers watched as people survived attacks which would have easily felled a normal person. Taggart slumped, resting his face in his good hand. Though not a total loss, he knew now that he had failed on some level. The Affliction was out there, and there was a high likelihood that it would soon spread beyond the confines of Hong Kong. The most he could do now was try to set things right before that was able to happen.

Kotova looked over at him, and the look in her eyes told Michael that they were thinking the same thing. They both knew that the best option was to retrieve the case containing the Affliction, if it was still hidden at the hotel. Getting there unscathed would be another matter.

They told Fang of their intentions, following which she nodded and wished them luck. She offered to watch after Alexey while they were doing this, but it was only halfhearted. It was almost certain to her that Kotova would decline, and this is precisely what happened. Fang couldn't say that she blamed her - after all that the two had been through, she wouldn't have let him go, either.

Wang Fang led them back into the building and down the stairs. The establishment was empty by now, all of its occupants either having been impacted by the Affliction or simply fled for safety. The lobby of The Last Resort is where they parted ways.

"Thank you for all of your help," Taggart said, shaking her hand.

"Yes," Kotova agreed, "thank you for taking such good care of my son. I don't know what I would have done if he wasn't put in such good hands."

Fang smiled, but it was a smile which contained almost as much sadness as it did joy. "We'll meet again," she said. "I've only known you two for such a short time, but it feels like much longer. I have no doubt that we'll be in each other's company before long.

"I hate saying 'goodbye,' because there's nothing good about it. I know you have to go as soon as you can, so I'll leave it with 'see you soon.'"

With these sentiments expressed, Kotova and Taggart parted her company and made four into three. The doorway of the brothel was devoid of any violent activity, but this proved to be a rare exception. In a roughly ten-foot radius around them, people from all walks of life were engaging in animalistic violence. Fists, pipes, bats, batons were coming in contact with flesh and bone. People who would normally be sickened at the thought of violence were participating in it as if it was their only function. The most disturbing thing about them was the unwavering intensity in their eyes; it gave them an almost inhuman appearance.

Taggart and Kotova looked for a way past the chaos, and the only possible avenue was over a stationary car and through an almost-empty shopping plaza. Taggart made a running jump onto the hood of the car and offered a hand to Kotova, but she was already climbing up with Alexey, unaided. Over the roof and trunk they went, looking down at the heads of the Afflicted. Most were bruised or battered, and the ones who weren't would soon have injuries of their own.

Some even grabbed at Taggart's feet as he moved past, but he was able to kick them away and reach the other side of the car. Kotova and Alexey were close behind, and the three were able to make their way out of the turmoil and into the openness of the shopping center. The only people who remained nearby were peeking out of windows to see what was going on. They were witnesses of a civil war with no objective or purpose.

The three foreigners bypassed these onlookers and indeed the entire area. On the way back to the hotel, the only calm one was Alexey. He was the only one able to carry the confidence that everything would be okay.

Most would chalk this up to the naïvetè of such a young child, but Taggart realized that he was the only one who knew how to emotionally survive this situation. Falling victim to worry and fear would just serve to drag them down and allow their worst fears to become realities. Alexey, without knowing it, was an inspiration to him.

Trying to maintain this mindset, Taggart followed Kotova across North Point, thankful that they didn't have to go the entire distance of the train ride that they had taken before. Similar scenes of chaos were occurring throughout the area, and they were forced to alter their route several times to avoid being caught up in it. Both of the adults were exhausted, but neither one of them complained. They had a feeling that their tiredness would be fixed soon. One way or another, it would be fixed.

Personal Journal of Michael Faust Taggart (Final Entry, No Date Provided)

I think this journal's just about had it. Not just because I'm about to be done with the Affliction and Interpol and all this mess for good... It's also because I just can't get used to it. Who knows, I'll probably start a new one when I have the time. Not if. When. Yeah. Perspective. I might as well take my own advice.

Anyway, these journals have been... better than I could have ever guessed they would be. I mean, it's not like any other treatment I've been through has gotten me to a point where I can... Since I can't come up with a better word, I'll just say it's a point where I can rationalize things a little bit. I used to be able to do that because it's a basic human function, but I'll take this over nothing any day. It's another thing to smile about, and I take happy moments like I take my coffee - any way I can get it.

...wow. That sounded a lot better in my head before I wrote it. Oh well, it's not like it's a communal journal. And besides, it's one of the more coherent thoughts I've had recently.

Speaking of which, I don't want to make this into a goodbye letter (I never believed in that kind of stuff), but if my mind decides to jump ship completely and someone finds this where I left it in that shoebox of a hotel room, just know that I went out fighting. Not fighting some bullshit weapon that a deranged guy dreamed up. It's true that I fought that, but it's not nearly as important as my fight for my mind. I've finally come to terms with this. I was so afraid of death when I was facing down Nikolai because I was defenseless. There was nothing that I could do. I think why most people fear death is because they feel like they should have taken better steps to prevent it. I don't have to live with that fear if my mind leaves me. I know that I've fought as hard as I possibly can, and I can face death or insanity as a worthy opponent.

Am I crazy for thinking this and writing this?

Maybe.

The point is, I finally don't care. I'm content.

Hong Kong, China (North Point) - 1:08 A.M.

It was with an unpleasant sense of deja-vu that Taggart and Kotova walked through the penthouse doors one more time. They retraced the steps they had made before, which also happened to be the path they were dragged through on their way to the island prison. The memories of this left the pair more cautious and paranoid than ever, which was probably a good thing in this case.

No one was manning the front desk, and this likely had something to do with the riots. When no one is talking in such a large area, the sound created by every movement seems to be amplified. Wood creaking underfoot and shallow breathing became the loudest things in the world. Their hearts beat a little bit faster each time there was a sound which might not have come from them. It was easy to imagine a third pair of footsteps accompanying theirs, even though no one else appeared to be there.

Room 878 was right where they had left it, Taggart sent the door crashing inward with a swift kick. Nothing inside the room appeared to be different since they had last been in it. He realized as soon as he did this that he could have picked the lock instead, but the time for subtlety was gone.

The interior, unlike last time, was fully lit. In all honesty, Taggart would have preferred the dimness of before to fluorescents shining down from every angle. Regardless, he checked around the suite for people who could be hiding there. Finding no one, Michael made his way back to the couch where Kotova was already searching.

With her free hand, she shifted the sofa's cushions to reveal a spacious compartment containing quite a few oddities. Different forms of currency were neatly stacked inside, each pile containing a small fortune. Beside these was a collection of syrettes, all of which had been used. Most importantly, there was a package wrapped in red cloth.

Withdrawing this bundle and casting the cloth piece aside, Taggart was met with the sight of a reinforced silver briefcase. His heart began to beat quite a bit faster, and he also felt his adrenaline working overtime. Michael knew that this must be what he was looking for, but he felt the need to check inside nonetheless.

Even though the danger of opening it was akin to playing Russian Roulette with a clip-loading pistol, Taggart disengaged both locks on top of the case, laid it flat on the table, and lifted its heavy lid. Both he and Kotova had expected an extravagant display, but there were no eerie, glowing lights or space age technologies. Instead, there were two rows of objects pressed into foam molds. The top row was comprised of clean, unused syringes, and the bottom was home to sealed vials of a dark-red liquid. This liquid was similar to the color of an Afflicted person's blood, and it didn't take much thought at all for them to realize its purpose.

Taggart was quick to close the briefcase, lock it, and pick it up with his good hand. Quickly reconsidering this, he moved it so that it was hanging on his right wrist. With his left hand, he drew his pistol and examined its sights. Like the transition from driving on different sides of a road in different countries, he did his best to adapt before any dangerous consequences could come of it.

He looked at Kotova, who nodded while keeping half of her attention on Alexey. "Alright. We have it now. The funny thing is, I have no idea what we should do with it now that it's actually in our hands."

Taggart chuckled in spite of himself. "You know what, me either. I'd been so focused on finding it and preventing it, but... I never *did* think about actually having it in my hands. I guess... we could pour it into the water around Hong Kong."

She gave a skeptical look. "Wouldn't that just cycle the disease to everyone when the water... Could it be that... I guess that since it's going to dissolve in the water, the other chemicals won't be present by the time the water's used for drinking purposes. But what about the fish? I mean, of course they aren't as important as people in the immediate sense, but what if the fish spread it among themselves and make that resource unusable. It might even be transmitted through eating fish. Then we'd have this all over again. It's far-fetched, but thinking of what-ifs is what's kept me alive."

Resting his chin on his hand, Taggart considered this for a moment. "I think it'll be alright on that account. I'm not really an expert on this sort of thing - hell, I'm not an expert on much - but if a fish manages to digest it, it'll still be fine. If the disease is spread initially through needles, that means it's being put straight into the bloodstream. The fish would just cycle it through their system and shouldn't be bothered."

Kotova nodded again, half-sighing, half-laughing. "We're really going to do this. We're really going to get rid of this fucking nightmare."

Taggart grinned, but this turned into a grimace when he tried instinctively to slide the briefcase from his wrist to his hand. Despite the moment of pain, he was quick to pick his smile back up and was filled with happy excitement. "That's the plan, at least! We'd better get going if we want this to work."

With that, he led the way out of the room. Behind him, Kotova had drawn her own pistol and was holding it at the ready. They looked like quite an odd couple, one with a disfigured hand and a comically over-sized briefcase and the other with a gun in one hand and a baby in the other.

Footsteps could be heard stomping up the stairs, and, after exchanging a knowing glance, Kotova and Taggart hurried into the elevator. The latter rapidly pushed the button for the ground floor until the doors decided to slide closed. As the box descended, they allowed themselves a brief moment of relief. Their muscles relaxed, and the two were at last able to let their heads fall - the effort of keeping them upright was even a strain at this point.

Not a word was spoken between them, but two people of similar minds are often able to communicate without making a sound. This had become the case with Taggart and Kotova, who were both thinking of what they would do if they were able to get out of this mess alive. They had both spent so much time and energy focusing on the immediate future, that this was the first time that they really were able to think any farther ahead.

An in-depth consideration of this would have to wait, as the floors ticked by and both of them were forced to ready their weapons once more. The door slid open on cue when they had reached the bottom, revealing three men who could have only been Triads.

Using the small amount of cover that the sides of the elevator provided, both of them opened fire. They must have caught the Triads by surprise, because none of them were even able to make a sound before two were already taken down. The next hail of bullets hit the third man square in the chest. It was impossible to tell who had killed him, but there was no doubt that he was out of commission for good. This left quite a scene - two dead men collapsed into heaps on the floor, the other one coming to rest with his face buried in an upturned chair. The blood that emerged from their wounds was the same consistency and color as the fluid in the case that Taggart was carrying.

After this, Alexey made his presence clear with quite a bit of wailing. Though Taggart's pistol was suppressed, Kotova's was not, and it was resonating painfully in their ears as well. Even though she had killed at least one person only moments before, Emelia contrasted this by rocking her son in her arms and whispering to him in Russian.

The wailing subsided into heavy sniffling from Alexey, with Taggart keeping his pistol trained on the stairs as Kotova handled the situation. She knelt to the bloodied ground and reloaded her weapon one-handed, and Taggart did the same once she was done.

They nodded at each other once more, this having become a universal signal for *let's get going*. Before moving out of the lobby, Kotova glanced over at Taggart. He had stretched out his mouth comically, held his tongue out, cocked his head to the side, and crossed his eyes for Alexey's amusement. After a moment's confusion, she laughed, causing him to look back up at her.

"What? Is there something wrong with my face?" he asked, still maintaining the goofy expression. Kotova shook her head, bemused but still smiling along with Alexey.

"For what it's worth, Taggart, I think you'd make a far better uncle than your Uncle Jeff was."

It was Taggart's turn to smile. He was already so overcome with stress and emotion, a tear emerged in the corner of his eye from the exchange. Wiping this away, he led the way out of the building with fresh hope.

Michael felt both relief and a bit of sadness at the thought of leaving the past few months behind. Though his experience in the country had been far from ideal, he had become familiar with the streets and the atmosphere and the people of Hong Kong. The normal people, that is. But Nikolai, his captors in the island prison, Kotova's ex... those were people who he would not hesitate to put behind him. Besides this, the people who had been a positive influence in his life would be there again. He didn't doubt this for a moment.

It was with these and countless other things on his

mind that he led Kotova and Alexey toward the coast. Leaving the country and dealing with the repercussions of leaving the Sentinels would come later. At that moment, the only important thing in the world was getting rid of that disease once and for all.

Surprisingly, the Afflicted mobs weren't much of an obstacle on their way to the bay. They were mostly concentrated in small groups and were fighting in out-of-the-way places. Some of them watched with animosity as they passed by, but they largely ignored Taggart, Kotova, and Alexey. This was fine with them, and it also sped up the process of reaching their destination. With circumstances being what they were, public transport was out of the question, but the walk was a mercifully short one.

They had arrived at a marina, which housed a variety of different boats. Taggart turned to Emelia and said, "I'm not usually an ends-justify-the-means type of person, but we really need to get out of here before we get rid of the Affliction. I don't think the Triads are thrilled to have their weapon missing. What do you think - should we take a boat?"

Seeming to have no objection to this, Kotova said, "Of course. Find one that you think will work, then I'll hot-wire it and get us the hell away from this place. Just a little skill I picked up in the FSB."

Taggart nodded, then made his way through the fleet of boats. The one that he ended up choosing was a speedboat which he hoped sacrificed space for top speed. Waving Kotova over, he said, "This should work. I'll hold Alexey if you need me to while you're working on starting it."

Without a word, she handed her son to Taggart, who placed the briefcase on the deck of the boat and readied his pistol. He hoped that this would be the last time that he would have to do so for quite a while.

He could hear Emelia swearing to herself, apparently having difficulty with the boat's starter. Doing his best to focus on spotting an ambush, Michael scanned the surrounding area. He had taken cover in the back of the boat so that only his eyes were visible above its edge, and Alexey wasn't visible at all.

Figures were appearing back on land, but it was difficult to tell through the darkness if they were of any threat. Steadying his left hand, Taggart aimed at the closest one with his finger still off of the trigger. He slowly readied to fire as the person came even closer.

Come on. We're almost home free. Not now. Not now.

Despite his pleading with the universe, he soon recognized the unmistakable outline of the strongman who had tortured him. Taggart was tempted to shoot at him with his mangled hand to prove a point, but he knew that this would only result in what the boat's warning sticker warned against - *Serious Injury or Death.*

Opting to use his one good hand, Michael lined up his target and fired without hesitation. The bullet met its mark in the strongman's center mass, but this did little to cripple his progress. In fact, it seemed to enrage him even more and cause him to charge at the boat as fast as he could. He had made it onto the marina and was less than a dozen feet away when three more shots from Taggart's pistol connected with his chest and neck. The look of rage still frozen on his face, the strongman stumbled backwards and collapsed into the water.

As this was happening, almost a dozen more Triads had appeared on the edge of the dock and lined up as if they were a firing squad. They might as well have been, in this case. Their shots came down at the boat simultaneously, and Taggart could feel them fly through the air just above his head. He buried Alexey near his chest to protect him, then reached his arm over the edge of the boat and fired blindly. There was virtually no chance that any of these bullets hit their mark, but Michael took whatever odds he could get.

Before long, he had fired off every single round he had. Turning to Kotova for a brief moment, he only managed to shout the word 'gun.' She got the message, sliding her pistol over to him without looking away from the boat's ignition system. It was an unfamiliar weapon used in his non-dominant hand, but Michael was able to fell two of the Triads in short order.

He couldn't hear it above the din of the gunfight, but Kotova had at last managed to turn on the boat's engine. It was only when she started to pull away from the marina that he did notice. What he did hear was a voice shouting in his ear.

"It's time to go! Untie the rope that's holding us back there; we can't have much longer before they hit us. Or they hit the boat!"

Transferring Alexey to her arms was no easy task, especially with the hail of bullets going by. The shots began to come closer to hitting them by the second, bits of wood and plastic being splintered on the boat's surface. Michael took a deep, rattling breath. Rising up to face Hong Kong for what would hopefully be the last time, he took aim at the Triads.

They had not slowed their attack in the slightest, only pausing long enough to reload their weapons. Taggart fired Kotova's pistol at them while he used his bad hand to untie the mooring line. The pain caused by this forced him to stop shooting for a moment, leaving him exposed while he tried to keep his senses in order. Dropping the pistol on the deck, Michael used his left hand to untie the craft.

As he did this, his gaze shifted from the rope itself to the Triads. Some of them had advanced closer, and one of them was fishing their fallen friend out of the water. None of them looked pleased with the situation. Taggart was fine with this, just as long as they were only able to hit his right hand. It had been through hell already, so he figured that it could be put through at least a little bit more.

If only the knot on the boat hadn't been tied so tightly. If only they had chosen a different boat. If only they had gotten there a bit sooner, it wouldn't have happened. It would have been fine. As it was, however, those things hadn't happened.

Taggart had just finished untying the knot and was watching as it slid into the water when it hit. *It* was one of the hundreds of bullets that the Triads were slinging their way, and this one made contact with the upper-left of his chest.

At first, he didn't even register the pain from this. It wasn't until another one hit him a few inches from the first that Taggart felt the increased rush of adrenaline and dropped to the floor. Screaming words that the hoped Alexey wouldn't remember hearing, Michael clutched at the holes in his chest and braced himself as the boat began to move.

Taggart's senses were disappearing one by one, but he thought he heard Kotova shouting his name. In vague, indistinct consciousness, he hoped that she would keep moving away from the shore. Away from it all. She could destroy the rest of the Affliction. She could inform the press about the incident. Nikolai wouldn't win out, even long after his own death. Taggart only wished that it didn't have to come at the cost of his own.

Michael reminded himself of his convictions from earlier - he was content with the life he had lived. He was content with the life he had lived. Taggart repeated this to himself, partially so that it would be more convincing to himself, partially because it was all that he could manage anymore. Two lucky shots. That's all it took. Well, not lucky for him, anyway.

With the last of his energy almost spent, Michael rolled onto his side in order to say goodbye and to thank them both. He didn't know what he would thank them for, other than just being themselves.

He wasn't able to stay on his side for very long, as a particularly rough wave sent him tumbling into a face-down position. He hoped that Emelia knew how much he appreciated her friendship and her persistence. Just how much he appreciated her as a person. Taggart also hoped that she would pass on to Alexey how much hope he had for him, and how he had been an inspiration to a miserable man, even before he was able to speak.

From his prone position on the deck, Michael could feel warm blood dripping past his face - his own blood. Through mostly-closed eyes, he could see more of his own blood than he had ever wanted to see. *It was dark, even when it came under the ship's lights. It was too dark, reminding him of the Affliction carried in the vials.*

In spite of the gravity of the situation, Michael gave one final, strained laugh. He wasn't too surprised. In fact, he found it to be quite fitting - if someone was to help 'cure' a disease, why not someone suffering from it himself? He would go out smiling. Smiling through things that no one would associate with happiness. He was determined to smile. For so long, he had wanted contentment and happiness. He had that now. It didn't even bother him that it had come so late. It was there, and that was all he needed.

Obituary taken from the New York Times, 12 December 2016

Michael Faust Taggart is presumed dead after a nine-month-long search for the man or his remains yielded no results. A closed memorial is to be held in Brooklyn in the coming week, its attendance restricted to the former co-workers of the deceased (all of whom make up the remnants of the enigmatic group of 'Sentinels'). Due to the inconclusive and mysterious circumstances surrounding the (assumed) death, little more can be disclosed at this time.

Michael Taggart was born on August 28, 1979 in West Chester, Pennsylvania to...

EPILOGUE

Adrift Between China and Macau (Exact Location Unknown) - March 28, 2016

The most emotionally conflicting moments occur at the end of a particularly long, arduous journey. On one side of this struggle is the relief and satisfaction from having completed something requiring such effort and attention, and on the other is the disappointment and a sense of deep sadness at losing a sense of purpose that had been present for so long.

Those were the thoughts going through Taggart's mind as he rested on the deck of the ship. Knowing that he must have lost consciousness for quite some time, Michael only tried to maintain his breathing and be thankful that he was still *able* to breathe. Waves were crashing against the side of the boat. He was only faintly aware that he was in a boat at all. Seasickness usually followed him on voyages, but the movement had become soothing somehow.

When he felt ready, Michael rolled onto his side and cracked his eyes open. The sight that awaited him was another pair of eyes, these ones bright and curious. They belonged to a very small child, and they were studying his face as if it was a new toy to play with.

"Alexey," he managed to whisper, putting on as convincing of a smile as he could. The baby laughed and crawled backwards, bashful.

Kotova must have heard or seen this, because she

was at his side a moment later. "Michael? God, you scared me there. I was hoping that I wouldn't have to give you mouth to mouth or something. I've seen a lot of disgusting things in my life, but I'm just not prepared for something like that."

In response, Taggart grimace-smiled and felt his stomach contract painfully as he laughed quietly. He pushed himself out of the pool his own blood and into a kneeling position on the boat's deck. He wiped his mouth with the back of his hand to clear it off, but this left his face even bloodier than before.

Brisk sea air cut against his face, causing him to grimace. Feeling and a sense of reality had begun to return to him, and with this came with a great deal of pain. But this pain was different. Somehow, it brought immense relief to him. Kotova had returned to the boat's steering wheel, but she was looking back at him with exhausted relief.

Pressing his hand against a wound in his chest, Taggart rose himself a little bit and was met with the sight of water on all sides - they must have drifted very far away from where they had set off.

"Wait! The Affliction... the case... is it... what happened?"

"Calm down: I really think you might hurt yourself worse. Everything is okay. I've smashed the vials; it's over. The syringes and the case are still here, just in case we need them while exposing the plot at some point. Everything is okay."

Letting out a massive breath of relief, Taggart

sank back into the corner of the boat. If he had survived long enough for the boat to be so far out at sea, chances were that he would make it to a hospital to be fixed up. With this in mind, the wounds in his chest felt almost insignificant.

It was after drifting in silence for some time that could hear a voice in the earpiece in his pocket. It was far-off and unintelligible, but he knew that it couldn't be his imagination. The words slid in and out of focus, but Taggart had heard the voice enough times to know that Colonel Grant was trying to contact him. How she had gained the frequency of the device, he didn't know. At this point, there was nothing that could make him care, either.

Michael ripped the device from his ear, crawled to the edge of the craft, and dropped it overboard. He was done. Done with destroying his own mind for the sake of someone else's agenda. Maybe he had helped prevent something terrible from taking place, but he was done. It was someone else's turn now. He was done putting his life in someone else's hands, done living in fear of dying at any time.

As far as anyone but Kotova and Alexey knew, he was dead. Taggart preferred it that way, especially since it meant that he could control the pace of his life for once. A feeling crept into the corners of his mind, a feeling that this wouldn't last. It told him that it *couldn't* last. He pushed these things aside, begging his mind to allow him a moment's rest.

After another moment's thought, Michael took the wedding band off of his finger, gave it one last pained look, and threw it as hard as he could. The ring gave a splash in the rough waters before sinking to the bottom for some treasure hunter to find. Hopefully it would have some value for them – it didn't carry any for him anymore. He felt that it was time to move on. Taggart's intention wasn't to forget about it, by any means. But he felt that dwelling on it had done him no good in the past, and he doubted that it ever would.

Kotova watched all of this happening, but she remained silent throughout. She had her own emotional weight to dispose of, so she let him get rid of his without being questioned. Even though this was never voiced by either of them, Michael knew that she was doing this on his behalf, and he appreciated it more than he could say. After he had finished with this, Taggart was the first to speak.

"Thank you."

Kotova turned from the controls and looked at him with a confused expression. "Thanking me again? For what?"

"For being one of the only people with their head on straight. I'd be a lot worse off than shot if it wasn't for you. I'd be... shot and stabbed, maybe? Who even knows. Just... thanks."

She smiled, closing her eyes for a moment and rolling her head back. "Well, thank you, too. I haven't told you before, but I should probably mention it - I really was on the verge of shooting you back in that bar in Moscow. Still not sure why I didn't. In any case, I'm glad I didn't kill you. I hope that counts as sentiment to you, because I'm exhausted and don't have any more words right now."

"I'll take it," Michael replied,

Head still spinning, Taggart stumbled to the boat's steering wheel and leaned on the stern, the uneven waves making his stomach give a nauseated lurch. He ran his eyes across the dials in front of him, noting that the fuel gauge's needle didn't even reach the large '*E*' printed above it.

Michael was too exhausted for that to be alarming, or even bothersome. He had done what he had set out to do, at least for the moment. So, as he let the boat take him to places yet unknown, he was content. Exhaustion and pain joined this, but, for the first time in a lifetime, he was truly content. He was done. If not forever, he was done for the moment.

The only thing that held him back from complete calm was the knowledge that the Affliction was coursing through his veins. It had been since who-knows-when. This caused his mind to generate question after question.

How have I managed to keep this in check? How long do I have left? Is my Affliction life-threatening? Is the sample we destroyed really the last of the disease? What about the scientist that Nikolai mentioned? Jesus, what about the Triads? Won't there be repercussions from this?

Kotova must have somehow noticed this internal turmoil, as she abandoned the controls of the boat and joined Michael in the stern. She didn't say a word, instead choosing to rest in contemplation beside him. Taggart preferred this to anything else - he held fast to the idea that silent thoughts were preferable to words without any thought at all. In addition, there was a sort of energy between them that made serenity and rest come much more easily.

It made Taggart forget about his concern of where they would eventually come into port, the fear of the future had dissolved. This was an unfamiliar sense of peace, and Michael was overwhelmed by it for a moment. After that moment had passed, however, he knew that this was the life that he wanted to live. It was a life in service to himself and those who he cared about. A life on his own terms.

For the first time in quite a while, he could fall asleep with tears of *joy* in his eyes. Alexey crawled over to him and curled up on his arm. Michael held him tightly, more by instinct than anything else. It was refreshing for Taggart to be with someone who was free from the needless worry and stress that maturity brought. He could only hope that Alexey would be free from those burdens for as long as possible. As soon as he was able to put these thoughts aside for the moment, they both fell into a deep sleep. Neither one felt regret over a single thing.

AFTERWARD

There were many sources of inspiration for *Regret* (*Blade Runner, The Bourne Trilogy,* and Ian Fleming's novels to mention a few), but the main driving force behind the idea was the simple fact that dehumanization of the main character in spy fiction has become far too commonplace. This book may be seen as a criticism of the *Bourne* and *Bond* franchises, and, as it turns out, that was the main motivation for this book. With all due respect given to those authors and their characters, I find their depiction of human emotion to be lacking in several areas. It is a glaring flaw which I find troubling, as it disregards the complexity and fragile nature of the human mind.

One critical thing that authors seem to have forgotten is that people conditioned to perform exceedingly dangerous and violent assignments are, in fact, still human beings. I endeavored to reinstate at least some of the humanity in such people throughout this novel, in line with the titular concept. In addition, it has become a taboo of sorts to reveal any iota of fear on the part of a protagonist in this specific arena of fiction, and this is something that I feel is an essential part of creating an honest, believable story. I would be terrified in many situations which Taggart faced, as would most other rational people, even those who are trained to deal with such matters every day. The reason that this is feasible is that such people have the unique ability to harness this fear into a drug of sorts – not one which is injected or swallowed, but one that the brain can create for itself in dire situations. Again, fear is something every human faces, and, in this novel, I wanted to emphasize that such characters, had they existed, would be no exception. Taggart is unique in that he has the power to harness this fear, but the lack of rationale behind this ability becomes apparent to him over time.

Another issue that I very much wanted to address was that of mental illness and its impact on a person's ability to function. Probably the easiest way to annoy me would be to make the argument that depression and anxiety *aren't* mental illnesses and shouldn't be treated as such. In truth, such a statement is akin to telling a person with a broken limb to "just feel better." Sure, it's possible for the afflicted person's condition to improve (whatever illness that might be), but this simply won't occur without a great deal of therapeutic attention. I will acknowledge, however, that situations differ and I wish to be respectful of people in all cases.

While writing *Regret*, I saw Taggart as a person who had suffered from an affliction of his own and had no option but to continue on in pursuit of those under similar circumstances. He was suffering to the point of being unable to recognize it as being different from how life is for every normal, average person.

A long way into the original draft of this novel, one disturbing fact occurred to me – the Affliction isn't a made up construct at all (at least the version of it which isn't manufactured into a weapon). It took far too long for me to realize that I was writing about my own experiences when I described the loss of control and irrational thoughts. It is a phenomenon which I have experienced more frequently than I would prefer, but, like Taggart, I force it to the side and move on with my life until it returns. I think everyone must face this difficulty, at least to some degree. Emotion overcoming reason to an extreme is a dangerous thing, and that's all the more reason that it cannot be ignored. I find it to be true of society that rage can manifest itself all too easily - it's quite simple to see it others, but it takes quite a bit of effort to see it in oneself.

In the interest of preventing this Author's Note from being a soapbox, I digress.

No matter what work of fiction you read, there are people other than the author who made the finished product possible. *Regret* is no exception, but I will keep my Academy Awards speech brief in the interest of… well, your interest in this afterword.

The final line of this book took me quite some time to finish, at least in a manner that I could be satisfied with. Like many things in my writing, the answer came to me late at night and in a period of pretty intense emotion, and I must attribute this concluding sentence to the same person to whom this book was dedicated – Mikaela Faust. I have nothing but thanks to give to her. In essence, she provided an influence which made *Regret* into a much more organic, honest, and valuable work of fiction. This ranges from letting me know what she thinks of my ideas and suggesting how they might be improved upon, to providing much-needed encouragement, and so many other things. Thank you so much, Katie.

Thanks must also be given to my dad, who remains a supportive force behind my writing, providing motivation when it is needed most. He continues to be a driving force behind literary minds, and this is something that the world needs much more of.

Someone who does the very same must also be mentioned, and this man is named Copper Wiezi. In addition to his humanitarianism and dedication to literature, he has also been an essential asset in the publication and distribution of this work. His input and unique perspectives have been wonderful to witness and utilize. Put in more simple and digestible terms, he's just a great guy.

Even though most people choose not to thank inanimate objects in their dedications, I've never been accused of being normal. The fact is, this would not have been able to finish this book, or anything else, without copious amounts of coffee. This leads me to my final words that I have to say for the moment -

Thank you, reader. Even though a great many writers do the same, I would like to give you my genuine thanks. Thank you for making it through *Regret* with me. It is my fondest hope that you have gained something out of this which extends beyond simple enjoyment of a story. What exactly that is, I'll leave up to you.

Take it easy - but take it.

--Andrew Kroninger

ABOUT THE AUTHOR

Andrew Kroninger was born in Paoli, Pennsylvania in 1996. Since then, he has developed a unique perspective and writing style, putting those to use in the form of his literary works. He is currently a student at Middle Tennessee State University. Following the acquisition of a doctoral degree, he intends to become an English professor and continue writing until the point that he can do the latter full-time. Whether or not that will occur before his retirement, the plan remains the same.